# MURPHY'S SECRET

A Second Chance Sports Romance (Murphy Family Saga Book #2)

CLOCKTOWER ROMANCE
BOOK 3

## BECKE TURNER

Special-T Publishing

# SUNBERRY, NORTH CAROLINA

*A place to call home.*

Welcome to fictitious Sunberry, North Carolina. Settle back, put your feet up and prepare to enjoy a basketful of southern hospitality. With a population of twenty thousand diverse residents, Sunberry is the small city Americans dream of calling home. This slice of southern comfort offers a four-year college, an historic opera house complete with second-level entertainment, and a full-service hospital. No need to feel like a stranger. Sunberry residents mingle with new inhabitants, especially service members returning to civilian life.

If you're a veteran from nearby Camp Lejeune, a local rancher breeding organic cattle along the river, or a dog trainer developing new puppies to assist the disabled, you're bound to find a happily ever after in Sunberry. After all, doesn't everyone crave a home?

I want more Becke Info!

# CHAPTER ONE

Losing was not an option.

Muscles tensed, Whit Murphy crouched on the thirty-yard line and checked the scoreboard over the stadium.

Twenty seconds. Enough time for a pass, catch, and score. *We've got this.*

At the snap of the ball, he exploded off the line. The Steeler to his right barreled his way. He cut to the center, found a hole, and sprinted toward the end zone, his breath expelling in rapid puffs of air. *Focus.* With the play running in his mind, the roar of the crowd dimmed, the odor of sweat faded, and the movement around him receded. Whit opened his stride and glanced downfield.

*Come on, Todd. Turn it loose.*

Under the bright lights, the ball spiraled toward him, and then faded left.

*Go, go, go.*

The blur of the cornerback on his right and the free safety closing in on his flank, flashed in his peripheral vision. Gritting his teeth, he sprinted three strides and leaped for the ball.

*Come on ... contact!*

A black jersey barreled toward him. Hugging the ball to his chest, he angled his body toward the goal line. Pain detonated in his side, turf rushed toward his face, and blackness swallowed him. Pads crunched; men groaned. The weight pressing on his chest, back, and hips increased.

Had he made it? With his lungs burning for air, he opened his right eye and searched the ground. *There!* One inch below his elbow—and the ball—the white line cut through the turf. When he smiled, his lip stung, and a blood-tinged victory filled his mouth.

Touchdown!

The whistle pierced in the distance, and the pressure of the bodies smashing him eased. Cool air fanned his face, and the lights blinded his vision. When he pushed to his knees, explosions flashed behind his eyes in sickening waves. Unsure if his legs would support his weight, he grabbed at the extended hand near his face. Pain shot through his side as the pull brought him to his feet, and he blinked hard to stop the spinning.

A fuzzy player in front of him jumped up and down like a wild man. "Amazing! When it went left, I thought no way. But you pulled that sucker right out of the air!"

Whit squeezed his eyes shut, then widened them. Todd, the Cougar's quarterback, broke through the cluster of white jerseys.

"Your throw was left." The words scraped Whit's throat. "Checking out my speed?"

Todd held up his fist for a bump. "You got there, man. You got there."

Ignoring the grind in his side, Whit maneuvered into the center of the players. They'd won and there was nothing sweeter than a comeback victory. Biting back the pain, he limped toward the locker room with his teammates, bellowing their victory.

"Media alert!" a teammate at the front shouted.

The deafening pandemonium and the nonstop camera flashes stirred the ache in Whit's skull.

"Lose the helmet." Ivan 'The Train' Traynor made a ridiculous face for the crowd. "They want to see our pretty mugs."

"Hiding the scar on my lip," Whit shouted over the noise.

"Right. Those camera lenses can magnify a pimple on your butt from the cheap seats."

Ivan's bawdy hoot faded, and hundreds of headlines scrimmaged through Whit's mind. His gut twisted, and it had nothing to do with the giant bruise he guessed covered his chest. He jerked off his helmet, wincing at the bolt of pain behind his right eye.

The press wasn't going to get a piece of him tonight. A headline beat like a drum through his head: *Dimwit Wide Receiver Suffers Too Many Hits*. He wiped the blood from his lip. That was one story he never wanted to read.

————

THE CLOCK in the Cougar's locker room read twelve forty-five when Whit eased into his leather jacket and jammed his hands into the pockets, his fingers seeking. The talisman brushed his fingertips and tumbled into his palm, the cool surface easing the tension in his shoulders.

Good game. After a week's rest, he'd be ready for the next one. He opened the door to the corridor and slammed it shut, scrambling back to the safety of the locker room. Why weren't the reporters following Todd? He was the star quarterback.

Cold sweat pasted Whit's shirt to his back, and the floor

undulated beneath his feet. He placed a hand against the wall and squeezed his eyes shut. *Come on.*

His vision cleared, and the wooziness subsided. For a minute, he thought he was seeing things. The hit had distorted some of his memories, but not the weirdest one: Talley watching the game with his hometown's Boy Scout troop. He'd spotted them during a time-out. At first, he thought he was losing it. And that was before the last tackle.

Now, she was in the hall? He rubbed a circle in the middle of his forehead. Of all nights for her to show up. In five years, she'd never come to see him play, never called, nothing. He fisted his hands at the memory of their breakup. His vision sharpened. He thought she got him, thought she understood how important it was for him to play, succeed. The only thing Talley *Quixote* got was her latest cause.

Still shaky, he squared his shoulders. *Face it, man, it's her.*

"Hey, Whit," Ivan called from behind. "Hold up. I need a chick magnet."

Despite his devil-may-care attitude, Ivan, with his curly red hair and massive size, always watched Whit's back and made him laugh. Just like his college teammate Jeff. Whit's mouth dried. Except Jeff hadn't made it to the league. One bad tackle had ended Jeff's career—and his life.

Jeff had been a great guy. So, why was his friend gone, and Whit was still playing after multiple bad hits? The shudder along his back intensified the ache in his head. The doc hadn't singled him out for concussion protocol. Disaster avoided. No injury leading to Chronic Traumatic Encephal ... opathy. He couldn't even wrap his tongue around it. Anyway, CTE was not a threat—yet. So why was his balance off?

He smacked the wall, embracing the pain in his side. No way was he going soft at this stage in his career. For once in his life, he'd claimed success, landed on top of the pack instead of under it. That's how he did amazing things for his family and his kid charities, and he planned to continue the course for as long as possible.

So, why was *she* here?

His practiced phrases could get him by the media, but Talley—she'd notice the strategic pauses. She'd helped him perfect the technique to hide his speech problems. One comment from her, and he'd be tomorrow's headline, which wouldn't help his contract-renewal negotiations.

So, superstar, are you man enough to handle her?

# CHAPTER TWO

Talley Frost paced the dimly lit stadium corridor with its odor of stale beer and nachos, waiting for Whit to resurface. She'd come this far. She wasn't giving up. Whit was talking to her. Tonight. Like it or not.

Despite the hollow sensation in her belly, she squared her shoulders. Whit better not mess with her. She knew darned good and well he'd seen her. She stood out in a sweater and jeans among women wearing heavy makeup, skintight clothing, and long hair done in elaborate styles. She smoothed her damp palms down her hips. At least she'd worn the team colors and wouldn't need a putty knife to remove her makeup tonight. Besides, she wasn't here to weasel her way into Whit's wallet or his bed.

Heat soared from her neck to the roots of her hair. There had been a time she'd have done anything to be with him. She shivered. That dream had died. She had one purpose—explain his sister Hope's latest escapades and get him to call home. After surviving the terror of watching his game for the last few hours, she intended to accomplish her mission.

One minute later, the door opened, and the crowd pushed

against her. Talley elbowed her way to the front. Beside her, a raven-haired, live Barbie doll held her ground. Talley braced. Barbie stood maybe five feet eight or nine and had a good three inches on her. Tough. Growing up a military brat had sharpened Talley's street smarts, including how to handle a crowd. She could grapple with the best of them—and come out on top.

"Whit," Barbie said in the perfect blend of volume and seduction.

Talley straightened. What an attention-getter, but not appropriate to use on her high school students. Still, she held the trump card. If Whit were the same guy she'd tutored through college, family came first—unless he was majorly horny. A flutter settled deep in her belly. In *that* department, he'd tutored her.

Whit, handsome as ever—even without the killer smile that had hooked her in high school, moved fast and purposeful in a blue shirt, jacket, and jeans.

Bright white flashes strobed the hall and cameras clicked.

"Spectacular play, Whit," called a tall man, poking a microphone between two fans in Cougar T-shirts.

"Have the Cougars renewed your contract?" asked a guy with a press card dangling from his neck.

Talley took a deep breath. "Winston Churchill Murphy, five minutes, please!"

A stunned silence fell over the group, and all gazes seemed to turn her way. To her right, Barbie's glare could toast a marshmallow. Talley pressed her lips together. Who knew Whit's fan club would be so touchy?

Whit's laser blues found her in an instant. Talley grimaced. Yeah, using his full name fell near the cheap-shot category. She lifted her chin. Dire circumstances required dire actions.

Barbie cut her off and grabbed his arm. "Hi, Whit. How

about coming with me to Ivan's? He's throwing one of his epic parties, and a bunch of us are meeting there."

Whit's gaze tracked Talley like Grandma's cat used to track bugs—no emotion, just watchful, waiting for her to make a move.

"Thanks for the offer, Lisa." He didn't blink, didn't look away. "I can't go tonight."

Barbie, aka Lisa, curled her hands, with Cougar-blue painted nails, around his arm. "Come on, Whit. We'll have fun."

"It sounds tempting, but I can't make it. I've got some personal business to handle." He kissed her cheek. "Have fun and watch out for Traynor. He's been hot for you for months."

Although Lisa didn't look pleased, she waved to the hulk of a man walking behind Whit. Whit's gaze narrowed on Talley.

"Hey," she said. "We need to talk."

Talley expected a hello, how are you, long time no see, something. Instead, Whit spun her around and towed her away from the crowd. Her heart fluttered in her chest. Which was crap. This wasn't her first act in the Murphy circus. Good grief, she'd been one of the Murphy tribe for most of her youth. She, Whit, and his two brothers, Kyle and Nate, had raised the blood pressure of every Sunberry, North Carolina resident with their antics. Of course, those adventures occurred before her college breakup with Whit.

A reporter thrust a microphone toward them. "Who's the mystery woman, Whit?"

Whit tugged her closer to his side and hustled her down the hall without responding. She sure as heck responded—at least her body did—to him. The heat of his lean, muscled torso singed through her clothes, a major distraction she would *not* act on.

"Whit?" Talley panted. "Slow down."

"Not here," he muttered, keeping a firm but gentle grip on her arm.

By the time they'd trotted through a side entrance to the player parking area, Talley's chest heaved up and down. A man of few words, Whit opened the passenger side to his black pickup, boosted her inside, and slammed the door.

While he circled the front end of the truck, she took a calming breath. That hadn't gone well. Who knew contact with her old flame would cause hormonal fireworks? Jeez, the man should come with a flash-fire panty alert.

He climbed into the driver's seat without glancing her way.

"Okay, I get you're a little upset," she said. If she could grovel to the guy who had broken her heart, he could endure a little embarrassment in front of his fans. "I'm sorry I had to call you out. But that doesn't give you a license to dump me in the seat like a sack of dog chow."

"If you wanted to talk, why didn't you call, let me know you were coming with the Sunberry Scouts?" Irritation laced his deep voice. "I answer my phone."

"Do you know any of the boys in the Scout pack you sent the tickets to?"

He didn't uncross his arms, but the thin line of his lips softened. "Not personally. The tickets came up so I grabbed them. I figured little boys like football, so I had my agent arrange it."

"That was nice, and the Scouts appreciate your generosity. But there was an incident a few days ago." Mercy, his nice gesture had turned into such a mess. "Two local Marines were killed in action. It made the national news."

He huffed out a breath. "Yeah, I saw that."

"The memorial service was today, which left the Boy

Scouts a chaperone short. I volunteered, so they wouldn't need to cancel the trip."

"So, you filled in? Nice. Where are the boys?" He looked over her shoulder like he expected them to materialize in the parking lot, like anything beat talking to her.

"On their way to the hotel with Rachel and Coach Cox." Right now, she wished she'd accompanied them.

When he glanced her way, his smooth brow furrowed in confusion. He had a high forehead and thick sand-colored hair that reminded her of ripe wheat. Correction. He used to have great hair. Now, he wore it cropped short, barely long enough to touch below the hairline. His hair wasn't the only change. What happened to his kind, compassionate eyes? Although they were somewhat estranged, they were still friends.

"Why are you here?" he said.

She slid her hands under her thighs to avoid wringing them. He'd just played a brutal game and was probably exhausted. But darned, there was no way to soften the news about his little sister.

"Hope's taking drugs." Her stomach rolled. It was bad enough to acknowledge it, but to say the words out loud, have them crash inside the small cab? She might be sick.

"I don't believe it!" The slash between his heavy brows deepened. "I called home last Wednesday evening, just like every week. Everything was cool. I may not live close by, but I don't ignore my family."

"No one knows. I filled in with the Scouts to have a legitimate reason for coming and forced Hope to come with me. I thought I could use the car time to talk. You know, just the two of us. I was hoping we could work things out. But I couldn't."

"So where is she?"

"She's with Rachel and the Scouts at the hotel."

He continued to shake his head, causing shadows to flicker across his abraded cheekbone. "You're overreacting. High school's tough, and Hope's always been a drama queen. It's probably boyfriend problems or a fight with her BFF. She called me last year when she got a pimple before the homecoming dance." A tentative grin grazed his lips. "Look, I'm sure it's a misunderstanding. I'm going home after the Thanksgiving game. I'll talk to her."

First, he doesn't believe her, and then he questions her judgment? Just because she couldn't work out Hope's problem on the car ride to the game didn't mean she'd shirk her responsibilities.

She smoothed her hands over her jeans, wishing she could iron out their problem in the same manner. "I'm not trying to wreck your game night. But I wouldn't be here if I thought boyfriend issues or a blowup with a friend drove Hope off the rails. The past week, I've seen unusual outbursts. She's hanging with a different crowd. Some of them are older, not in high school. She's cut class a few times and even missed basketball practice. That's not like her."

Those weren't her only concerns. Through the darkened glass of the passenger window, the parking lot's straight white lines intersected the asphalt so unlike the curves in life's road. She sucked in a breath to steady her rattled nerves. She'd broken Hope's confidence and possibly destroyed her relationship with the teen. Losing what she shared with Hope would be like ripping off a limb, but she'd sacrifice it in a heartbeat to save her. Something inside her chest clenched. She'd experienced that feeling before—after losing Whit.

Talley moistened her lips. "I know your career is important. And I know you're coming up on the playoffs. But we're talking about family—your family." She drew in another breath and released it. "Hope needs you, and so do I."

## CHAPTER THREE

Whit suppressed a laugh as bitter as the night's chill and turned up the truck's heater. Hot coils and leather cleaner warred with Talley's distinctive scent. His mind fogged like the windshield condensation.

Talley needed help? With his sister, no less. Except it wasn't funny. When Talley's chin quivered, he'd almost put his arm around her shoulders. Almost. He gripped the steering wheel. Knowing another person was hurting—and not just a little but a bad hurt—twisted his insides.

This was serious stuff. Talley had never been one for drama. In the fifteen years that he'd known her, she'd cried two times: the night Jeff died and the night she'd broken up with him.

When his stomach rumbled, he pressed his palm to his abdomen. Get it together. His agent's instructions had been simple—stay healthy, follow the team rules, and play his heart out. Family and former girlfriend issues would have to wait until he had a signed contract.

But what if she were right about Hope?

The pound in his head sharpened with the insistent gurgle in his stomach. He needed to eat, decompress, avoid unnecessary drama. Except Hope and Talley weren't thinking about his needs. In the dash lights, the challenge in Talley's dark eyes burned, daring him to blow her off, blow off his family.

He unclipped his cell and pressed Hope's number. This was an easy fix. He'd talk to Hope, work out her latest drama, and finish his night as if this never happened. The second ring raised the hairs on the backs of his arms. He'd donate his truck to charity if he could move, act, do anything but sit beside Talley and choose between his career and his family.

Hope's cheery recorded message filled his ear. "Love your call. I'm really busy right now. Leave a number, and I'll call you soon."

"What the ...?" Hope never ignored his calls.

He jabbed the call button. The phone purred. Once. Twice. He thumped the screen. If he had to listen to Hope's chirpy message again—

"She's just busy," he muttered. But his lame excuse probably wouldn't convince Talley any more than it slowed his sprinting heart. "Probably helping with one of the Scouts. You know how she likes kids."

He swiped the screen. No texts, either. Win or lose, she never missed contacting him, no matter how late the hour. Whit thumped the cell against his palm.

"She watches me play just so she can pick at me. I swear she's more critical of my game than the coach." He turned down the heat but didn't remove his coat. At least Talley hadn't stated the obvious: he was dead wrong. She didn't have to. His unanswered calls said it all.

*Face it, dude, you've got a situation here.* Talley was pushy, but she'd never lied to him, never jacked him around, and had never gone hysterical like some of the women he dated.

Although the security lights illuminated the parking lot, the truck's interior shadowed her features. He expected her signature look of confidence. Instead, she'd tightened her lips into a straight line and kept wringing her hands.

He lifted his arm to rub his scalp. "Augh!"

"You okay?" She leaned toward him, her scent messing with his already messed-up brain.

"Forgot to brace the ribs. I hate being blindsided." He forced a smile past the throb in his side. Her frown didn't soften. "Sucks, on and off the field."

Her dark eyes narrowed as though she were reading his mind. That was no trick, except on the field—his confident zone. No one could read him there, which is why he earned the big bucks—if the Cougars re-signed him.

When the silence threatened to crush him, he jabbed the hot key for Hope. No answer. He tightened his quad muscles to stop his foot from tapping the floorboard.

*Answer the blasted phone!*

The black screen mocked him. Hope was a good kid, she'd call. He'd be happy if she'd pick up the phone when *he* called.

Closing his eyes, he sucked in a steadying breath. A scent tinged the air—Talley's shampoo? Not flowery. Fresh—a vegetable, a long green one. Zucchini? Nope. An image flashed in his mind, but the word didn't accompany it. He waited, slowing his breaths. It would come to him, just like Hope would eventually pick up. Long green, long green ... cucumber, yes!

He drew in another deep breath and released it. The shakiness dissipated, and his heart rate slowed. Forcing a confident grin, he turned to Talley. "Maybe she took a shower after they returned."

He pressed Hope's number again. His cell whirred, once, twice. *Come on, Hope. You're killing me here.*

"Obviously, something is going on with her." But drugs? Not his little sister. If she'd answer the phone, he'd prove it. And if Talley were right? Despite the ache in his joints and the burn from his peeled knuckles, he gripped the steering wheel.

Talk about poor timing. Why couldn't Hope derail during his off-season when he had time to drop everything and help her? Because that's what he'd do—in a heartbeat. He loved his funny, smart-mouthed little sister, would die for her. But dropping everything tonight translated into losing a chance at the playoffs, a chance to stay in Charlotte, a chance to prolong his career.

Coach had picked him out of five wide receivers to dress for the game. One in five! More impressive, he'd scored the winning touchdown. He showed his boss he still possessed the hands and the speed. This was it. He needed every spare minute to commit plays to memory. When he hit the field, he had to be ready, every play on speed dial in his brain.

"Hope's not answering my texts." The rapid tap of Talley's fingers filled the silence. "I'm checking with Rachel. Hope was mad because I wouldn't let her meet you tonight. But I wasn't going to let her spin out of this one. I had to talk to you first."

Where was his head? They were talking about his sister, his blood, and he was whining about his career. He'd been in the NFL far longer than most guys, and he was complaining? Whit massaged his temple.

"Hope helped Rachel with the room check fifteen minutes ago," Talley said, her gaze on her cell. "Rachel says Hope silenced her phone a while ago, but Rachel thought it was because of boyfriend issues."

"Ask Rachel to make her answer." The echo of his voice bouncing around in the cab intensified the ache in his body.

"She's in the shower." Talley shook her head. "I'm sorry. I wasn't trying to ruin your game night. Hope's always had a good head on her shoulders. I just thought once you understood what was going on, you could call her and swing her back on track."

"What makes you think Hope has a serious problem?"

When Talley didn't answer, he glanced her way. She was staring out at the vacant parking lot. What a disaster. His teammates had already left to celebrate. Twenty minutes ago, it was game night as usual—except for this train wreck. He enjoyed the player/family gatherings but avoided the late-night bachelor scenes with the baller babes. The dash clock rolled forward, and Talley shifted. The hair on his forearms lifted. Three minutes had passed since he'd asked the question. Although she faced him, her gaze remained fixed somewhere over his right shoulder—which was seriously wrong. Talley met challenges head-on. Nothing rattled her.

"Friday night," she started in a low voice. "I came home late. I found Hope sitting on the front porch, in the dark, trashed."

A knifelike pain exploded in his right calf. "Augh!"

Shoving open the truck door, he hobbled onto the asphalt.

"Come on." He pounded the hard ball of muscle contracted beneath his jeans. "Let loose, let loose!"

When the cramp finally released, he staggered against the fender.

"Muscle cramp?" Bundled in her sock hat and puffer coat, only Talley's narrowed eyes showed beneath the lot lights.

He forced a nod. "Yeah. Occupational hazard." He raised a palm when her brows scrunched together. "It's a good thing. Considering I got to play and scored, I welcome a minor cramp."

When her head canted to the side, he bit back a laugh.

He'd never forgotten Talley's expressions, especially her skeptic look.

"Injuries are part of the job. They're expected and *temporary,*" Whit added just to get a rise out of her.

"Just the minor ones," she said.

"Yeah, well, they beat the pain caused by people." He moved closer to gauge her response. "Especially people you love. That's a whole different game."

Based on her sharp gasp, he'd scored on that one. But he didn't want to score marks; he wanted her to understand. He braced, waiting for her comeback, wanting it to be a well-deserved one. Instead, she spun toward the back of the truck, circled to the passenger door, and climbed inside. Guilt, like he'd kicked a puppy, washed through him.

"Forget I said that." He leaned against his open door. "When I'm tired and frustrated, I make mistakes. The game forces that lesson on you."

"I didn't want to believe Hope might be using too. But I couldn't take that chance." Her voice shook. "That's why I'm here."

Talley could handle anything, but she wasn't handling the issue with Hope. She was scared, really scared. The hairs along his neck lifted. "We need to put our past behind us and focus on Hope."

"Agreed," Talley said.

She didn't have to be so quick on her come back.

"It's just ... I don't know." That was the problem—he didn't know. Hope had never pulled anything like this. "It doesn't make sense. Not for Hope."

"I understand," she said. "I went back and forth on my decision to come to the game."

"It's got to be something else." He reached in the door well for water, but he'd forgotten to bring a bottle with him. "High school is a sketchy time. We all engaged in risky behavior. Beer in the woods, smokes in the alley. No big deal."

"It wasn't alcohol, and your mom has an assortment of painkillers in the medicine cabinet. I checked."

"That doesn't mean—"

"One of Sunberry's graduates overdosed on heroin last month," Talley said.

"Heroin! Hope wouldn't ..."

Talley's features blurred and then sharpened. He pressed his hand against his abdomen, but it didn't stop the pitching inside him. He needed to eat.

"Something's happened to her." Talley's shaky voice vibrated through him.

She knew the score, could help him work through Hope's mess—whatever it was. He curled his fingers into a fist. No way. It was *his* family not Talley's, and he'd be there for them. Helping Hope wasn't the same as the stupid college exams Talley had helped him with. He'd left that loser image behind when he became a professional athlete.

In the truck's shadowy interior, he couldn't gauge what drove Talley. But he could feel it. As crazy as that sounded, he knew her emotional status as sure as he knew the contact point of a thrown ball. Something had drained her self-confidence, and that just didn't happen—not to Talley Frost.

"Hope's been all right," he said. But was it true, or did he want it to be true? "I talk to her at least once a week, sometimes more."

Talley's chin trembled again. He hadn't seen that haunted look on her face since they'd taken the wrong path in the woods. They'd been twelve years old. By the time he'd found the trail, dusk had shrouded the forest. She'd clung to him, so he'd kept it together—for her. On the inside, he'd been shaking in his sneakers.

Whit fisted his hands to keep from pulling her close.

"That's the problem. I don't know what's wrong," she said in a raw voice barely above a whisper. "I know strong-willed girls like Hope. She thinks she's got the world figured out. She doesn't realize how one bad decision can screw up her life."

# CHAPTER FOUR

*If you fail to plan, you plan to fail.*

Talley leaned against the stiff leather seat of Whit's truck, overwhelmed by his spicy aftershave and her mother's favorite quote. Breathe. Focus on the reason she had to succeed, not on him, not what was happening to him. Jeez, she'd never get the sound of the players' grunts and groans out of her head.

Her muscles froze. She couldn't breathe, couldn't think. No! She squared her shoulders. Talley Frost would not concede after one football game, a fan encounter, a recalcitrant ex-boyfriend, and a wonderful teenager who had suddenly lost her mind. Nope. Not happening. She'd been taught by America's finest Marines—her parents. While Colonels Noah and Michelle Frost were committed to country, she'd committed to community and loved ones.

*Breathe.* She could do this. It wasn't like she was a stranger to success. Number one for blood donations, Toys for Tots donations, and Teacher of the Year—teaching high school, no less, was nothing to sneeze about. And neither was the attraction to her ex. Gads, which was worse, her fear for him or her attraction to him?

So, why couldn't she put her feelings for football and Whit aside to help Hope? Whit believed her. Now, she had to convince him to come home, so they could work out the best way to help his sister.

She leaned her forehead against the cold window glass. She'd known coming into this Whit represented the wild card in her plan. Not only had she miscalculated his response, but she'd also underestimated hers. Why? Nothing had changed. He risked his life to play ball. No big secret. No big surprise. No big change.

Still, the scrapes across his knuckles, his pained movements, and his cut lip scratched at her stomach, made it pitch and cramp. He'd made his decision to play football. He'd also decided her opinion of the sport didn't matter. She couldn't care about him. But she did, and she couldn't stop those feelings any more than she could stop the last few minutes of the game from playing in her head. The roar of the crowd, the crunch of equipment, and then Whit disappeared under those big men. Had that play resulted in a head blow hard enough to cut his lip?

Another time the crowd had cheered, another pileup, pressed to the surface of her mind. Beads of sweat erupted along her hairline and skittered down her cheeks.

She couldn't see what football was doing to the inside of him, but the outside? The training had transitioned him from a lanky college star to a toned, jaw-dropping man. She unzipped her coat and pulled her sweater away from her sweaty flesh.

"I've got to pick up something to eat, and Roscoe's will close soon." Whit turned down the heater. "Do you mind riding along?"

Absolutely, she didn't sign up for this. At least she didn't think she had. "Sure."

"The ride will give us time to catch up about Hope. After that, I'll drop you off at the hotel." The engine whirred as he eased off the clutch. "Are you hungry?"

"No, thanks. I got full watching seven boys pig out on stadium food," she fibbed.

"Glad they enjoyed it."

The weight smashing her soul shifted. The media always pegged Whit as a ladies' man, but he was really a kid's man. She swallowed. Although enthusiasm lifted his tone, his body position suggested a different story. He drove at an odd angle with his arm clutched close to his side.

"Before the game started," he continued. "I contacted Ralph, a vendor I know, to take care of the Scouts."

"He did," she said, squinting in the low light.

Was that a weird smile or a grimace? Something about him nagged at her. After his college games, he'd always been on a high. Tonight, he looked exhausted, beat-up. Her unexpected appearance probably hadn't helped.

*Don't panic.* Whit avoided change. No doubt, she'd caused a huge adjustment to his post-game schedule, so she needed to go along with his routine. Let him relax. Get something in his stomach. Hunger used to make him irritable. He believed her, believed Hope needed him. Once he talked to his sister, they'd come up with a plan like—No, it wasn't like the past. Tonight was supposed to have been a five-minute talk to get his help with Hope. If Hope would answer and confide in him, Talley could manage the home front until he could break away. She needed to know what she was up against.

The turn signal clicked in the silence, and Whit exited west from Charlotte to U.S. 29. A road sign welcomed them to Belmont, North Carolina, which seemed an odd destination for a super jock after a big game. Too many unanswered and critical questions circled her mind. Despite the heat pumping from the vent, a chill shook her shoulders. She couldn't keep avoiding it.

"How bad are you hurt?" She tried to keep her tone casual like the answer wasn't twisting inside her.

"Just banged up a little." He stared straight ahead. "Nothing major."

"Then why are you wearing sunglasses at night and massaging your head?"

"Sometimes the light bothers my eyes," he said, giving her a quick glance.

When her students pulled that move, they were usually fibbing.

"I saw the team doc after the game," he continued as though he'd memorized his answer. "He taped my ribs. The tackle wrecked my side, not my head. I'm not on concussion watch."

Although she silently ticked off numbers, her heart pounded louder and louder in her ears. "You don't have to get hit in the head—"

"Let it go!"

"I did." She fought back the waver in her voice. "Five years ago, when you signed your Cougar contract."

A thick silence settled around them, emphasizing her loss of control.

She had to say something, start that losing fight, whip that dead horse. Worse, their old battle would not help Hope.

By the time she'd moved on from her internal rant, Whit had parked in front of a neighborhood café. Squeezed between a nail salon and an insurance office, the timeworn establishment sported a blue OPEN sign in the window. Over the storefront, the peeling red and white letters declared that Roscoe's offered a homestyle Southern menu.

"I didn't mean to raise my voice." He set the emergency

brake. "I appreciate your concern for Hope. I'm tired and ... processing the news."

"I'm edgy too," she said, eager to return to a less-volatile discussion. "Hope's the little sister I always wanted. I've let her down and betrayed her trust by coming to you."

"I'll talk to her." He placed a big hand on her shoulder with a tenderness she'd missed. "If I have to beat down the hotel room door, I'll talk to her."

She forced a grin. "After you eat."

For a moment, he looked like something more occupied his mind. When he nodded, a sense of loss assaulted her. Worse, she hadn't a clue as to what she'd missed. It was like them and what they'd once shared: gone.

"Roscoe has a huge flat screen. His regulars remind me of the guys at the Sunberry Diner." Whit opened his door. "You could depend on the diner to serve a few beers, attract good company, and show the local game. Roscoe's has a similar vibe. He's also open late and always bags up the special for me. He has awesome food like Mom's."

His lopsided smile emphasized the shadows beneath his eyes and fine lines bracketing his sensuous mouth. In addition to his cut lip, an abrasion colored his right temple.

"Roscoe makes fantastic pie." He raised his brows in the comical way that had once made her laugh. "Are you sure you don't want a piece?"

Afraid a tear would leak free, she shook her head. The minute he turned toward the diner, she pressed her palm against her lips. Hope wasn't the only Murphy who needed her help.

Fifteen minutes later, Whit re-emerged through the glass door carrying a large bag and beverage cup. When he opened the driver's door, the scent of spicy meat, creamy chocolate, and clean man swirled through the cab along with a blast of cold air.

"Hot chocolate for you and dinner for me." Whit lifted the bag. "Now, where to?"

The chocolate called to her, but she needed to hook him up with Hope then get out of Dodge a heck of a lot more than she needed her favorite cold-weather beverage.

He turned the key. "Did you get Hope?"

"Not yet. Rachel's supposed to prod her again." Despite her heated cheeks and racing heart, her voice came out cool and calm—as long as she didn't count the wobble at the end. "Hope told Rachel she had cramps, and only a hot soak eases them."

Whit massaged his forehead.

"I'm sorry," she said. "I thought one call from you would end our problem. I had no idea she'd behave like this."

"It's not your fault. Hope's gotten her nose in a snit before but has never clammed up." He huffed out a breath. "I only live a few miles from here. Do you mind hanging out at my place while I eat dinner?"

*Mind?* Of course not. She also didn't mind someone extracting her fingernails with pliers. "No problem." She gripped her cup with both hands to keep from spilling it in her lap. Maybe scalding her thighs would burn some sense into her since her thoughts had run as rogue as Hope.

She'd once loved him. They'd planned a life together, a future, and he'd trashed everything for a big paycheck. If she let him into her heart again, she'd end up broken like before. Whit took risks. She didn't. Tonight, he'd resurrected her feelings with one crooked smile. She couldn't chance hanging out in his house. And she sure couldn't admit that to him.

# CHAPTER FIVE

Talk about a train wreck. His sister was doing drugs, and he was running head porn, starring his old girlfriend. Next time, he'd think twice before talking the doc out of concussion protocol. At least he'd have a valid excuse.

Whit jerked open the entrance door to his high-rise condo.

"Home sweet home," he bellowed to cover his groan.

Maybe he'd underestimated his recovery time. Dang, he hurt. And that was the last thing he'd admit to Talley. When he pushed the elevator button, he sneaked a glance at her and paused. She looked kind of cute with her eyes round with wonder. He guessed his digs looked fancy to most first-time visitors. No doubt, he could get her attention if he took her hand or snuggled her close to his side. He grinned, and his body's aches dissolved.

When the elevator slid open, he waved her in. He had 8.5 seconds, with no other stops, to get his thoughts from Talley's tight jeans to helping his sister, a tall order considering Talley's proximity. Her fresh and enticing fragrance tickled his nostrils and scattered his thoughts.

Inside his condo, Talley moved toward the bank of windows with her lips forming an *O*. He bit back a grin. The Charlotte cityscape often affected visitors like that.

"Wow!" She rotated in a small circle, her voice as hushed as players enduring a coach's rant after a botched play.

His heart performed a fast-footed maneuver, and he sucked in a sharp breath of air. So much for his game high. He'd feel better once he'd eaten.

"Your living room is bigger than my three bedrooms combined," she said with a hint of awe in her sexy voice.

"Family room." He flipped on the lights. "Why do people call it a living room? Sounds weird. Don't we live in the other rooms?" And how did a man find comfort in a room with polished wood floors and stainless-steel accents? The place felt cold as a tomb. Dang, he was grouchy. "Kitchen's back here."

He skirted the granite countertop, longer than the bar at the Rat Hole, their favorite college dive, and opened the refrigerator. The cold air blasting his face sent a shiver down his spine and sharpened his thoughts.

"Can I get you anything?" He poured a glass of milk. "The fridge is stocked."

She lifted her cup. "No. Roscoe's chocolate is perfect. Thanks."

When he straightened, his body ached to the tick, tick, tick of the clock in his head. "I better call Hope."

Talley turned toward him with an odd look, but who knew what that meant. Since he didn't run his mouth, he was good at reading people—until now. Tonight, ideas kept bouncing in his head like a fumbled ball.

Careful to keep his face blank, he moved to his favorite chair in slow, measured steps and placed his dinner on the end table. Old Mr. Tibbs used to move the same way. He stifled a snort. More good news. His big game night had just aged him forty years. Good thing his aches were temporary. After fuel and rest, his body would return to normal.

Across from him, Talley sat on the corner of the sectional and rubbed her forearms.

"Are you cold?"

He retrieved the afghan from the basket near the fireplace.

Talley's smile seemed to light up the room. "I remember this." She snuggled beneath the soft wrap. "Your grandma crocheted it. I bet you think of her every time you unfold it. I cherish the few things I have from my grandmother."

When a lady talks, a man should respond. But not one word could crowd out the memory of her burrowed in his dorm-room pillows. He blinked. Five years evaporated, and just like that, Talley was back.

An itch to act on the once-buried attraction tugged at him. He slid his hand in his pocket. The stone warmed his palm. Yeah, Talley possessed an intense passion for causes that made him crazy, especially if he were the target. However, he could go for a healthy dose of her passion between the sheets tonight. The sexual release would be a fair exchange for the dizziness and blurred vision.

The light from the overhead fixture danced in her auburn hair. She'd worn it down, the way he'd always liked it. During the short walk across the stadium parking lot, the wind had tossed it around her face, giving her a just-laid look. His desire jacked up another notch, confirming his head was messed up worse than he thought. Talley wasn't the one-night stand he went for. She was the real deal—the wrong deal because he loved the game she hated. They were distant friends, but friends. That's how it had to stay.

Tonight, he needed someone he trusted to help him sort through Hope's latest drama. He tore off the corner of the ketchup packet and spread it over his meatloaf. In high school, Talley had been his savior. Unlike the kids in their class, she'd accepted him and his problem the same way as his parents. Talley never made him feel stupid, never made fun of him. Without her help, he wouldn't have finished high school or gotten into college. He owed her the same way he owed the rest of his family.

He checked his phone and tapped the hot key for Hope. When it went straight to voicemail, he bit off a cuss. Since he always drew the kid promotions, he limited cussing. It was bad enough navigating a speech problem. He didn't need to slip up and cuss like his teammates in front of the kids.

Across from him, Talley dug through a purse big enough to hold two footballs. Without a word, she extracted a phone, touched the screen, and then handed it to him like it was perfectly natural for her to be in his place, his life.

The irony of the situation floated through his thoughts with the whirring of the connection.

"My phone was out of juice. I couldn't respond until I charged it at the hotel," Hope answered in a gush of words.

"Hope?"

He clenched the phone, praying she wouldn't hang up on him.

"Why are you using Talley's phone?" Hope snapped.

"Why are you ignoring my calls?"

"News flash, big brother. I was busy. You're not the only one with a life."

He moved the clamshell to the end table and stood. "So you answer and tell me you'll get back to me."

*Silence.* He locked on Talley's gaze. At least *she* was on his team.

"You found me," Hope said with an attitude he'd never heard from her before. "What's so urgent?"

"You tell me. You're having school problems, you don't

answer my call, and now you're giving me attitude. I thought you and me ..." He hesitated, scrambling for the right words.

"You and me *what?*" she said. "Used to be close? Used to talk? Used to watch each other's backs? The operative words are 'used to.' We no longer circle in the same orbit, Mr. Football Star."

"I have to make a living, Hope." He kept his voice low, praying his little sister would pick up on the hint and reciprocate. Her shrill tone was going to pulverize his brain. "You know that."

"I'll tell you what I know. I know you have no idea what I'm dealing with. Nobody knows, and nobody cares unless I don't jump when they call."

When the edges of Talley's phone cut into his flesh, he eased his death grip and leaned against the sofa cushions, waiting for Hope to finish her rant.

Keep chill. Little Sis would wind down if he didn't antagonize her. Yelling at her had never worked, the same as inactivity didn't work for him. He stood and paced to the kitchen, then retraced his steps to the fireplace.

"You're right," he said, once he could trust his voice to remain calm. "I don't know what you're dealing with. So, fill me in."

*Silence.* A trickle of sweat oozed along his side.

"Talley told you about Friday night?" Hope finally said.

"Yeah. Why, Hope?"

"I was just having fun, like you. It's not like I was hurting anyone. I didn't drive."

She might as well have opened his chest and cut out his heart. "You can't fix your problems with drugs."

"Really?" she shot back. "What are you going to do, call the police?"

"I'm your brother, not the enemy."

"There's nothing wrong with me wanting to have a life

too. You know I don't have to do something just because Mom and Dad think it's a good idea. It's my life."

Whit dropped to the edge of the couch. He didn't know what had changed with her, but a single call wasn't going to fix it. Talley was staring at him, worry creasing her brow. Man, she didn't know the half of it.

"Why haven't you told me about these changes?" He wasn't sure he wanted the answer—at least not tonight.

"When are you available to talk to me?" The defiant tone had returned to Hope's voice in spades.

"I've always been here. All you need to do is call."

"Not during your season."

He shoved to his feet. "Anytime." However, the way he'd choked out the word, he doubted if she'd believe it. He sure didn't. "We're coming up on the bye. I'll be home tomorrow."

Coach would have his hide with the playoffs coming up—which wouldn't help his contract negotiations. Not to mention his injury. Talk about a train wreck.

When Hope sniffed, he wished he were there to hug her, protect her from life's knocks. His career didn't mean crap without his sister, his family.

"You're coming tomorrow? Like that will happen," she said, but the resentment had left her voice.

Some of the guys on the team had talked about attitude swings with girlfriends or kids, but he'd never encountered them—until tonight. Add her bizarre behavior with the pound in his head and he'd traveled from a great game to a nightmarish rollercoaster ride.

"Hey, little sis. I'm coming home, tomorrow. Promise."

Silence invaded the connection. Whit tapped the screen. "Hope?"

"I'm here," she answered, but her tone didn't ease his concern.

Talley touched his arm and opened her hand for the

phone. At first, guilt tightened his grip. He'd screwed up. He needed to fix it. The pounding in his skull intensified, and his vision blurred. Talley held his gaze but not in challenge. Her liquid dark eyes softened with understanding. Although the game had beat him down, she had his back.

He'd once trusted her, but that was five years ago. Those shared secrets, dreams, love had faded with time. His frown intensified the spike drilling his forehead. She cocked her head, and he released the device, hoping she didn't notice the way his hand shook. Hope might be his sister and his responsibility, but he could kiss Talley for covering his blind side.

His grin opened the cut in his lip. Talley was using the same don't-mess-with-me tone with Hope she'd used with him during his tutoring sessions. She'd been tough, but he'd passed every class.

He eased back in his chair and let the cadence of Talley's low but firm voice wash over him. How could he let this happen? If Hope had given clues about her unhappiness, he'd been too distracted to notice. But he'd stayed in touch, made sure his family's needs came first. The season was insane, but he called twice a week, always. It wasn't enough.

When a hand, warm and soft, stroked his shoulder, he blinked.

Talley's concerned gaze made his throat tighten. "Are you okay?"

He shook his head. For a minute, he was back on the playground with Aaron chanting: *dimwit, dimwit, dimwit.*

Talley stooped by his chair. "Rachel's staying in Hope's room until I get back."

Although he didn't want Talley's pity, he couldn't stand, couldn't be strong and courageous like his dad and stepdad. Why hide the truth from her? Sure, he'd worked his tail off, taken brutal hits, but he'd failed the most important people in his life.

"Talley Quixote." Thank goodness she hadn't given up—even when he'd been a jerk. "Thank you for making me see."

"I'm sorry. Hope's popped off a few times but nothing like tonight." Talley glanced down at her hands and then returned his gaze. "Your parents, Hope ... they're my family too."

The sparkle of her unshed tears melted his resistance. He didn't give two flips what had happened five years or five minutes ago. Standing, he pulled her close, breathing in her essence. She smelled ... fresh. Baller babes always smelled like flowers or fruit. Not Talley.

He rubbed his cheek against her silky hair. *Fresh* didn't accurately define her scent. The beat of her heart throbbed against his chest. Her flesh rippled beneath his hands, causing his breath to hitch. Yeah, the ribs still hurt like sin, but he'd break them in two before he released her.

With his cheek pressed to her temple, his body aches eased. The murky, underwater feeling dissipated, and his vision sharpened. Maybe he *could* fix the problem. He just had to go home. Home? Something inside him shifted. That was it. Talley smelled like home.

He stepped back, and she lifted her chin. Bright eyes wet with tears seemed to look through him. When she moistened her lips with the tip of her tongue, he froze. Her eyelids drooped, and her breath, scented with chocolate, fanned his cheek. Few things scared him, but the moment seemed ... fragile, as though it might slip away if he didn't grab it.

With his index finger, he lifted her chin. "Please tell me I can kiss you."

"Thought you'd never ask." She lifted to her toes to meet his lips.

# CHAPTER SIX

Talley breathed Whit in, accepted him, encouraged him to step up the pace. He moved back and sank into the chair, pulling her onto his lap. When his big hands drifted toward her hips, her thoughts blurred. Hard muscle rippled beneath her palms. His insistent tongue, with its faint taste of milk, dueled with hers, tempted her.

The whine of an ambulance in the distance shot her eyes open. She'd lost her mind. Whit probably seduced women at the snap of his fingers, but she was no football groupie. She had a reason to be in his condo—an important one. And it wasn't a prelude to falling into his bed or back into a dead-end relationship.

As if sensing her withdrawal, he released her and leaned back against the cushion. She ignored the chill from the loss of his body heat and retreated to the corner of the couch, burrowing beneath the afghan.

"Sorry. That's been brewing a while," he said, his voice smoky from the kiss.

*For sure!* But there was no sense in denying her desire after that kiss. If the siren hadn't cleared her sex fog, there's no telling what would've happened. She could take a stab at the results and really hate the answer.

"Chalk it up to the crazy night," she improvised. "Your food's getting cold." *Too bad, she wasn't.*

From the downward turn of his lips, she wondered if Hope or their kiss had spoiled his appetite. As usual, Whit kept his thoughts to himself, so she checked out the twinkling cityscape outside the window.

"Nice place," she said. "Did it come like this, or did you hire a decorator?"

"Mom and Hope picked out the furniture." He cut the meatloaf into pieces. "I wanted leather loungers with cup holders."

A snort popped out of her mouth before she could stop it. "I like the blue."

"I had two choices: blue or orange." He gave her the cutest eye roll. "And when the Murphy women double-team a guy ..." He turned his palms up.

"The colors work." *Like they once had.*

"The realtor said the wood-planked walls give the place a contemporary jive." The familiar twinkle returned to his gaze. "My teammate Ivan swears women love the wood. It makes me twitchy, like I've overdosed on sugar."

A rosy blush brushed his cheeks before he ducked to eat his mashed potatoes. Although Whit had always attracted women, his speech difficulties made him shy. But that was the old Whit. Now, he'd attained superstardom with all the perks of fame, including crowds of adoring women. And yet, he'd seemed embarrassed. A mushy sensation settled in her belly.

"I wanted to paint the place, so Mom and Hope said they'd pick out a color for me. We were in Chicago playing the Bears and took a beating that night. Hope must have set her timer. Called me ten minutes after I fell asleep." He chewed a big bite and washed it down with the last of the milk. "Then boom, she lays it on me! She's scheduled a crew for six a.m. to paint the place Barney purple. Said it would go with the couch." He wiped the milk mustache from his lip.

She suppressed a groan. He looked so cute with a milky lip. And she really got off on the fantasy of removing the stain with her tongue. She shook it away, focusing on Whit in a purple living room. Her lips twitched. She suppressed her giggle. Between his dimples and those amazing blue eyes, the man was so darned endearing with the halting way he shared the story. A guffaw loud enough to shake the window glass honked past her fingers. With other dates, she might have been embarrassed. But not with Whit. Just like their college days, he made her forget her problems, have fun, enjoy life.

"Hope loves to hassle you," she said. "She told me she'd make sure the fame didn't go to your head."

"Hope's joke ended the painting idea. Mom swore I'd get used to the wood. I was glad the walls weren't purple."

"I was glad to see you don't live in a house decorated in black velvet, chrome, and glass." She gulped her chocolate and coughed. *Filter, Talley!*

Silence filled the room. The last thing she needed was to fan the desire simmering beneath the surface. A peculiar expression distorted his face. Well, maybe not peculiar. More like smoldering, like she was naked, and he was enjoying the view.

"I better get back and relieve Rachel." She cringed at the husky quality of her voice.

He pushed from his chair and rolled upright. "I'll drive you."

Talley bit her lip. What was wrong with her? While she'd regressed to a self-centered groupie, he was hurt and in pain.

"You've done enough." She retrieved her cell. "I'll call an Uber."

When he didn't protest, disappointment squeezed her

belly. "They'll be here in twenty minutes." She tapped her phone screen and pasted on her brightest smile.

"Do you want the nickel tour while you wait?" he said.

*Heck no.* "Sure."

With his shy smile and the upward lift of his brows, he almost looked like he wanted her to stay. Whoa boy, and she wanted much more than a tour. She nodded, despite the do-not-go-there warning bell jangling every nerve in her body. However, touring his house was a safer action than touring beneath his clothes. *T-minus nineteen minutes.*

"Guest room is in here." He opened a huge door measuring at least a foot higher than the top of his head.

She blinked, breathed in, breathed out, and then snapped her slackened jaw closed. "This is the guest room? Holy smokes, how big is the master?"

"Big enough." He raised his right brow, which sent images skittering through her mind: Whit tangled in the sheets, Whit touching her, Whit making love to her.

She shook her head hard enough to rattle a few fillings loose. *Seventeen.*

"This button closes the blackout curtain." While a wall of fabric extinguished the outside lights, a low whir filled the silence.

"Nice." Yikes, her voice sounded like a dog's squeaky toy.

"The comforter is gray." He winked. "Not black and not velvet—at least, I don't think it's velvet. Whatever that is."

He flipped on the light in the adjoining bath, and a funny sound erupted from deep in his chest. Or maybe the noise came from her. She blinked away the image of Whit in the shower. *Fifteen minutes.*

"The bathroom's in here," he continued.

His ginormous bathtub sent more hot images bubbling in her brain. She waved her hand in front of her face. Amazing that a place like this had an inefficient air conditioner. In late fall?

"Weird tub, huh?" His gaze drifted to her mouth. "Remember the water trough at Grandma's farm we used for our tadpoles?"

Her lips twitched. "The tub's trendy—and big."

*Twelve minutes.* Sweat trickled along her ribs.

"I'll notify Tony, the desk guy, to call when your ride is here." He turned to leave and hesitated, making her wonder if he might try another kiss. "I've also got to call my agent about my unexpected trip home."

If he winked one more time, she might act on her sex-starved thoughts.

"He'll be furious," Whit said. "Right along with Coach, but they'll get over it."

She resisted the urge to fan her face. *Ten minutes.* "Big game coming up?"

"Yeah, playoffs, plus contract negotiations." He rubbed his hand across his side. "But we're coming up on the bye week. It's late for us this year."

"I heard you mention it to Hope." *Nine minutes. For Hope. For the plan.* His gaze could roast a hot dog, and the way his lips moved—

She blinked. *Focus.* "Just so you know, I tried everything to turn Hope around before interrupting your schedule." *And seeing you again—even for eight minutes.* "I think a little brotherly persuasion will do the trick."

"I hope so." He hesitated. "My free time is limited until the season ends."

"So, are all the Cougars off this week?"

"Heck no!" Whit massaged his forehead. "Doc benched me because of my injury. But that doesn't mean I do nothing. I've got plays and opponents to study and a charity luncheon on Tuesday. I'll have to get out of it."

"Thank you," she said. "For the help, the chocolate, and especially for the explanation."

His brow wrinkled.

She rested her hand on his sinewy forearm. "I hate the silent treatment." Like she hated slow stinking time!

"Mom told me a man should listen more and talk less."

She followed him to the hallway. "When people and lives are at stake, you need to say something."

He glanced over his shoulder at her. "You've got the cause thing covered."

"Hope's important to me."

The right side of his mouth lifted in a sexy half smile that raced her heart. "She's at the top of my list too. But talking? You know about me. Not exactly my skill set."

Really? Mr. Superstar still carried the old baggage? "If we're discussing your learning issues, there's a lot going on."

The words flew from her mouth fast and pointed before she could stop them. Dang him, every time he disparaged his natural intelligence, she wanted to thump him on the back of the head. He'd worked hard in college, and so had she— before he threw it all away.

"It just took work to interpret it," she said. "Everything worthwhile requires work."

He nodded. "Sounds like Mom."

"They're her words." She softened her tone. "Like I said, your family is my family too."

"So, what are we going to tell Mom?"

"Ugh. Just poke me in the eye with a sharp stick."

Whit ran his hand along his neck. "I feel the same way, but this is too big to keep hidden."

"I hope Ava won't be mad that I came to you first."

"She will be, but she'll understand—after a good blessing."

"Hope, you booger!" First, the game, then her reaction to

Whit and now Ava. She'd rather watch that awful game again than tell Ava about the drugs.

"Hey." His hands warmed her arms and were way too soothing for her own good. "We'll do it together."

His shoulder looked really good about now. But she wasn't going to cry, and she wasn't going to start leaning on him again. He was taking a few days off to go home, not retiring.

"We have to leave at oh-dark-hundred. Hope has school, and I have to go to work." No matter how she worked it, the upcoming meeting would be dreadful. "Hope has cheer practice after school. I'll cut out early and meet you at the house."

"I'll plan to arrive after school," Whit said. "I'll text you when I'm fifty miles out."

"Thanks. No matter how old I get, I still despise reporting bad news to people I care about."

"We've had our share of confessing to Mom over the years."

She swallowed, but it didn't help the dryness in her throat. She didn't need additional reminders of how close they'd once been.

His gaze drifted to her mouth, and he leaned toward her. She needed to step back, say something, do something. Her fingers curled into fists, and her legs grew roots through his expensive hardwood floors.

He reached for his wallet on the side table. "I'll pay for the Uber."

"Don't insult me." She cringed at the harshness of her tone. Darned it, he shouldn't still tempt her. His money had never been a consideration—and now, neither was he.

"That's not—"

Talley drew a line across her throat. "I'm here because I love Hope." *And used to love you.*

He turned over his phone. "Your ride is here."

There is a God. She rocked back on her heels. Whit

seemed to have sucked the oxygen from the room. In the dim light of the hall, his eyes glittered with ... what? Resisting the urge to run her hand along his neck and press her lips to his, she collected her purse.

The decision to come to him on Hope's behalf had rekindled a long-banked fire. If she maintained her present course, she could guarantee heartache would follow—again. That's why she wouldn't let it happen.

# CHAPTER SEVEN

When Whit passed the "Welcome to Sunberry, North Carolina" sign the following afternoon, he breathed through the aches in his battered body. *Home always eases the pain.* With its twenty-thousand people, Sunberry offered the best of small-town charm and big-city amenities. He couldn't put a word to it, but he felt whole here. Well, as whole as he ever felt. Way better than knocking around in his Charlotte condo. There, he felt off, as if he couldn't quite get the rhythm of things. Sounded like homesickness. He snorted. Best keep that from Ivan. His bud's Alabama drawl echoed in his head: *wussy weakness.*

The combination of Atlantic salt and forest pine scented the air drifting through his open window. Although he loved football, the team, and a good postgame celebration, he missed Sunberry. Which was crazy considering he'd hated the place, right along with his brothers, Nate and Kyle, when Mom moved them there. Of course, teens created more drama than groupies at a party. After Dad was killed in Afghanistan, he and his brothers were bent on making life miserable. Exactly the reason he was cutting his little sister some slack.

He gripped the steering wheel. "Hope, you better be home and sober."

At Calhoun Street, the steady click of his blinker kept time to the thud in his head. The ache dulled with the familiar tree-lined street and historic homes. Memories of riding bikes, playing cops-and-robbers, and leaving chalked clues on the sidewalks warmed his belly.

The yellow two-story, with its twin porches and balcony, created the perfect backdrop to the red and yellow leaves. He huffed out a breath. If his side improved, maybe he'd rake the lawn. He used to enjoy working in the yard.

The truck bumped over the curb into the drive, and he rolled toward the detached two-car garage. Today, the closed white doors hid the bikes and sports equipment. He cradled his injured side and slid out of the truck. Sparse weeds peppered the lawn between the Murphy home and Talley's place, a blue single-story to his right. The Frost and Murphy residences still side by side, just like the day he'd met her. His family moved to the gracious yellow house the week after Ryan had married Mom. One month later, the Frosts had purchased the little blue house—and the rest was history. Good history but still history. He'd mow for Mom and Dad—just like old times. The memory eased the pressure on his shoulders.

His step lighter, Whit grabbed his duffel from the back seat and slung it over his uninjured side. The American flag whipped above the redbrick stairs leading to the front door.

In high school, he'd considered a military career. But since Mom had lost Dad in service, he didn't want her to worry about losing a son. The football-military comparison twitched his lips. His job had its risks, but the government wouldn't value his hide like the Cougars. Plus, the team followed up their contracts with plenty of green. Although he worked to keep his feet grounded, his chest grew a few inches every time he thought about paying off his folk's mortgage. Helping people, especially kids, made him feel good. Football made that possible. He fished his house key from his pocket.

*Pop!* What the—

He turned toward the sound. His duffel dropped to the ground. "Holy—."

"You're staring, Murphy," Talley hollered from the adjacent driveway.

*Ya' think?* Her red Miata almost gave him a hard-on—until Talley straightened beside it. Talk about eye candy. Tight denim covered fine hips, and the puffer coat and shoes that matched her car drew his gaze. His grin faded. He'd kind of gotten off on those boots she wore last night.

"Forget the dreaded meeting with Mom." The stiff brown grass separating the houses crunched beneath his feet. "Let's talk about you buying my dream car."

"I couldn't resist."

"Tell me about it." He ran his hand along the rear fender when he wanted to run it along her jeans.

"Most things don't tempt me. This little jewel"—she patted the latte-colored convertible top— "called my name, extra loud."

Yeah, he knew about wanting, except he gravitated to warm, curvy bodies. He opened the door and checked out the leather interior to keep from taking what he'd yearned for all night—Talley.

"Sweet," came out in his groan. "Was Hope at school?"

"She was. Now, she's at practice, and the basketball coach promised to keep an eye on her. If she leaves, I'll get a text. If she behaves, we should have an hour before she gets home."

"Right," Whit muttered, but he was more irritated with his lack of focus than with Hope.

He shouldn't have kissed Talley last night. Sex screwed things up, and he couldn't afford to mess with their friendship. Not with Hope jacking up the landscape.

"I can carry those bags in for you," he said.

Her grip on his arm surprised him. Maybe Talley lifted weights too.

"I haul my books and laptop back and forth to school every day." She pulled at the canvas bag. "You can drop the act. I know you're hurt."

Crap! Nobody wanted to hear a player whine about an injury. He turned on the smile that had distracted Mrs. Wiggs in fifth grade. "Only when I move."

Instead of reciprocating, she planted her hands on those curvy hips. "You've been playing for five years. How much money do you need?"

"Are we going to do this again?" Why had he let down his guard? "Football's the way I make a living. I'm good at it."

He *was* good at it. Same as he was a rotten prospect to give her what she wanted—a family. At one time, he'd wanted to. He still thought about it. But the genetic cards for a guy with expressive aphasia and a mixed bag of deficits scored a goose egg in the primo-daddy department. End of story. End of romance.

"You're good at a lot of things." The unforgettable fire flashed in her eyes. "I'm sure you could find a job that doesn't cause brain injuries."

"I appreciate your help and your concern." He sucked in a breath to tamp the frustration curling his toes. "The league's changed the rules, and I'm careful. I'm still running strong and want to play another two years."

For once, she remained quiet. No comeback. No argument. A man could get lost in those big brown eyes—once he overlooked her stink eye. He rubbed at the back of his neck.

"I like buying things for my family," he babbled like a girl.

For some reason, he needed her to understand. She'd walked out years ago without giving him a chance to explain. "I'll never be able to repay them but making life easier for them makes me feel good inside."

"Families are about love, not payback."

"Are you an expert on my family?" Whit squeezed his eyes closed. He hadn't meant to sound defensive, but she should know better. Know him better. "The bad crap came before your time."

He shifted his weight. He'd expected to feel better today. But with the drama, limited sleep, and car ride, he hadn't improved. Add in Talley hitting his pressure points, and the throb in his head caused his words to dangle out of reach. Worse, his speech came in starts and stops while he fumbled for them. He squinted at her huge eyes that took over most of her face. She blinked, frowned, and nodded.

"That's how you pay it forward. Admirable." She squinted, her features screwed into the tutoring mode, except she was learning, and he was teaching. "But when's enough, enough? You've been playing for five years."

He shifted his weight to his toes, but there was no place to go. Besides, he had no reason to question his choices. "I'm aware of the risks. All of us know them. We do our best to avoid injuries. But hits like last night happen. Besides, no one wants to hear about a player's pain. Not with all the money we make."

Her huff of air ruffled the hair covering her forehead and heated his blood hotter than the fire around his ribs. He couldn't say why her quirk attracted him. He'd even seen guys do the same thing. But Talley was no guy.

"Did they strap those ribs for you?" she asked.

He hated it when she changed the subject and forced him to scramble for an answer. "Yeah, but the tape itched worse than sand fleas, so I pulled it off."

"I've got some hypoallergenic tape in the house."

Like he was going to feel better with her hands touching his skin? No, ma'am. Not with the way he'd been reacting to her. He had enough trouble with Hope.

"Maybe later." He wanted her to stick around but needed to keep his distance. "Are you hungry? I'm going to grab a snack. We can work out our strategy before Mom gets home from the shop."

When she continued to stare at the pavement, he leaned down to crowd her. "You're also avoiding confrontation."

Talley glanced at the front door of his parent's house. She held up her palm. "Guilty. The ride home in complete silence with Hope was bad enough. But compared to telling your mom that I went to you first?" She drew a line across her throat, and her mouth pulled down.

He'd bet a kiss would make her feel better. Wouldn't hurt his feelings a bit. As a matter of fact, he could use a little mood-lifter.

He couldn't keep his mind straight. "When I got jammed up at school, I used to walk my bike instead of ride home. The delay never changed the outcome."

He turned toward his house and moved. When she hurried behind him, he almost bit a hole in his lip to suppress a grin. Misery loved company.

"Come on. We'll brainstorm a way to break the news." He dug out his house key. "Mom will be upset with you, but nothing compared to how mad she'll be at Hope."

"I despise ratting out Hope. I'm her surrogate big sister. I'm supposed to guide her, help her navigate life, not get her in trouble with her mom."

"And I'm her big brother. I've run interference for her for years. But this time, Hope needs to face the full consequences before something bad happens."

Inside, he stopped in the foyer. The aroma of chocolate

chip cookies brought his stomach to life with a growl loud enough to scare a cat.

"Uh-oh," he whispered. "I can count on one hand the days Mom hasn't gone into Robey's Rewards."

"Well, add today."

"Anybody here? Incoming!" He followed the sweet scent of chocolate and pastry. If stuff was going to hit the fan, he might as well take it with a cookie.

Sounds filtered from the back of the house. Talley trailed behind him through the family room to the back door leading to the screened-in porch. In the corner, the patio furniture was stacked nearly to the ceiling. A small table with an assortment of paint cans and brushes occupied the right side. In the middle of the enclosure, a wooden chest rested on old newspapers. On her knees beside the chest, his mother, Ava Murphy, painted a farm scene on the chest's surface.

"Whit!" Ava jerked her brush away from the scene she was painting.

"Prodigal son and Murphy gang member on the scent of homemade cookies."

Ignoring her frown, he pulled her into a bear hug. Man, he'd missed her. The aroma of chocolate and paint overpowered her peach fragrance. It wouldn't matter if she smelled like a locker room. He missed her. Missed the way this proud, determined woman filled his heart with joy.

Yep, he and Talley were in trouble. His heart scrimmaged in his chest, and the air thinned. He blew out a breath. Mom did that to him, probably did it to everyone she met. That was the thing about his mother. She was firm and loving and smart, and an overall super mom.

She pushed against his chest, and he released her. Above her nose, her brows joined. His goofy smile hadn't impressed her. But danged if he could straighten it.

"You're looking good, Mom. No one would ever know you launched three ornery boys into manhood."

She capped her paints and dropped the brush in a jar of clear liquid. "Sweet talk will not get you off the hook. How is it I didn't know you were coming home?"

"Bye week, Mom. Besides, I needed a good dose of home, chased with a few cookies and a cold glass of milk."

Like two bad kids awaiting punishment, they followed Ava into the kitchen, which served as the hub for the Murphy clan. A large tray of golden-brown treats cooled on the dark granite countertops. Saliva filled his mouth, and his stomach grumbled again.

"I'll have to make another batch. Those are for cheer practice tomorrow." Ava rolled her eyes and shook her head at him. "I'll pick up more chips after I check on the shop."

Over his dead body. He hadn't come home to create work for his mother. Considering she wasn't at the store on a weekday, something was up.

"Not necessary," he said. "I'll go to the store and check the shop for you on the way home from school. Bennie's wife still working for you?"

"Yes, and Bennie's putting in a few hours, too." Ava narrowed her gaze on him. "Why are you going to school?"

Jeez, he couldn't think. He massaged his temples. "Time out. We've got too many things going on at once."

Mom touched his cheek. "Are you okay? That tackle last night was dreadful."

Great. Now he had two women mothering him. "This is not about me."

"It's certainly not about me." Ava removed a magnetized notepad from the refrigerator.

"I thought you always paint your scenes at the shop," Talley said.

Whit's shoulders drooped. It was about time she helped

him out. Although she'd never been a coward, she sure was standing back today.

"I had some appointments this week, so I brought the table home." Ava smiled but didn't meet his gaze. "It saves time to work from home."

Since when? She loved the shop. He moved closer. "What aren't you telling me?"

First, his sister decides to be a druggie, and now Mom was sick? All that in addition to the fact he hadn't heard from his agent. Life would've been easier if he'd volunteered for tackle practice—as the dummy.

Ava wrote two lines. "I was going to ask Talley to watch Hope, but since you're home—how long do you plan to visit?"

"Through the end of the week."

"I'm so sorry, son. If you'd given me notice, I could've rearranged my schedule."

The hammer came to life behind his right eye. When he glanced at Talley, she shrugged. Great. Mom clearly had a secret about her health. She'd always been slim but wasn't gaunt, nor did she have a sickly pallor. Maybe she had more grays in her hair, but she was still an attractive woman. He'd always been so proud of her every time she came to a school function. She still turned heads. The guys were just a little older. So what was wrong with her?

"Don't change your schedule. But is there something wrong? Are you sick?"

Ava added more items to the grocery list. "Chill. When I have something important to share, my family will be the first to know. I'll be staying with a friend in Durham for a few days."

It didn't make sense. Mom never visited friends in Durham—even when Dad was deployed. He needed a snack; his head worked better on a full stomach. He turned to Talley. "Milk?"

She shook her head, looking as clueless as he was.

He retrieved a glass from the cupboard. "I won't eat the cookies."

"Better keep an eye on him," Talley said. "He's still got that sneaky fade."

Ava opened the refrigerator, but the way she narrowed her eyes made him want to hunch.

"Anyway," she said, disappearing into the pantry, "I'll be back for the weekend."

She placed a box of graham crackers on the counter, and Whit snatched her pencil and paper. With a frown line marring her brow, Ava opened the crackers.

"I always created the grocery list with you," Whit said, the memory easing his headache. "You'd tell me the items, and I'd write them down. You said it helped me with spelling. I just wanted to help."

Mom's face lit up the room and eased the pinch in his neck. "You boys were my salvation after your dad was killed." She scooted the box of graham crackers across the counter and turned toward the coffee maker. "Talley, coffee?"

"Let me get that for you," Talley said, but her thin voice sounded as though she expected the final hit to come in seconds.

Whit removed a packet of crackers. "Sorry I haven't been home more, especially with Ryan deployed."

While Ava moved to the pantry and then the refrigerator, Whit's thoughts spun. Mom opened her shop, Robey's Rewards, to honor his real dad, Josh Robey. Although the shop barely scraped by, she refused to let Whit buy the building for her, and she'd never let it go even if she risked her health.

The ache behind his eyes sharpened. After the Green Bay game, the throb had lasted a few hours. This one was harder to shake.

"That should do it," Ava said. "Oh, pick up a package of chicken breasts. I'll make that dish we like this weekend."

"I'll do the cooking while I'm home. I want to try a recipe Todd's wife gave me." He tucked the list in his pocket. "If I make the cookies, will you keep me company this evening?"

"I'd love to." Ava poured two cups of coffee and settled on a counter stool. "Now that the niceties are over, you can tell me why you're home and Talley's not at cheer practice?"

Beside him, Talley's cup clattered against the counter. Whit tapped her thigh from beneath the table. It was a dumb move, but he wanted her to know he had her back. Although not up to his usual game, he'd give it his best run.

"Murphy huddle," he said. Which was partially true. They'd come over to tell Mom what they'd found. It just wasn't a smooth play.

Mom had raised five kids, so she wasn't buying his delay tactic. Her usually loving gaze narrowed on them. "So, what's going on with Hope? It must be significant, or it wouldn't take the two of you."

A shudder inched down his spine. He didn't envy Talley's position. Although Talley had traveled to Charlotte and enlisted his help, Mom wouldn't like the pass. For now, all he could do was support his friend. As soon as Mom blessed her out, they'd have to navigate a conversation about drinking and drugs.

# CHAPTER EIGHT

Ava: one. Whit: nothing.

Talley suppressed the urge to lick the tip of her index finger and draw an imaginary check in the air. Now she was in the Murphy matriarch's sights. Walking a plank held more appeal.

Talley broke a graham cracker in two but couldn't eat it. Not with Ava's pointed stare boring into her. How could such a kind and generous person sport such a scary look? Talley swallowed a gulp of coffee and winced as it burned a path from her throat to her stomach.

"After raising four children plus one stray"—Ava's index finger shot out at Talley— "I've developed certain techniques. You are very dedicated to your students and don't take days off—unless something's up. Although Whit goes more on instinct, he always calls to share his plans. He avoids surprises like the plague."

Humor had helped Whit earlier, so Talley bumped her forehead with the heel of her palm. "There you go. Dead giveaway."

Ava nodded, her lips set in a flat line. "It's your pattern,

Talley. On weekends, you come over after you run and shower, usually about nine. Workdays, you're here in the lonely hours before bedtime."

"Okay, now I sound pitiful." *Try loser.* Talley swallowed. Based on Ava's grim look, the conversation had veered around a sharp curve and was plummeting downhill. Not good. Not good at all.

"We all slip into a routine, and mothers get better at reading their offspring's cues." With a lifted eyebrow, Ava's stare continued to laser through her forehead. "It's like there's a secret code and each child comes with a decryption key."

"I'll keep that in mind with my students." Talley bit her tongue, but it was too late. When her nerves tightened, her tongue loosened.

Ava's gaze traveled from Talley to Whit and back. "So, what's going on with Hope?"

"She's scaring me," Talley said, forcing the words past her parched throat.

"That makes two of us," Ava admitted. "I've noticed a change in her over the past month. I've tried to give her a little room, but it hasn't worked. Since we're having this discussion, it worked worse than I anticipated."

The breath lodged in Talley's lungs squeaked out. "She acts like I'm the enemy. We used to talk. Now she avoids me."

"So, you called in Whit?" Ava held Talley captive with her hard stare.

Ava didn't really interrogate. She read minds. When they were growing up, Talley, Whit, Kyle, and Nate had commiserated about Ava's skill. No one, not even brainiac Kyle, had figured it out. At present, nothing came to her, so Talley forged ahead.

"I worried if Hope found out I had come to you, it might fracture the relationship I have with her." Ava's look of hurt and disappointment made Talley's eyes burn with tears. "We need a link to her, especially now. I didn't mean to disappoint you. I just wanted more facts before I talked to you."

Talley inhaled a breath and released it. "We think she's stealing meds. Maybe from your medicine cabinet? That's a common source."

A chill raced across her shoulders despite the cozy kitchen. Most of the time, Ava maintained a steady, easygoing demeanor—unless something or someone got on her very last nerve. Based on her reddened cheeks and flared nostrils, anger might be an understatement.

"I thought I'd seen it all with the boys. I rarely take the pain meds I've been prescribed, and neither does Ryan. I've always kept them just in case. Sometimes, Ryan throws his back out. I should've pitched them." Ava stood. "One of you bring your cell. We've got work to do."

Talley exhaled, fanning her long bangs. Knowing she'd disappointed Ava ruined her pathetic hopes of relief. When the mean girls had humiliated her, Ava had hugged her and taken her shopping. When she'd bombed her first attempt at standardized college tests, Ava had bought her hot chocolate. Every time she'd needed a shoulder and her own mother was deployed, Ava stepped up to the plate to nurture her. Talley climbed the stairs to the Murphy's second level. So how did she repay Ava for her kindness? Secrecy.

In the master bath, the frosted glass doors on the cabinet creaked with Ava's jerk. "Kyle lied to me. He always had to be perfect. If he made a mistake, he never wanted to admit it. Nate was sneaky. If I turned my back, he was doing exactly what I didn't want. It was like his mission to get away with something without me figuring out it was him. Hope's a diva and my drama queen. If she scraped her knee, she'd tell me her leg was falling off. But drugs ..."

Ava pulled out a prescription bottle and read off the label, emphasizing every syllable. "Google that to see what it is."

"Pain medication," Talley read after thumbing through three screens.

Ava tossed it in the small wicker wastebasket and read off the next label.

"Muscle relaxant," Whit reported.

Ten plastic bottles rattled in the trash before Ava snapped the doors closed.

Talley followed Ava down the hall. "What was Whit's tell?"

Ava stopped outside Hope's bathroom. To open the door, she had to kick aside gym shoes, two blouses, and a pair of jeans. The vanity looked like a bomb had detonated in a makeup aisle. Foundation, lipsticks, shadows, and a variety of nail polish bottles littered the counter.

"Since you two are—" Ava scrunched her face. "Forget that. I don't have a description for your relationship. For that reason, the Mom Secrets shall remain for my eyes and ears only."

Whit dropped the trash can, and the clatter of plastic containers rattled the momentary silence.

"We're friends." Talley's voice sounded like the cabinet hinge. She swallowed. Fine time for her voice to poop out on her. "Estranged friends, but friends."

Ava gave her a pointed look, then stared over her shoulder —at Whit, no doubt. Ava followed an equal-punishment code for all family members.

"That's what gave the two of you away." Ava turned back to the messy bathroom. "You would've moved heaven and earth to avoid calling Whit for help."

Talley squirmed, and she'd bet her car Whit wasn't all that calm, but no way would she turn around to check. Of course, that didn't stop his body heat from warming her back.

Regardless of the fallout, she'd repeat her decision to go to Whit. Hope needed help, and Talley had to save the girl. Too bad helping Hope turned out to be so painful.

"Whit's always had a special bond with Hope," Talley said.

Ava opened the drawers on the right side of the vanity. "But not as strong as the link between you and Whit. That's why I can't tell you his inside story. But I'll tell you something I've learned about *you*." She narrowed her gaze. "And it's something that won't give him an edge if you two ever ..."

Heat flamed up Talley's neck. What did that mean? Did Ava think— Talley slapped her hand against her chest. No thinking. Thinking was not her friend today.

Ava inspected a prescription bottle hidden behind an acne cleanser, and Talley picked up where Whit had faltered and held out the trash basket.

"Hope, you're in so much trouble," Ava said.

The basket wobbled in Talley's trembling fingers. Focus. Today, and the rest of the week, was about helping Hope. She and Whit were history. Been there. Done that. Sported the cracked heart for her trouble. Whit eliminated all chances for reconciliation the day he chose the Cougars over her.

"You have an incredible sense of equity," Ava said, rummaging through the second drawer. "If there's a wrong, you battle to make it right. I'm sure that comes from your parents. That strength often runs in military families."

*But?* Talley followed Ava to Hope's bedroom and froze. "Whoa! I'm no neat freak, but ..."

Clothes littered the bed, the floor, then trailed into the closet. The color-block comforter and two pillows covered the bedside table, and the lamp teetered at the edge.

"This is disgusting," Whit said.

Talley grimaced. Harsh but accurate.

"How does she find anything?" Talley finally managed.

"A mother has to pick her battles. She only cleans when

she wants to go somewhere," Ava said. "That's my leverage. If there's a dance or a party, she cleans the room so she can go. Check it out on a Friday night before she leaves. It will be spotless. Other than that ..." Ava shrugged. "This is pretty much status quo."

"Our locker room never looks this bad," Whit said.

"You're a neatnik." Ava opened the curtains, and sunlight flooded the room. "Kyle's average. Nate's a little sloppy. Miss Hope?" Ava waved her arm like she was presenting a new subject. "Hope is my slob queen."

"This gives new meaning to the term shabby chic," Talley said.

"More like something from a Stephen King story," Whit muttered.

"Take the mattress off," Ava directed.

Based on the glance he gave her, Talley guessed Ava's request had surprised him. She'd bet boys stashed their contraband outside. Not her. Between the mattress and box spring had always been her go-to place for her mom's racy, off-limits romance novels.

Grunting to maintain a hold, Talley wrestled up the corner near the head of the bed while Whit elevated the lower end. They turned the queen-size mattress on its side. A wrinkled and very lumpy pillowcase rested on top of the box spring.

Talley removed a pack of cigarettes, a half-empty fifth of whiskey, and another pill bottle. She read the label and hesitated.

Whit moved closer. "What? Bad drug?"

Her hand shook as she showed him the bottle.

"What!" He sucked in a breath. "She took these from my place? I got them after that pileup in Dallas but didn't need them. I should've thrown them away."

"It doesn't matter where she got them," Ava said.

From the way Whit's brow furrowed, he didn't agree. Talley noticed the expression every time a professor gave him a low score after he'd busted his chops studying.

"Yesterday, I would've gone to my grave stating none of my kids got into drugs. After this?" Ava's shoulders slumped, and she slowly shook her head. "I better go to the ATM."

"Excuse me?" Talley said.

Ava dropped her chin to her chest and stared over the top of her reading glasses. "Bail money to get me out of jail after I'm arrested for assaulting my daughter."

"We'll form a line," Whit said. "I never thought my baby sister would pull something like this. Yeah, she's no angel, but drugs?"

"How do you respond to this behavior?" Talley asked.

Ava scooped up the contraband and dumped it into the trash. "Suspending her in the closet by her leggings might be too harsh, so I'm open to suggestions."

After they'd righted the mattress, Talley smoothed the sheets. Not that Hope would notice in her disastrous bedroom, but Talley needed to do something constructive. Life had taken a serious turn when she'd found Hope trashed and had continued one loop after another since that time.

"At this point, abuse seems conservative." Whit still looked as shell-shocked as she felt.

Ava checked her phone screen. "We've got about thirty minutes to strategize before Hope's due home. I've had my coffee limit today. Anyone want a cup of tea with me? We can use Hope's stash to spike it."

Whit tied the garbage bag. "I'll stay with milk."

While Ava prepared tea, Whit poked at the fire and then added a log. The flame crackled, and pine scented the room. Talley slumped in a striped side chair. If a fire was Whit's attempt to set a cozy mood, it wasn't working. Her heart ached. Since the day she'd wiggled her way into the Murphy family, their home equaled comfort, generosity, and love. But Hope's latest banished the usual sense of peace.

Ava brought in their beverages on a tray. "I'm thinking no car and no extracurricular activities until she goes to college."

Talley winced. "Two years?"

The right side of Ava's mouth twitched. "Too lenient?"

Talley's breath rushed past her lips. Leave it to Ava to add a hint of humor in the dark moments.

"I can give her a ride to school if you let her stay on the squad," Talley offered.

"I should have never bought that car for her," Whit said. "It gave her too much freedom."

"If you hadn't bought it, your dad would have." Ava touched Whit's sleeve, love burning in her gaze. "This behavior is not about freedom. It's about choices."

"Bad choices." Talley had made her share of toxic decisions at Hope's age. For that matter, she continued to make them. Maybe that's what made her sway toward leniency. "So, how do we make Hope realize the decisions she makes now can impact the rest of her life?"

Ava sipped her tea, and twin furrows creased between her brows. "It's a fine line. If I make the punishment too restrictive, she could rebel more."

Talley's heart hammered in her ears. "Do you think she'd run away?"

Whit groaned and massaged his forehead. Poor guy. He hadn't seen any of this coming, which was normal considering he was in the middle of the season. However, Hope had left clues. Talley hadn't recognized them, or maybe she couldn't accept they were valid—not with Hope, not with a kid surrounded by love.

"Hope's too smart and too much into the diva persona to leave home. Still ..." Ava stared at the flames. "I need to give her something to work for rather than take everything away."

Ava always seemed to know how to manage her kids—even when they made horrific choices.

"If she attends school and keeps her grades up, can she stay on the squad?" Talley leaned closer to her mentor.

Ava nodded. "I think that's a good plan."

"And her cell?" Whit said.

Ava exchanged a look with her son. "I took Kyle's away once."

Whit pushed away from the mantle. "That day is seared into our memory."

Talley nodded, making the connection. "Absolutely. It was the same day I was initiated into the Murphy gang. Maybe me initiating them into the Frost gang would have been more accurate. My braces started the incident."

For the first time that day, Whit grinned, and the room lightened like the sun had appeared after a terrible storm.

He pointed at her. "The tomatoes were your idea."

"How was I supposed to know Colonel Schmidt had a fetish about that stupid Porsche? I mean, really. It was a piece of steel. And it's not like we were aiming at the car. It was collateral damage in our feud with his bully son."

"I thought the colonel would haul us straight to jail," Whit said.

Ava's dark brows lifted in that knowing look that silenced most kids. "Thank goodness Ryan came to your rescue. I nearly went crazy because you boys were out on bikes long after dark. And, of course, you couldn't call me because I'd confiscated Kyle's cell. That ended my phone restrictions," Ava muttered. "Hurt me more than the boys. I better cancel my trip."

"No, Mom. Talley and I can handle it. Besides, you said Hope wasn't listening to you. Give me a chance." Whit shrugged. "Hope has always been my ally. If it's just me and Hope ..."

Ava massaged her temples. "It's not right dumping this on you. I'm the parent."

"And I'm her brother. You've done so much for me through the years. Let me at least try to do this for you—and Hope."

"Go on your trip. I can watch Hope at school, and Whit will cover the evenings."

"Durham's not that far away," Ava said. "But if anything happens—"

"You'll be the first one to know," Whit said.

Ava nodded, but the furrows in her brow remained. "I hope you can help her. I never keep anything from Ryan. But I haven't told him about Hope's latest. Like you, I was hoping she'd come out of it. Besides, he's got enough on his mind."

"We've got this," Whit said.

"One other thing on the punishment. What if you let her keep her cell only at school if her grades stay up?" Talley said. "If she stays out of trouble the first week, give it to her for one hour after school."

"A reward." Ava gave Talley a two-fingered salute. "Great idea."

Warmth radiated through Talley. "I'm happy to do anything I can to help." She paused, stunned at how much Ava's praise touched her. "You've done so much for me. There are so few ways for me to return your kindness."

"Hey." Ava stood and held out her arms. "Come here."

The minute Ava embraced her, Talley could actually breathe. They were going to get through this. With Ava in her corner, she could slay dragons. That's why she'd never thought of moving or even selling the house her parents had given her. This family, this community, meant home.

Ava's small hands gripped Tally's upper arms, and her hazel eyes glittered almost golden in their intensity. "You've already given me something," she said. "Another daughter."

Afraid her voice might shake, Talley nodded. Ava gave all of them purpose: Kyle and Nate through their grueling medical educations, and Talley through her various causes. Behind Ava, Whit watched, his features unreadable.

What was he thinking? And why, with Ava in his corner, did he risk his life playing sports? Ava and Ryan had always supported him. Only his brothers occasionally referred to his speech problems, and that was to keep him grounded. After all, siblings had to keep the ego in check.

"Throw Hope's stash in Talley's dumpster," Ava said.

"Really?" Talley blinked. "You think she'd resort to dumpster diving?"

Ava's bark sounded like a cross between a grunt and a chuckle. While Whit hauled the trash to the dumpster, Ava stood in the doorframe, her body dwarfed in the opening. However, her spirit held the strength of ten men. And her intensity? Talley smiled. Whit had inherited that trait from her.

"I always thought you and Whit were right for one another," Ava said.

Talley stepped back, and her bootheel sank into the mud at the edge of the Murphy porch. She covered her open mouth with her fingers, but her efforts were pointless. Ava often knew more about her thoughts than Talley did.

The sparkles on Ava's sneakers caught the late-afternoon sun. "Part of loving someone is accepting the traits that make them unique—even when they steal drugs from the medicine cabinet."

Although Ava was referencing Hope, Talley understood the matriarch's message. Her throat tightened again as she sifted through her feelings. News flash—she still cared for Whit, a lot.

# CHAPTER NINE

W ho knew a visit home could turn into a train wreck? Whit turned into the Murphy drive and hesitated. One hour and three minutes had passed since he'd escorted Hope to the house, then escaped to the grocery store for cookie supplies. Seemed like plenty of time for Mom to talk sense into his sister. Or not.

Loaded with groceries, Whit entered the house. The silence intensified the burn in his chest, not from his injury, but sorrow. What he wouldn't give for the raucous voices of men mingled with Mom's laugh. With a little luck, everyone would be home for Thanksgiving—everyone except Dad. His stepfather wasn't due to return from deployment for another six months. Mom always made the holidays special, so maybe Hope would snap out of it.

He placed the last box of cereal on the pantry shelf, and his cell vibrated against his side. His brother Kyle dressed in his lab coat, populated the screen.

"Hey, bro." Whit stepped onto the deck for privacy. "Thanks for getting back to me."

"So, what's really going on?" Kyle said.

His big brother didn't have the time or patience for small talk, so Whit gave him the skinny on Hope's latest and waited for him to process their hot mess.

"I can call Hope if you think it might help."

"She might not answer." Whit explained about his ambush with Talley's phone. "Plus, Mom's going to limit cell use when she's at home."

"It's about time," Kyle said after a huff of frustration. "Hope's always gotten off too easy."

"Mom's starting to see it as a problem. I talked to Nate while I was waiting for Hope at the school. He agreed." But Whit's gut told him something deeper haunted his sister. He'd acted out as a kid because he couldn't communicate his fears. Hope could talk the devil out of his pitchfork. That didn't mean she'd share deep fears any more than he'd talk about brain injuries. Besides, talking didn't fix things. Action did.

"We're seeing more and more problems with teens and drugs," Kyle said. "Actually, we're seeing more problems with all ages and drugs. But Hope?"

Whit paced the enclosure. "I hear you."

What he didn't hear was confirmation that Mom was visiting Kyle, which didn't make sense. She wouldn't go to Durham and ignore his brother, who attended medical school at Duke. Mom had a secret. Although Kyle hadn't mentioned it, he could be in on it with her.

"Keep me posted," Kyle said. "And Whit?"

"Yeah?"

"Thanks for covering for us."

The tension in Whit's shoulders eased as he picked up an armload of wood for the fireplace. Kyle had a different way of dealing with stress. However, Murphy blood ran in his veins. He'd come through, as they all would.

Inside, Whit added a log to the fire to keep the chill out of the air.

"Did you remember the chocolate kisses?" Mom asked, joining him. "Since I'm leaving tomorrow, I thought we'd have a late dinner and bake cookies first."

"Hope?"

"Sulking upstairs." She waved a hand. "Enough drama for one day. Let's enjoy some time together."

His shoulders drooped. Got that. Besides, cooking always eased his jitters.

The expansive kitchen included the usual stainless-steel appliances, except bigger. Big family. Big stuff. Big sticker price. The granite countertops looked purple to him, but Mom loved them. She'd put a girly flower-and-butterfly wallpaper in the adjacent breakfast area. Every time he cooked a meal in her kitchen, with its pinkish-gray backsplash, an image of that decorating lady, Martha somebody, flashed in his mind.

His mom reached for the turkey apron he'd given her last year.

He caught her elbow. "Nuh-uh. I'm baking today."

"You're serious?" A hint of humor glinted in her hazel eyes.

He nodded, and she handed him the apron. Careful not to rip the fabric, he struggled into the tiny garment. The strings dangled at his chest. Mom giggled when he tried to tie them behind his back.

"Hold on." She swatted at his hands. "You've got to let the neck down."

The apron dropped a few inches. Still ridiculous.

"I don't need it," he said. "I can wash."

"Got it." She tugged at the strings, tightening the fabric across the front of him. "No sense in messing up your clothes."

Still giggling, Mom turned him to face her. "Nice. Maybe I should take a photo and post it to my Facebook page."

Whit groaned. "Just what I need." He pointed at the counter. "Sit in my old place."

"Good gracious, Whit. I'll feel foolish."

Like he didn't? But he'd probably walk in high heels to hear her laugh again. "Humor me. I don't get enough family time."

*Way to go, Murphy.* He boosted her up on the smooth granite but avoided her gaze. Mom knew him better than he knew himself. If she picked up on the longing in his voice, he was toast.

In the space between Mom and the oven, he assembled the cookie ingredients and then opened the cupboard and removed the large mixing bowl.

"Preheat the oven," Mom suggested.

"Good catch." He pressed in the temperature. "I remembered to leave out the butter to soften."

"You're homesick."

He opened the drawer and rummaged through the measuring cups. Did the recipe call for two cups of flour or two cups of sugar, or two cups of both? Why couldn't he remember? He'd been making the cookies since second grade.

"Whit?"

"Yeah?"

"Is everything in Charlotte going okay?"

Near panic, he opened Mom's recipe box and flipped through the cards until he found Peanut Butter Blossoms. The small print blurred on the card. "Did you see I caught the winning pass?"

At least his voice stayed steady.

"I did. You always were ahead of the curve on motor skills." She tapped his chest. "I'm more concerned with your heart. Are you happy, son?"

Right now, happiness ranked rock bottom of his worries, but he dialed up a big grin for her and held his breath.

Her brow lifted, and her lips screwed into that mother-knows-everything grin.

He breathed, but it didn't release the tension coiled in his back. The team medicals had passed around pamphlets with warning signs of a concussion. Visual disturbances and memory lapses were on it, but so were a lot of symptoms he didn't have. He needed to take it easy.

"No special girl squeezing into your spot," he told her. "You're a hard act to follow. And please ignore what they print about me."

"If I believed the tabloid nonsense, I'd be concerned about STDs."

"Jeez, Mom." Heat singed his neck and cheeks. "A guy doesn't talk about that stuff with his mother."

Her laughter had always made him feel like he could do anything. Not today. Sprinkles of sugar trailed behind his shaky hand from the canister to the mixing bowl. Sunday night's game injured more than his side.

In two more years, he'd have enough saved to cover the Murphy educational bills and help set up Kyle's practice. Then he could move back to Sunberry and look for a second career. Right. What did former NFL players with no skills do? He had enough money, but he still needed work. Although he liked working at Robey's Rewards, it wasn't full time. Besides, the artsy-fartsy gene skipped him, and a man had to produce, contribute.

A fist formed in his belly and twisted. Talk about a gauntlet. With his thoughts colliding in his head, he couldn't make his tongue work. Not that Mom would call him out. She knew how his brain worked, and she accepted his silence. While he added the dry ingredients to the peanut butter mixture, she filled him in on Hope's last few months.

By the time she finished, his brain felt like the cookie dough clogged in the beaters. "Was I that bad in high school?"

She shook her head, but the terrible sadness in the downward turn of her mouth hammered at him. "You gave me very little trouble after the age of five. By the time you hit your teen years, you had Talley."

"But we got into all kinds of trouble together."

"Kid trouble. Fun trouble. But the emotional ups and downs skipped you because you had Talley for a companion."

He retrieved a spoon from the drawer, scooped out a tablespoon of dough, created a ball, and dropped it in the sugar. The heat from her stare warmed his face faster than the oven.

"I've never wanted my children to worry about me like I worried about my mother," she said.

His hands froze around the dough. Mom had been sad the days before Grandma died. But she'd also been ... silent. He remembered being scared because Mom was different. He'd come home from school, and she'd be sitting in her chair, staring. Didn't ask about school or his day. Just stared at the wall like he didn't exist. A chill raced along his spine, and he worked the dough faster.

"Of course we worry," he said after a moment. "We love you."

"We can't keep loved ones safe." She shook her head again but didn't make eye contact. "Heaven knows, I didn't want you to go pro. But playing has given you something I couldn't —pride in yourself."

Put that way, he understood. "I went to college because you expected me to. I didn't want to waste your money if I couldn't make it. When the football scholarship came through, I thought it would be okay. Talley and the school gave me lots of help. But I was barely getting by. Then the Cougars contacted me."

She smiled and nodded.

Whit placed the sugared balls onto the second cookie sheet. "I'm good at it, Mom. Plus, the money is crazy. I love buying things for you guys, making life a little easier for all of you. That makes me feel good."

Reaching up, she cupped his chin with cool hands. "I was proud of you long before you played football. But it's not what *I* think. It's how you see yourself. That's why I never tried to talk you out of going pro." Her radiant smile widened. "I love you. I would never do anything to take the joy of giving away from you—even if it means I might lose you."

The muscles in his neck tightened. Not trusting his voice, he nodded.

Mom pinched a piece of dough from a ball and popped it into her mouth. "Remember to keep evaluating your choices. Make sure your heart is your motivation. If you ever lose that, you have the means to find a different career, a different life."

A little blindsided, he ran her words back through his thoughts. Did she suspect his doubts about his life after football? "I'm good. I like my life."

Although she didn't say anything, her long gaze made him second-guess his words, like he'd missed part of an important play.

"You and Talley were so in love. Those women I see you pictured with in the tabloids ..." She shook her head. "Not your style."

"She wanted a family."

Mom's soft palm warmed his jaw. "She wanted *you*."

# CHAPTER TEN

Talley's life ran like a car with four balding tires. She'd fix one, and another went flat. Today, validated that theory.

With her index finger, she cracked the front drape. Whit had returned to the house ten minutes and thirty-three seconds ago. She bumped her hand against her forehead. *Get a life, Talley Frost.* Actually, she had one, and it included dinner with Ava and Hope ten minutes ago. So, did she stay true to her routine or play the stalker neighbor?

She wouldn't fail Hope or Ava, and she wouldn't fail Whit's friendship. Her commitment to the Murphy family included him. Resolute, she straightened her shoulders and left her tidy house for the place of her heart.

Talley knocked once and opened the front door. "Something smells heavenly."

"Kitchen," Ava called.

Like a hound on the trail, Talley followed the aroma of peanut butter and chocolate. She halted, her heart fluttering in her chest and every muscle in her body on instant freeze. With her legs swinging like a schoolgirl, Ava perched on the kitchen counter, forming dough balls, and rolling them in sugar.

A nice, fun, and wholesome picture, but not the reason for her mini heart attack. Bent at the waist in front of the oven, Whit served up a fantastic view of lean hips covered by tight jeans. When he stood, her gaze traveled from his lopsided grin to his child-size apron. Gorgeous.

"Want to help us bake cookies?" he said.

Oh, she wanted something all right—something a heck of a lot more satisfying than a peanut butter blossom.

She blinked away the obscene thoughts of Whit. "Only if I can brew a cup of coffee to go with it."

Ava popped a broken piece of cookie in her mouth. "Mm, the cooked ones are almost as good as the dough. I guess we're doing a cookie dinner."

Comfortable in the Murphy kitchen, Talley retrieved a mug from the cupboard. "Whit? Ava?"

"I stop drinking caffeine at noon." Ava pressed chocolate to the last cookie on the pan.

With a mitt in hand, Whit picked up the baking sheet and transferred the warm, lightly browned cookies to a plate. "I could go for a glass of milk."

"One milk coming up. Ava?" Talley said.

"Sure. I need the calcium and protein. What food group includes cookies?"

Talley placed a pod in the coffee maker. "Happy foods."

After filling two glasses of milk, she collected her brew, and together, they moved to the breakfast bar.

She raised her cup. "To great treats and greater friends."

"Great family," Ava corrected.

Warm, delicious cookies couldn't compare to the joy of being with the Murphy family—her family, even if they were adopted. Although Whit would always possess a special place in her heart, she had to contain her feelings to friendship or a brother-sister relationship.

Whit popped an entire cookie in his mouth, chewed, and swallowed. "I should open a bakery."

And she should focus on the Hope problem instead of the Whit temptation. "Did you come up with anything new?" she asked.

Ava shook her head. "Just moving forward." She snatched another cookie from the plate. "I think Hope's good mood will be a stranger until I lift her restrictions. And that's why I'm having a sugar dinner. Tough love stinks."

Talley bit into the warm cookie and held up her index finger. "Can we put off the details of your mom-talk for a minute? I need a few selfish minutes to be one with this delicious cookie."

Ignoring Whit's smirk, she savored the rich flavors. The impending drama stopped clouding her thoughts. Although she wanted to devour her treat like Whit had done, she nibbled around the edge, enjoying the blend of peanut butter and sugar. She popped the chocolate center into her mouth and licked all trace of the snack from her lips.

"Okay, I'm fortified with caffeine and chocolate," she said.

After Ava gave them a brief rundown of her conversation with Hope, the cookies lost their appeal.

Whit massaged his forehead. "Wow! Sorry, Mom. I should've stayed to back you up."

"No." Ava glanced at the stairway as though looking for Hope. "You needed to know the highlights so you can help. However, some conversations between a mother and daughter should be private."

Talley swallowed. Thank goodness she'd stayed home. "What's the plan?"

"If it's okay, I need to leave early tomorrow." Ava patted Whit's muscled shoulder. "You two will be on your own. Who knows? Maybe a star will rise in the east, and the camels will march by, and Hope will miraculously see the light."

Whit drained half of his glass, leaving a milk mustache on his upper lip that made Talley consider licking it off. Heat danced through her body in a variety of rowdy cheers. She sipped her brew—as if she needed more heat. What was wrong with her? Hope had a serious problem, and Ava was depending on her.

"Enjoy your time away," Talley said. "We'll watch the home front." If she could keep her eyes off Whit.

"Talley has the school front covered. I'll go to practice and then make sure she comes home. Maybe she'll open up about what set her off."

"I've always been able to depend on you." A loving glow highlighted Ava's smile. "You were a special boy who grew into a very special man."

"Okay, Mom," Whit said.

"Well, it's not like Talley's a stranger."

"No, ma'am." Whit captured Talley's gaze. "We're not strangers."

A lustful gleam sparkled in his hooded gaze. Talley swallowed past the hum in her head. Holy smokes, every cell in her body begged to snuggle near him, and her girl parts didn't give a flip if Ava saw her reaction. Since she couldn't cross her legs, she curtsied, like an idiot.

Halfway through her bob, it hit her like an arrow. The love between Ava and Whit wrapped around her heart. Tears stung her eyes.

"Are you okay?" Ava asked.

"Sorry." Talley pressed her palm against her chest. "It's watching ..." She huffed out a breath. "The love in this house fills me up inside. It's like my heart is going to float out the top of my head."

"What a lovely thought," Ava said, giving her a hug. "You

look so much like your mother. I'll never forget how devastated she was after she decided to let you remain in Sunberry."

"You talked to her about that?" Talley said, trying to imagine her in-control mother sobbing in Ava's kitchen.

"She didn't tell you?" Ava sighed and shook her head. "Your parents always struggled between duty and family. But letting you stay behind broke their hearts. You were their little girl, and they were determined to make you happy."

A strange, disoriented feeling swallowed Talley, and she couldn't balance. She knew it was her perception that was warped, but she couldn't get her head around it. They'd left her for their careers. At least that's what she'd always told herself. Her version made more sense. She'd been a sulky teen, concerned about her friends and her life. They'd been committed to the country, a bigger, more important worldview. The idea that leaving her behind and honoring her wishes had hurt them had never occurred to her.

"Why would my mother keep that a secret?" Talley's voice was almost a whisper.

"Because a mother will do anything to protect her children," Ava said gently. "I'm so sorry. I didn't realize you were unaware of your parent's feelings. Take some time. If you want to talk when I return, we can. Besides, we've had enough drama for now. Whit, since you did the baking, I'll clean up. Oh, and there's soup in the slow cooker, but it will keep if you're full of cookies."

"I'll pass on the soup, but I can take a turn with the cleanup," Talley said, thankful for the diversion. "At least you added the chocolate to the cookies. All I did was eat the end results."

Ava removed a clean dish towel from the drawer. "I'll dry."

"No, ma'am." Whit took the towel from Ava and followed Talley to the stainless double-bowl sink. "This was my party, and I remember sitting in that spot, thinking you got to do all the fun stuff."

Talley squirted soap in the sink. "Washing dishes?"

"Are you kidding?" he said. "Bubbles and water?"

"And more on the walls, floors, and counters than in the sink," Ava added. "When he was three, I told him no and left to put in a load of laundry. I returned all of ten minutes later, and he'd filled the sink with bubbles and water and then submerged every dish in the house."

Talley washed a cookie sheet. "The helper."

"The problem child," Whit said in a sobered tone.

"You were my spirited son," Ava corrected. "When you looked at me with those big blue eyes and said you were helping ..." Ava shook her head. "I couldn't get mad. You were so excited about doing a chore for me."

Whit winked at Talley, and the pan slipped from her fingers, splashing bubbles in the air.

He wiped a small mound of foam from his cheek with his shoulder. "Spirited? I'll have to remember that one."

Talley rubbed at the bubble on her nose and popped the one floating in her mind. She liked standing side by side with Whit and listening to the cheerful banter—too much. It wasn't just her reemerging feelings toward Whit. This family had given her a second home, an open mind, and an open heart.

ONCE THEY'D WASHED, dried, and stored the dishes, Whit lifted his arms to remove the tiny apron and froze. A sound between a croak and a curse filled the air.

"Are you still suffering pain?" Talley said.

"I need to move." He checked his wristwatch. "And turn in early tonight. Can I walk you home?"

She snorted. "I think I can find the way next door."

"I think you're afraid to be alone with me."

The stinker knew she couldn't pass up a taunt. "After last night's wreck, I doubt you can keep up." She forced out a little laugh, but her attempt at humor had done little to defuse the bomb inside of her.

Outside his house, Whit shoved his hands in his pockets, and Talley threaded her arm through his.

"I miss what we had." He stopped at the drive. "I miss you. But we can't go back. I'm not leaving the NFL. It's the only thing that makes sense for a guy like me."

"Wait." Talley stalled somewhere between him missing her and football. "Translation, please."

Whit's mouth, warm and welcoming, covered hers. She leaned into him, seeking the elusive something instinct told her he could provide. His big, wonderful hands slid down her back and snugged her so close she couldn't tell where her body stopped and his started. He angled his chin, and his tongue probed for entrance. She accepted him with a sigh, savoring the taste of peanut butter and chocolate.

When he released her, she wanted to protest, needed to. Then there was the problem of her rubbery legs. Without Whit's hold, she'd probably be on her bum.

"Was that clear enough?" His hoarse tone matched the desire filling her veins.

"Heck, no." She tugged him closer to get another taste. "But I'm too aroused to argue."

He flashed a dimple, and she abandoned all resolve to resist him for a minute, a day, a year. She didn't care. She'd be with him for as long as he wanted.

"Do you know how hard it was for me to let you leave last night?"

"Stop," she whispered. "You had me one second after that kiss started."

He teased the side of her mouth.

"Whit," she said on a sigh.

"Only forty yards to your house, give or take. I'm betting you have a nice bed." He worked his brows.

What had she done? Talley dropped her forehead against his chest, and her cheeks burned with embarrassment. "I can't believe we kissed like that on the front walk. What if your mother was looking out the window?"

"You seemed to enjoy it. I know I did."

Good gravy, yes, she'd enjoyed it. Just thinking about what he'd suggested made her brain turn to mush. She needed to laugh, or at least, giggle. Turn the offer into a joke before she grabbed his hand and hauled him into her bed. Instead, she closed her eyes.

He tilted her chin and held her gaze. "So, do we have time? We're only a few minutes away."

"If it were only that easy."

"It is easy." He winked. "Focus on what your body needs and keep your head out of it."

But what about her heart? Despite her physical needs, that question cleared her thoughts. The sidewalk intersected behind them—right to her house, left to the Murphy's. Too bad her decisions weren't that easy.

His hand drifted from her shoulder to her elbow. "I want you," he said, the earlier playfulness gone from his expression and tone. "But I've never lied to you. I love the game, and I'm not ready to give it up."

Since she couldn't get her mouth to work, she nodded.

"So, think about it. Us." He squeezed her hand. "See you tomorrow."

"Wait!" She licked her lips.

He reeled her in so close she could feel the whisper of his breath against her cheek. The sky blue of his irises deepened, darkened.

"You're aroused." His husky tone amped her hormonal

response up another notch. His scent, mingled with sweet pastry, lured her closer. She drew in a ragged breath of fresh air, which was a good thing because she sure didn't have any words to fill the void.

When he kissed her forehead and released her, she almost melted to the ground like some goofy cartoon character.

A sexy grin lifted his lips, but his gaze remained hot with promise. "Now you're definitely thinking about it."

# CHAPTER ELEVEN

He had this. With a scrape of his knife, Whit slid the vegetables over the meat and lidded the pot. Although in the final countdown, he believed he could turn Hope around. Mom's secrets still bothered him, but she'd come clean soon. He just hoped her revelation wouldn't be bad news. As for Talley Frost? He set the timer and resisted snapping the dish towel. She was coming around too. All he had to do was get her in his bed and keep her out of his head.

He checked the time on his phone. Hope's practice would be over soon. After that, game time.

Fifteen minutes later, Whit parked across the street from Sunberry High. His position provided a clear view of the side exit despite the chain-link fence surrounding the school. The tap, tap, tap of his fingers against the steering wheel filled the silence. Practice ended five minutes ago, but still no sign of Hope. The dash clock progressed one minute with the ooze of sweat trickling along his hairline.

The school door opened, and a group of teen girls emerged. They looked so young, talking and laughing. Straggling behind them, Hope walked out. She'd always been the

Murphy social butterfly, dancing from one group of kids to the next—but not today. He blinked at the face-slapping change in her.

Although he loved his sister like air, today she looked like a guy could buy her with a nickel and get change. Whit stepped to the street and raised his hand to draw Hope's attention. Tension coiled in his muscles with each step she made toward his truck.

*You've got to be kidding.* He squinted. Since Hope had been to basketball practice, he'd expected a warm-up suit, not jeans two sizes too small for her curvy frame and a skimpy red top under some guy's letter jacket. Top? That didn't describe the scrap of fabric. It looked more like underwear. Pain raced up his face at the force of molars on molars. Whit worked his jaw and tried to relax before he broke a tooth.

With her big brown eyes and dark curly hair, Little Sis was a knockout. According to Mom, she looked like some old movie star named Audrey Hepburn, so he'd googled the starlet. Sure enough, his sister resembled the actress. Except the woman had been shorter. At five feet eleven, Hope could look him in the eye—if she stood on her toes.

Her height had never worried her, and it wasn't twisting his shorts at the moment. Yeah, she was tall enough to stand out. But it was her dangerous curves, long legs, and come-on look that burned his pipes from his throat to his stomach. If she continued her present trajectory, he'd have to leave the team so he could guard the blasted house. Guys would be all over her, especially with Dad deployed.

"It's chilly out." He held her gaze but didn't doubt every boy in Sunberry would zone into the way that scrap of red emphasized her breasts beneath the open jacket. His fingers curled into fists, but he refrained from zipping the jacket to her chin the way he'd once zipped her snowsuit.

Hope placed her fists on her hips. "Got something to say about my clothes, big brother?"

"More like the lack of them." He slipped behind the wheel. "Has Mom seen that top?" Dad had missed it because he would've used it to kindle a fire.

The slam of the passenger door shook the truck. "I thought you were coming home to hang with me and recover, not nag about my wardrobe."

"I came home to talk to you." He bit off his words to keep from raising his voice. "Find out what's going on."

She shrugged and rolled down her window. "I'll catch up with you at Hot Cups," she hollered to the girls climbing inside an aging Honda.

Whit thumped the console. This was not looking good. Since Mom had laid down the law last night, he'd felt guilty about his extra precautions—until Hope strutted out the gym door. Plus, his precautions made it hard to get her to open up about her need to self-medicate. He swallowed. Call out the problem for what it is. His sister was using drugs.

Hope checked her cell. "This isn't a good time for me, but I can give you ten minutes. Then I'm meeting my friends."

*Ten minutes, and she was heading home—even if he had to tie her Subaru to his bumper.*

She glanced at him, the beginning of a smile twitching her lips. "I could be late if you wanted to take a side trip to the Jacksonville Mall. I saw a great pair of knee boots there, and I'm low on cash."

Yeah, well, he was dangerously low on patience. "First, we talk."

He locked the doors with a click and ignored her narrowed eyes. His sweet little sister no longer inhabited the body beside him.

"How much is the Women's National Basketball Association paying players?" Hope asked.

He gripped the steering wheel. Her lateral questions were more challenging than an offensive play. "I don't know. But it'll change by the time you graduate college. Why?"

Her complexion turned one shade lighter than that skimpy blouse she wore. "I've decided to follow in your footsteps, except for the degree. The player I talked to said if I was good enough, I might get an offer my sophomore year."

"Wait." Whit's head careened like a car on ice. "What about vet school?"

Hope waved her hand. "Too hard and too much school."

"But you're smart. You can do anything."

"Smarter now since your stunning example." She beamed at him. "It was right there in front of me. I don't know what I was thinking."

She was talking too fast. And she was so happy—that was coming through loud and clear. He had to be missing something. Next time, he'd make sure Talley joined them.

"Slow down, sis. I'm still recovering from a rough game."

"Boy was it ever," she said. "They creamed you. I'm so glad basketball is my game. Football is too rough."

"Me too," he said. Except he wanted her to have a career, not a game. "But I love football—"

"Duh. The money is awesome," she said. "So how much will you get the next contract? Will the Cougars stiff you since you're getting older? I read your contract's in the air, and you may end up going to the West Coast."

He massaged the sore place on his head. His entire body still ached. And her perfume, some thick, flowery fragrance, had to be swelling his brain. He pressed the window lever, and the cool breeze fanned his face.

"You know the science on concussions is pretty scary," she was saying.

He held up his hands. "Time out. We're talking about you. Your future."

"It's a conversation, big bro."

"Just listen to me." Dang. How did he have a conversation with her without yelling? Her idea was insane. "You're smart. You don't need to get beat up to make a living. Besides, a sports career is short, so you need a degree to earn a living after you retire."

"I told you I was following your lead."

Her agreeable smile and demeanor raked down his spine like a cat's claws.

"You've taken care of our family. I won't make as much, but I'll save my money. When the body gives out—" She stopped and studied him. From her scowl, she wasn't impressed with his appearance. "You really do look wrecked. If you've got enough money, maybe it's time to retire."

"Thanks for your support," he muttered. It was like talking to the dog. Although she kept smiling and nodding, he wasn't getting through.

Hope's phone pinged. "Oops. Got to go. The team's meeting at Hot Cups. You should join us. You look like you could use caffeine."

He blinked, collecting his thoughts. That was the sanest thing she'd said in the last ten minutes.

She opened her door. "What time's dinner?"

"No Hot Cups." Whit firmed his voice despite his murky thoughts. "Mom grounded you."

"Well, Mom is out of town."

"I'm not."

At least she'd stopped smiling. When she pulled the door back closed and placed her hands in her lap, his thoughts spun like he'd had too much to drink—or too much of Hope's stash.

"It's not fair. I'm not a big druggie if that's what you're thinking," she said.

"Yeah, li'l sis, that's exactly what I thought." When his two remaining brain cells rubbed together.

Hope shrugged. "I'm an opportunist."

If she smiled one more time, he'd probably blow a blood vessel.

"When I find something interesting, I check it out," she continued. "I've only tried Oxy the one time Talley busted me. I can't believe she ratted me out."

He couldn't believe this conversation.

"I could see a beer once in a while. Maybe a wine cooler. But drugs?" The strain in his voice seemed to echo in the truck's cab.

"One Oxy chased with a wine cooler," she said.

*Since when were opioids no big deal?* "This makes no sense. You have everything rolling your way. You're smart, pretty, have a wonderful family who loves you—"

She gave him a dramatic eye roll. "It's not supposed to make sense. It's supposed to be a new experience."

When had he gotten so old? "Kids who experiment with drugs end up dead or addicted."

"And I'm supposed to be the Murphy drama queen. Listen to yourself. It was *one* time." She held up her index finger for emphasis.

"It better be the last time." He gripped the steering wheel so hard his hands cramped.

"It probably will be," she said. "I'm not going to be a druggie, so get over it, big bro. This has been fun, but my friends are waiting for me at Hot Cups."

"Only if you plan to walk there."

Although she looked like steam might come from her ears, she maintained control. "I experimented one time. It wasn't cool. It won't happen again." She removed her keys from her bag. "You wanted me to talk. I talked. Told you my plans. Which aren't that different from yours." She opened the truck door. "Now, I'm going to Hot Cups for thirty or forty-five minutes, and then I'll join you and Talley for dinner."

He'd hoped things wouldn't come to this. He and his brothers had been rowdy teens, and they'd tried everything at least once—except drugs. They'd never crossed that line. And he couldn't just let his sister experiment and ignore it. Not on his watch. Mom was depending on him.

The confines of the truck cab seemed to diminish. Sweat moistened his brow. He slapped his hand against his knee to stop his heel from tapping the floorboard. Hope walked around the chain-link fence to the student parking lot. Even through the links, her features were clear, her step almost jaunty. Whit suppressed a smile. *Wait for it.*

Through the driver window of her Subaru, Hope's head canted down. Although he couldn't see her movements inside the car, he ticked off how it would go. She'd get in. Fasten her seatbelt and power the engine. She'd try to start the car twice before it sunk in. His lip twitched. When she finally turned toward him, her pretty eyes narrowed.

*Gotcha'.*

Although he loved winning on the gridiron, his success with his sister left a nasty taste in his mouth. If this was an example of tough love, he wasn't a fan. Ignoring the stiffness in his muscles, he stepped to the pavement, walked to the truck bed, and lifted Hope's battery for her to see.

"Get in unless you want to walk home."

He had to hand it to her. His usually hot-blooded sister kept her cool. No cussing, no foot-stomping. She strolled back to his truck and slipped into the passenger seat.

"This is wrong," she said.

He squinted in the afternoon sun. For a minute, he could've sworn she'd smiled. Like the whole thing was a big joke. Anger rolled his stomach. They were talking about drugs—bad drugs.

"Consider it an insurance plan," he continued through a clenched jaw. "You, me, and Talley are going to share a nice evening at home."

"I'm home almost every night, and so is Talley," she said. "Unlike you, the millionaire who always wants one more year, I'm happy with my life. This disagreement isn't about my one big experiment. It's about my career decision. Pretty hypocritical if you ask me. A sports career is fine for you, but not me."

Although her words hurt more than the effort to lift the battery, he waited for her to fasten her seat belt. He'd figure out a way to get her car home later. For now, he couldn't wait to continue the discussion at home with Talley. Man, did he need someone trustworthy to back him up.

# CHAPTER TWELVE

At the quacking ring of her phone, Talley spilled the contents of her purse on the black granite counter to locate it. Her friend Rachel's name appeared on the screen. No, no, no. She needed a report from Whit about what happened after practice, not a social call.

"This is really bad timing," Talley said instead of hello.

"Sorry. I know you and Whit are up to your Buster Brown's in alligators reeling in Hope. But I've got an important request with a teeny-weeny runway."

Talley ignored the way Rachel had used baby talk for the teeny-weeny part. It was kind of funny, and her best friend rarely made requests. But doggone it, since the moment Whit kissed her, her life had gone sideways.

"O-kay." Talley leaned against the counter. "But I'm awaiting a call. If it comes in, I'll have to take it."

"Got it. I'll be fast and to the point. I need Whit to speak to the Scouts."

Talley groaned. "That's not a request. It's a miracle."

"But he'll do it if you ask him," Rachel persisted.

"He kissed me." The words erupted from her mouth like a warm, shaken soda.

Rachel whistled. "No wonder you sound crunchy. Was it good?"

"Do not encourage my lascivious thoughts."

"It was worrisome leaving you alone with him after the game," Rachel said. "But when you talked him into coming home, I figured the risk was worth it. Guess I figured wrong."

"The kiss was a momentary lapse in judgment." Talley grasped the feeble excuse like a lifeline—with an anchor at the end.

"A lapse with lingering effects," Rachel said. "Not a good sign."

"You're supposed to be giving me encouragement."

"As your friend, I'm giving you honest feedback."

Talley slapped her palm against her forehead, delighted Rachel couldn't see the action. Of course her friend had to provide the honesty slap.

"Talley?" Rachel's voice raised in concern. "Are you sure you're okay? Maybe you're not over him. I could fix you up with my cousin's friend. He lives in Wilmington and supposedly is one smoking fireman."

Talley stifled another groan. The last hot fireman she'd dated had an entourage of old girlfriends.

"No matchmaking, please." Talley slipped down the wall to sit on the floor.

"At least Whit's a good brother," Rachel said. "He picked up Hope from practice. That's a good sign."

"I was so sure I was over him."

"Aw, hon, I'm so sorry," Rachel said. "But the two of you were always the perfect couple."

"Don't remind me."

"Maybe he'll retire soon."

"I'm not hopeful." Talley blew her bangs from her forehead.

"It's been five years. That's a long time for football."

*Like she didn't know the statistics.* "Whit loves the game."

"Not all players die," Rachel whispered. "If the spark's still there, give it another shot."

She did, every night in her nightmares. In the first clip, Jeff goes down. Second clip, the team surrounds him. A trickle of sweat oozed in front of her ear. Third, the players cover the body with a sheet. Talley shuddered. But it wasn't Jeff's face in her dream; it was Whit's. She swallowed to staunch her nausea.

"I can't go through that again," she whispered. "Worse, he's hurt."

"I know," Rachel soothed in her southern drawl. "It was on the news."

Talley straightened and wiped her eyes with a tissue. "So, you need a speaker? I've got a plumber friend in Emerald Isle." Their short relationship had fizzled, farted, and died before the second date. "He'd probably talk to the boys."

"A plumber? Seriously?"

"Are you kidding?" Talley said. "Boys love toilet humor. He can tell the Scouts about the bizarre things he's fished out of commodes."

"The plumber is not what I'm going for." Rachel's defeated sigh cut through the cell's reception.

"Policeman? I know—"

"The sheriff visited last month," Rachel said. "If you could ask Whit ..."

Since the Murphy driveway remained vacant, Talley trudged to her bedroom. "Rachel, Whit's a good guy. He'd probably donate. But he doesn't like public speaking. That's why you rarely see him interviewed."

"Can't you ask? I know I'm being pushy, but it's for a good cause."

They were *all* good causes.

"You know the little redheaded boy, Parker Evans? He was with the Scouts at the game," Rachel continued.

How could Talley forget? She'd almost lost the little booger in the men's room. "He's the live wire?"

"Exactly."

"Good to hear because he nearly gave me a heart attack," Talley said. "And that was before the game started." Of course, the boy's antics in the stands helped distract her from the game. She loved his energy and enthusiasm—as long as he didn't hide from her.

"His mom was thrilled he was so active," Rachel clarified.

"Oh, I can attest to his activity level." Talley pulled her sweater over her head.

"Until he arrived at the stadium, Parker hadn't spoken since his dad was killed."

Talley's fingers froze on the zipper to her skirt. Come to think about it, the boy had been quiet in the parking lot. She thought that was the reason Coach had assigned him to her.

She pressed her hand against her forehead and squeezed her eyes closed. "Please tell me his dad wasn't a—"

"Parker's dad was killed in Afghanistan three months ago. That football game in Charlotte worked as a light switch for him."

"Poor little guy." Talley's chest squeezed, making it hard to breathe. "I didn't even think. I just knew he turned into ADD kid the minute we joined the line to enter the stadium."

"He's nearly back to normal," Rachel said, her drawl picking up speed. "His mom's doing everything she can to keep him engaged. She started taking him to the high school football practices."

"Is it working?" Talley asked, but she already knew the answer.

"He's all about football. On the internet, library books, you name it."

"And he would be over the moon if Whit showed up at your Scout meeting?" Talley guessed.

"We don't schedule meetings this close to the holidays, but I couldn't turn Pam down. Bring Hope with you. I could use help with the Scouts. That would give you and Whit a break for the evening." Her strained laugh crackled over the connection. "It's a solid trade."

Talley switched the phone to her other ear and stepped out of her skirt. "What if Whit visited Parker at his house?"

"I thought about that."

Talley believed her friend. Respectful of others, Rachel didn't abuse favors. But when it came time to help a child, Rachel turned into a tiger.

"Pam's afraid a one-to-one home visit will be too intense," Rachel continued. "With his buzz cut, Whit kind of looks like Parker's dad. Pam thought in a setting with his peers, Parker would do better."

Talley searched through her hanging garments. Whit might be a tough NFL player, but he'd be vulnerable to Parker's circumstances—maybe too vulnerable.

"Tell Whit he doesn't have to make a speech," Rachel continued. "Just conduct a Q and A with the boys. You know, how he started playing for the Cougars, what practice is like, stuff like that. It's scheduled for the day after tomorrow. We'd planned a little holiday party, so if he could come, it would be great."

Talley kicked off her shoes and wiggled her toes in the plush carpet. She loved the barefoot feel, couldn't wait for days to end so she could indulge her aching feet. But her favorite ritual didn't relax her. Her mind retraced the memory of Parker jumping up and down in the stadium after Whit's big play. The urge to shelter her head between her knees washed over her just as it had at the game.

Between Hope and his contract negotiations, life had overfilled Whit's plate. But Parker? Whit knew what it was like to lose a dad.

Talley plopped on the mattress. *Why was life so hard?* "I'll ask him."

"Thank you." Rachel's voice raised in a rush of relief. "That's all I'm asking. Really. I promised Pam I'd ask."

"I'll get back with you tomorrow." What kind of person could turn down a boy after such a tragedy? Although Whit would feel the same, Talley hated to put him in the situation. She'd give up her summer vacation to avoid asking Whit this favor despite the incentive of an evening without Hope's snarky remarks.

After ending the call, Talley stood in her walk-in closet. She shouldn't dress up. Tonight's dinner wasn't a date and the last thing she needed—they needed—was additional drama. Her new black leggings and soft orange turtleneck sweater might work. A volunteer at the Red Cross complimented her on the way the sweater emphasized the burnished gold high-lights in her hair. Considering she'd tied her locks into a tail, the color was moot.

When Talley moved toward the front of the house, car lights illuminated the hall. She ignored her favorite baseball cap perched on the closet shelf and slipped into a fleece jacket.

She hesitated with her hand on the door handle. Maybe they'd decided to go out for dinner. Maybe the lights were from a delivery truck. Maybe she was losing her mind and her nerve. Nope, she'd lost her nerve an hour ago. She didn't have a good feeling about the evening.

With her breaths panting out, she peeked through the

crack in her dining room curtain to view the front yards of their houses. Talley wrinkled her nose as Whit and Hope vacated Whit's truck. More surprises. She was starting to hate surprises. The expressions on Hope and Whit's faces didn't inspire confidence.

A few minutes later, Talley stepped inside the Murphy foyer, and the heavenly aroma of seasoned meat and yeast momentarily banished the fear over the impending conversation.

She entered the kitchen and halted, her heart stuttering in her chest. "Yum, what can I do to get that food on the table?"

Whit looked up from the oven wearing an odd smile that displayed his dimples. Her thoughts spun. It wasn't exactly his happy look. Maybe, relief? He'd admitted his toothy smile had gotten him out of a lot of jams through the years. But she couldn't be a jam, especially during a casual meal. It had to be Hope.

"Did you talk to her?" Talley whispered.

Whit glanced at the empty hallway leading to the second story. "I need a lift to the high school after dinner."

*Not the answer to ease her nerves.* "And?" Talley prompted, raising her hands.

"She wants to skip college and go pro in women's basketball."

"What!" Just what they needed. Another Murphy risking injury in a sport's career. "She wanted to be a vet."

"Are we going to eat in this century?" Hope's waspish tone cut through the kitchen.

"You set the table." Talley stepped away from Whit. "I'll start drinks."

The energy in the room sent a chill along Talley's arms. Beside her, Whit leaned forward almost as though he was on the line waiting for the ball snap.

"We haven't shared a meal in a while." Talley tried for her best cheery-teacher voice. It wobbled. "Do you think we should get out the china and eat in the dining room?"

The suggestion was ludicrous, considering the current atmosphere.

"I vote for paper plates and sitting at the counter," Hope said.

Talley glanced at Whit and raised her brows. He gave her a slight nod.

Minutes later they sat at the table and Hope jabbed her fork toward Talley. "I don't know why you two have to act like jerks. Mom will never know if I go out. I'm sure not going to tell her—unlike you."

After shooting Hope a disgusted glance, Whit provided their parking lot discussion, blow-by-terrible-blow.

"He left my car in the lot," Hope added.

"Talley and I will get it later," he said. "You won't need it for a while."

"Whatever," Hope said. "But I'm going to the dance this weekend. I've already accepted."

"Un-accept," Whit said.

"The dance is a fundraiser for the basketball team," Hope said. "Mom agreed that I made a commitment to the team. People should honor their commitments. Don't you agree?"

While Talley squeezed her glass so hard it was a wonder it didn't shatter in her hand, Whit stared at the ceiling like he expected someone to beam him into the heavens.

"Ava gave us explicit instructions about your activity during her absence." Talley forced a civil tone to her words instead of the rant trying to blow the top of her head off.

When Hope slumped in her chair, Talley froze. Was she finally going to talk about the real issue? The grandfather clock in the hall ticked. After another beat, Hope stacked her utensils on her plate and stood. "You know you two are overreacting. But I'm not changing my mind. The recruiter for North Carolina State called the coach about me. If I get an offer, I'm taking it."

"Programs are looking for healthy players, not druggies," Whit said, but the fight had gone out of his eyes.

"What part of 'one time' don't you understand?" Hope said. "I was home, not driving, not out in public. No one knows except for you. Thanks to our not-so-awesome neighbor."

"And I'd do it again in a heartbeat," Talley said. "But, please, enough fighting. I usually eat alone. For once, I have awesome company and a home-cooked meal. Let's enjoy it."

Except they didn't enjoy it. They endured it. Hope answered her attempts at casual conversation with monosyllabic responses. Although Whit tried, it was clear his heart wasn't in it. The poor guy had come home to endure another killer tackle on the home front.

"You're a good cook, big bro," Hope said fifteen minutes later.

Talley forced a smile. At least that was a nice gesture.

The teen carried her dirty plate to the dishwasher. "I hope you've made a good dessert. I'll be in my room."

"It's going to be a challenge holding her in line," Whit said after Hope disappeared upstairs.

"It's going to be a challenge getting her to adulthood." Talley scraped her plate with a clang of glass. "She's right about your culinary talents. Amazing meal." She ran her plate under the water. "You saved me from a depressing selection of frozen chicken potpie or leftover pizza."

Whit squirted dish soap in the sink and swung the faucet to fill the basin. "You don't need an invitation. Dinner's at five thirty. Come on over. If I'm home, we'll have plenty to eat."

"You only cook here?"

"I'm on the road a lot." His frown wrinkled his brow. "It doesn't make sense to cook for one."

He motioned her away from the dishwasher and slid the top rack in and out of the machine. She shook her head. Good try, but she taught high school. Her students had given her ace lessons on diversion tactics. Although fame, fortune, media, and women surrounded Whit, tonight he almost sounded ... lonely?

"That must get old, traveling from one city to the next." She rinsed a plate and handed it to him to load. "For me, it's the quiet at night. I loved coming to your family home. I craved the noise, the chaos, the love." She paused, letting her words settle. "After growing up like that, don't you get lonely?"

He didn't take the dish in her hand. His gaze held hers, and she thought a shadow passed his features. She and Whit had once shared values, wants. She swallowed. Love? The back of her neck itched. Just because they found pleasure in a family meal didn't mean they had couple-potential.

"I miss my family, especially during the season." The usual firmness in his tone softened.

Talley searched his gaze. He missed them more than he wanted to admit.

"Your home was so busy and ... full. Someone always spilled their glass or wanted ketchup," she said, keeping the family memories working on him. "But there was more at your table. There was always a connection. A knowledge that a Murphy had your back."

Although he didn't respond, she believed he was thinking back to the many shared meals, the same as she. Memories wrapped around her shoulders like a warm blanket. Like Whit. They'd shared so much. Maybe they still could if he'd retire.

Many of their old connections remained. He preferred the

family home over his place in Charlotte, something she'd noticed during her visit. Although his condo would earn a spot in a decorating magazine, it also seemed cold—especially compared to here.

"I can wash the pot," he said.

Talley started. "Sorry. I kind of zoned out. After a big meal, my blood abandons my brain and goes south to digest."

He ran the scouring pad around the bottom of the ceramic pot. His long, sexy forearms—her weakness—flexed. Right on cue, her body responded. Holy cow, zero to hussy in one point two seconds. Thank goodness, she was far from her classroom.

Of course, the rest of him wasn't hard on the eyes. Built and toned for a professional sport, only a crazy woman would fault his physique. Thus, the reason for his groupies. Her gaze drifted to his face, tense with thoughts.

He didn't look up. "You're staring."

Her cheeks heated. "Busted. But I was also thinking—"

"I'm good at cleaning too?"

She laughed, but not because of his comeback. Unlike his quick-witted brothers, sarcasm rarely tainted Whit's voice. With Whit, you got honesty. You had to look deep into the man, but he didn't put on the macho mask. Whit merely remained silent and let people apply his personality. But he could do something other than risk his health.

"You could open a restaurant. The roast and vegetables were wonderful, and that soda bread—" Talley groaned. "That was to die for. People would come on your name recognition and curiosity. Then you would roll them over with the food. Shoot, I'd buy stock."

He paused as if considering her idea. "I've never cooked for anyone but family."

"But you enjoy it?" she pressed.

"Sure, but I only cook the meals we've always eaten.

Upscale restaurants change menus all the time. I know a few of the chefs in Charlotte. They're always trying something new." He handed her the insert for the slow cooker. "And they make that stuff up. I don't even know how to pronounce some of those crazy ingredients."

"People in Sunberry like home cooking. Everybody's too busy to cook these days. If it weren't for your mom, I'd exist on yogurt and fast food."

"Fast food is poison." He drained the dishwater. "My body pays the bills. I try to feed it right—most of the time."

Oh, those toned muscles were well fed. Her girl parts twirled with the image of sliding her hands along his arms, his legs, his abs. *Focus!*

"That's why I run." Her voice sounded like she'd sprinted a mile.

Whit wiped down the counter but remained silent. When she'd first met him in high school, the holes in their conversations had bothered her. With time, she'd learned they were part of Whit's processing.

"Do you think you could teach me to bake bread?"

He gave her a sidelong glance that spun her heart. "That could be arranged."

An image of Whit with his sleeves rolled and hands kneading dough slithered down her middle and pooled in an indecent place. Her breath hitched, and she shook off the inappropriate thought. Her darned senses were clouding the job at hand.

"I've got this request," she started.

Whit straightened.

"It's not bad. It's just not something you're comfortable with." She was making a mess of this.

Whit had turned to face her, his arms crossed in front of his chest in a look that clearly said whatever she was selling, he wasn't buying.

"It's for one of the Scouts who attended your last game." She blurted out the words and cringed. But it wasn't like she could suddenly develop a soft approach.

He didn't uncross his arms, but the thin line of his lips softened. Not as soft as when he'd kissed her. *Focus.* Heat raced up her neck to her cheeks, and she prayed they hadn't reddened.

At least he wasn't totally opposed to a new idea. She took in a deep breath and gave him a short version of Parker's story. When she got to the part about the father's death, Whit's big shoulders sagged, and his long, expressive hands hung limp at his side.

"Ah, man, that's tough," he said, his voice hoarse and raspy. "I'm glad the game helped him."

"That's just it." She hated pressing him since the boy's plight mirrored one of Whit's wounds. "His mom's hoping you could keep his progress going."

"Sure. I'll give it a shot. I was close to Parker's age when my real dad was killed. I remember how lost I felt."

When he didn't continue, she glanced at him. He shrugged.

"I always had this hole." He rubbed his belly. "Like I didn't know where I belonged. Football filled that void for me too."

All this time, she'd never known. She and Whit had shared a lot of personal information over the years, and she'd assumed his stepdad had filled the loss of his biological father. The connection between football and loss never occurred to her.

She resisted the urge to smack a plate against the granite to relieve the frustration bubbling inside her. Why did people have to be so complex, especially the ones she cared about?

"Talley?"

She blinked and focused on the third button of Whit's cotton shirt.

"How am I supposed to help Parker?"

She got the feeling he'd asked that question more than once.

"They're having a special Pack meeting tomorrow evening," she said in a hurried stream of words. "They want you to talk to the boys about football. What it's like to be a player, how you practice. And answer questions from the boys."

Just poke her in the eye with a sharp stick because that had to be easier than watching Whit make the decision. To her, Whit had always been quiet, often hard to read. But, oh boy, had she been wrong. The sequence of sadness, anxiety, and finally, acceptance changing his chiseled features hurt her heart.

"The Cougars require guest appearances." He huffed out a breath. "I always go to the kid functions, usually at hospitals. Little people don't seem to notice anything different about me."

She placed her palm against his cheek, her fingers twitching to soothe the lines of anxiety from his features. "I didn't know that about you."

"You should meet those kids," he said, his eyes moist. "They're so brave, and some are really sick. Too bad that kind of story doesn't always make the big news outlets."

"Human interest stories are the best ones." She paused. "So, you'll do it?"

"When I was a kid, the garbage collectors were my heroes." The right side of his mouth lifted. "I thought they had the coolest job riding on the back of that truck. I always ran to the front porch and waved. The guys probably thought I was a dumb kid, but they always waved back. For a while, I thought they came by to wave at me. I never minded taking out the garbage on Wednesday morning."

Talley closed her eyes, mentally noting yet one more trait about Whit she'd missed. "Why don't you ever set the record straight?"

Although he didn't look up or speak, she knew he'd heard her question.

"Never was one for talking," he said after a few moments. "You know that."

"Yes, but I could always count on you for honesty."

He opened the cupboard and put away the slow cooker. She waited, giving him time to frame his thoughts because that was the best way to score points with him. She always struggled to rein in her objective, but she'd managed—most of the time. Every now and then, if he delayed too long, she'd push him, help him see the way.

"The media does spin," he said.

"So, you haven't turned into a womanizer?" She caught his pause from the corner of her eye. When she turned toward him, his face brightened. Which should've been a warning. Instead, she brushed aside her annoyance and bam! He gave her a full-wattage smile that made women beg—including her. Still, they needed a drama break.

"Define womanizer," he said.

Whit flirting? Be still my heart. "A man who goes after any available skirt."

He cut a pointed look her way, his lashes shading his blues, and just the hint of a smile on his kissable mouth. "No standards?"

"Clarification." Dang, she would not cave to this heart-stopping attraction. "A man who goes after any available woman who meets his predefined criteria."

He poured detergent into the dishwasher and snapped the door closed. "Then, the answer is yes."

Yes? Her hand raised to her face. So, she was another pretty face to him. Wow, time to step out of the fantasy and head home while she still had a little pride. She pivoted on her toe, but he caught her and pulled her to his chest.

"One adjustment." His eyes burned with a fire she hadn't seen in years. "The women in my life, they're only one-night stands."

"Sex for bragging rights. How dreadful," she managed to squeak out.

"They circle me because they want to bed an NFL wide receiver. They don't know me. I don't let them know me."

Talley cringed. "Why?"

"Because I'm not the man they think I am."

Her chest tightened. "Who are you?"

"You know." His gaze dropped to her mouth. "You've always known."

He found his target, executed the play, and claimed her lips like he claimed the gridiron. She struggled to maintain her equilibrium as he savored. Her knees wobbled, but his strong arm at her back held her tight. His lips teased hers apart. She accepted him with a sigh, unable to resist his touch, his warmth, his promise to treasure her and bring her pleasure. In one wonderful moment of passion, he owned her, and she so wanted him to.

"About dessert." Hope's voice sounded behind them.

Talley straightened, her arms falling from Whit's neck. He tightened his grip around her, his mouth insistent, deepening the kiss, wiping out her thoughts, her embarrassment. His scent, his taste, his warmth shut out the world. Her heart raced, and her lungs burned for air.

When he ended the kiss, she sucked in a breath. Her brain hummed. Thank goodness, his arms still held her because she wasn't sure if her feet were still planted on the floor.

"Dessert will be served in five minutes," he said in a tone as smooth as melted caramel.

"No problem, bro," Hope said. "I'll, ah ... wait in the family room."

Talley pushed on his shoulders. "Whit!"

This time he savored her mouth like she was the dessert, and he wasn't going to waste a morsel.

"Breathe." His low, sexy voice strummed her ears almost as sensually as his kiss.

She battled the basement floozy who wanted to drag Whit upstairs and make him finish what he'd started.

His heavy right brow lifted. "Dessert?"

"Only if we have it in my bedroom," she whispered.

He blinked.

"That's right, darn you." She jabbed her index finger against his rock-hard chest. "I can play too. When you kiss me like that, all I can think about is getting sweaty with you. So next time, don't light my fire unless you plan to fan the flames." She moved from his embrace and turned back one last time before exiting the kitchen. "I'll take three cookies. Warm them in the microwave for ten seconds, please."

Talley marched to the family room, plopped down on the end of the couch across from Hope, and picked up a magazine. Why was the house so hot? She shoved up her sleeves.

Whit loved a fire, and he'd built a blaze hot enough to melt glass. But no way was she heading home—not after their display in front of Hope. She'd done the crime, so she'd serve her time. Un-freaking-believable! Where had the man learned to kiss like that? Duh, lots of practice.

"No dessert?" Hope complained.

"The chef's working on it," Talley said in a clipped but shaky tone.

Her cheeks flamed, and she couldn't meet Hope's gaze. From the tone of Hope's voice, the diva was having way too much fun after catching them in a lip-lock. Talley gripped the magazine. It was upside down.

Hope's smirk grated Talley's very last nerve. The last thing she needed was comments from the teen. The man responsible for her internal fireworks entered with a tray of cookies —a freaking tray like Rachel Ray. With a flourish, he set them on the coffee table and worked his way behind her.

Whit bent over her shoulder, his breath tickling her ear. "They're *all* warm." The turd had to get in the last word.

"Coffee?" he said with a wink.

"No, thanks. I think I'll have cold milk. I'm cutting back on caffeine." Talley ignored Hope's snort and Whit's smirk.

When Whit's phone chirped, Talley pushed to her feet.

"Answer your call," she said. "I can get my own glass of milk."

By the time she returned, Whit was standing in the hall, and Hope looked like she could gnaw the fire poker.

"Did I miss something?" Talley took her seat on the sofa and prayed the teen hadn't decided to turn her mercurial mood on her.

"His agent." Hope jerked her chin toward Whit. "He's talking to someone in Phoenix and San Diego."

Whit returned to the room. "Talley, I need you to take over here. I've got to head back to Charlotte tomorrow."

# CHAPTER THIRTEEN

Talley jerked awake at her cell's ring, patting the bedside table for her phone. The clock progressed to 12:32 a.m. Only bad news came after midnight. She snapped her jaw closed and peered at the screen. Whit's name sent her heartbeat scampering in her chest.

"Is everything okay?" she said.

"Hope's gone."

Talley pushed to a sitting position. Gone? She jerked open her bedroom curtains. "Her car's in the drive."

"And I have the keys."

Few things rattled Whit. He'd always been a steady force in the Murphy household—unlike his sister or brothers. Tonight, his voice pinged like a high-tension wire stretched too tight.

"Something woke me up, so I checked her room just to make sure she was all right," Whit said. "Her bed was empty, and she's not in the house, the garage, or the yard."

Talley rushed to her closet and jerked down a pair of yoga pants. "Don't panic. One of her friends must've picked her up after you went to bed. Did you try texting her?"

"Only every two minutes while I searched the house."

"Take a breath." Although she maintained a calm tone for Whit, a spiked ball bounced in her belly. She tapped a text to Hope.

"Talley?" Whit's tinny voice sounded from the speaker. "Are you still there?"

"Right here," Talley said. "I'm dressing. Give me five minutes, and I'll come over."

While Talley tied her shoes, a text pinged.

"Holy crap, Hope," Talley hissed, reading the message. "You're pushing the limits now."

She started to text Whit, then pressed the hot key to call instead. "Just heard from Hope. She's on her way home."

Although he didn't reply, the rush of his breath huffed through the speaker. "What'd she say?"

"You're not going to like it." Talley turned on the front porch light. She sure didn't.

"I haven't liked a whole lot my sister has had to say lately."

"She wants to meet at my house." Talley held her breath.

"I don't understand her. Hope and me ... we were close."

Tears stung her eyes, but she had to tell him. "Hope was pretty upset about your plans to return to Charlotte. I don't know if that's why she sneaked out of the house, but it's a possibility."

His hiss shattered the silence.

Five minutes later, Talley pulled open the front door. Whit stood on the other side, his phone pressed to his ear. "I can't be there. If they make a good offer, go for it. That's what I pay you for."

He ended the call and stepped into the entryway shadows. Worry etched grooves in his forehead and bracketed his handsome mouth. He might as well have opened her rib cage and squeezed her heart. She'd tried so hard. But she couldn't stop what her heart yearned for, no matter how great the personal risk. With every warning bell blasting in her head, she opened her arms. Whit stepped into her embrace.

"I canceled my trip." Whit hugged her close. "It's not fair to leave you alone with her, especially with her latest escapade."

His long hands stroked down her back.

*Don't look up. Look into those blues, and you're doomed.* With a fortifying breath, she straightened. Whit released her.

"Let's talk in the kitchen."

While he straddled a barstool, she rummaged in the bottom cupboard for her glass pan.

"What are you doing?" he asked.

"I don't have snacks." She cringed at the sound of her statement.

Talk about dumb, but she needed something to do. One piece of her wanted to lead him back to her bedroom, and the other wanted to shake something—like Whit.

The man was concerned about everyone but himself. That was the thing about him; he always put others first. Maybe that was why she had fallen for him. The pan clattered to the floor.

No, no, no! Talley shook her head. She *used* to be in love with him. Now, they were friends. Friends cared about friends, worked to ensure their happiness and safety. Whit deserved to enjoy the rest of his life, even if it couldn't be with her.

She stooped to retrieve the pan, but he beat her to it and handed it to her.

"Hey, I'm here." He rested his palms on her arms. "We'll straighten this out, together."

When his big hands caressed her shoulders, her heart quivered from his tenderness. And his look? Oh my, the way he looked at her did crazy, insane things to her heart, her lungs, her wobbly legs.

"I'm making brownies." She slapped her hand over her mouth, but a bubble of laughter erupted through her palm. Where had that come from? Why did she have the stupid urge to cook?

He gave her an endearing, crooked grin. No doubt, he thought she'd lost her mind. She tried to stop the laughter, but she couldn't.

"I know it's absurd," she said in between bouts of giggling. Tears filled her eyes.

"We're going to talk, not eat," he said.

"That's right. You, me, and Hope are going to *talk*. Keep that in mind. Based on the way you charged to the front door, we'll need chocolate."

"Chocolate?" he said. "Food fight?"

She giggled.

His brow furrowed. "O-kay. How can I help?"

"Got it covered." She held up the box delighted the movement helped her control the inappropriate giggling. "Whit?"

He frowned. "What?"

"We've got to think this through. About Hope." And after she stuck her head in a sink full of ice, she might, *might* think about what he was doing to her. Because there was no Talley and Whit. There could be no Talley and Whit.

"You're right." He sobered. "Where did Hope call from?"

"Private party."

"Party! She's in so much trouble. She sneaks out of the house to attend a party? Even if she wasn't grounded, she's too young for wild parties that end after midnight." His eyes widened. "Crap! How long has she been gone?"

Talley held up her hand to steady him. One of them had to stay cool, and she'd already failed that requirement. "Just because *we* went to wild parties doesn't mean she does."

"Yeah, it does. I know how the wheels turn in her mind like I know how a play will work."

She'd always wondered about his process. But she couldn't think. Right now, cracking an egg was proving to be a challenge.

"Hope's been held back too long." Whit's eyes narrowed. "She's coming into her first wind. My bet, she's one step away from a smackdown—if this isn't it."

Talley blinked. Smackdown was an interesting word choice.

"She's a good kid," Talley said. *Just not at present.*

"I should've seen this coming. Mom and Dad don't need more kid drama. Me, Kyle, and Nate put them through enough."

Car lights passed across the wall of the family room.

"That's her," Whit said. "We'd better come up with a play, quick."

While they strategized a plan, Talley finished the brownies and placed them in the oven. However after fifteen minutes, a sweet, chocolaty smell filled the kitchen, but Hope didn't enter the house. Whit plowed through the back door with a bang and returned with an armload of logs and enough fire in his gaze to ignite the house.

"Fifteen freaking minutes," he muttered, adding a log to the already blazing fire he'd built. "She's messing with me, running the play for all it's worth."

"Don't check the drive," Talley said.

Whit's gaze darted between her and the front window. "Why not? Nothing seems to bother my little sister."

Talley tamped her racing heart. Hope had pushed Whit too far, and if Talley didn't spoon-feed the information to him, he might blow a blood vessel—which would not help their cause or anything else.

"Did you check the drive while I went outside for wood?"

"I thought I heard a car door," Talley said. "I peeked out the side of the curtain after I checked the brownies."

"And the car windows are steamed up, right?" Whit paced in front of her. "How can you stay so cool and calm?"

"I teach high school."

"If she doesn't walk through that door in two minutes, I'm going outside."

"Just the drama Hope wants." Talley kept her tone even, reassuring. "Think about it. It's like a reality show. Famous brother races to the car. Tires screech. An engine roars. Sister locks door and glares out window as car pulls away. Fade to black."

The fire popped and hissed.

Whit raked his hand over his head. "Yeah, yeah, yeah. I get it. That's the kind of thing she'd get into. It's our fault. She's the only girl, so the whole family babies her."

Talley picked up a magazine when she wanted to toss it across the room. But one of them had to remain cool.

Whit paced to the front window without moving back the curtain and then stomped back to the fireplace. "I need to think. The next forty-five minutes might be the most important speech of my life. But Hope's got me so wound up—"

"Sit." Talley pointed to the floor in front of her. "I'll work on your shoulders like I did before college finals."

He sat between her legs, anger rolling from him in waves. Beneath her fingers, the muscles in his shoulders bunched and strained like steel ropes.

"Breathe," she said, as much to soothe him as to tamp the desire boiling inside her. This was not the way to resist the sexual attraction between them.

"We can't lose her," he said, a hint of desperation in his tone. "Hope's always been too smart, too talented, and too headstrong. But now? The world's a dangerous place for that kind of girl."

Talley squeezed her eyes closed. "When you visualize a play, you don't imagine dropping the ball, do you?"

His shoulders lifted beneath her hands. "No."

She concentrated on slowing her breathing and kneading his taut muscles. The aroma of rich, warm chocolate blended with the pine logs burning in the fireplace. If she kept cool, she could help him get through Hope's drama and help him see the light to retirement. "Try to get in her head. Think like she thinks."

"Seventeen minutes!" he said through gritted teeth.

"Seventeen minutes. That's it!" Talley blinked at the simplicity of the plan. "The same as her age. No doubt, she's had an eye on the dash clock the entire time she's made out with the guy. Poor schmuck probably doesn't have a clue you're mere yards away. Hope had it all planned."

The door closed with a soft thud, and light footsteps sounded in the hall. Whit stood.

"Hey, Talley," Hope said in a cheerful tone that sounded a tad wobbly.

Whit stopped in front of the mantle and casually leaned against it—casual as a big snake ready to strike.

"I thought you were coming home an hour ago. I was worried," Talley said.

Hope sat on the love seat beside her, her gaze darting to everything but her big brother.

"Was it that long?" Hope waved her hand in a carefree gesture that didn't match her thinned-out lips. "We were having such a good time, I guess I didn't notice."

"What's the guy's name?" Whit's grave tone raked the room.

"None of your business," Hope snapped.

"Hope, come on." Talley said. "Everyone here loves you and has your best interest at heart."

"Best interest?" Hope tucked her blouse in her waistband. "Really?"

"Do you always dress like that?" Whit said.

The small hairs along Talley's neck lifted and a sick feeling settled inside her. The buttons on the teen's blouse were mismatched, making the garment hang haphazardly. Why hadn't she noticed? Maybe it was a guy thing, or just that she hadn't considered Hope would go so far. There was only one reason why a girl had misaligned buttons: she'd redressed in the dark car.

A rosy stain flushed Hope's cheeks. She straightened the hem of her shirt but didn't attempt to fix the buttons.

"We were just fooling around," she said defensively. "It's not like I'm pregnant."

*What's wrong with you?* Talley glared at Hope, trying to tell her with her look what she couldn't say out loud. "When you deliberately worry and hurt the people who love you, it's a problem."

"You're seventeen," Whit said.

"Really?" Hope jabbed her finger at her brother. "You have no right to question how far I go with a guy. Not when your sex life is broadcasted on every grocery-store shelf in town. Do you know how it feels to have your friends talk about your brother?"

Whit's heavy exhale broke through the crackle of wood. "You know better than to believe that tabloid stuff. Besides, I'm not seventeen."

"I'm mature for my age," Hope said.

"Says the girl who throws away a brilliant mind for a sport that might support her for five years," Whit said. "*If* you make it to the pros. If you don't, what will you do without an education? The competition is fierce. There are ten guys who will play for half my salary waiting to replace me."

"I'll make it," Hope said. "I'm a Murphy. Coach says I've got real talent."

"Of course you're talented," Whit was saying. "But so are a lot of young women. I'm not saying don't play. I'm saying you need a backup plan."

"Like yours," Hope said.

Talley closed her mouth before her gasp choked free. Before she screamed for them to stop.

"I got your boyfriend's license number," Whit said. "I'll look him up tomorrow."

"He's not my boyfriend, and you can't intimidate every guy I like."

"Please don't disrespect yourself." Talley gave the girl a pleading look, but Hope turned away.

"I'm done here." Hope's neutral tone had picked up a rasp of raw emotion. "I'm going to bed."

The storm door swished closed, and the teen disappeared into the night. Whit stood at the door until she'd disappeared into the house and then turned back to Talley. "What just happened?"

A bell dinged from the direction of the kitchen, and Talley turned. "The brownies are done." Talk about ridiculous. The whole world just blew up, and she was taking brownies from the oven. "Are you up for drowning your problems in chocolate?"

Whit followed her to the kitchen. "Beats a bottle."

He settled at the driftwood table with yellow padded seats. Although she longed to snuggle up to Whit and indulge in a treat near the fire, she placed the pan on the table, cut a slab for Whit and a smaller one for herself.

Whit covered her hand with his. "Thanks for helping me with Hope tonight."

"I wasn't much help."

"You kept me from going viral."

She pinched off a corner of the warm, fudgy cake. "Considering Hope's behavior, I think you should be commended."

"I expected a problem." Frustration laced his voice. "I didn't expect that one."

"At least she's on birth control. I saw it during our raid."

He placed half the brownie in his mouth, chewed, and swallowed. "I got the famous 'mom chat' at fifteen. But Hope's too young ..."

He polished off the rest of the brownie within seconds. Any other time, she might have been amused. But Hope worried her. Standing, she pointed at the pan, and Whit shook his head. Talley collected their plates and loaded the dishwasher. She'd already given Hope the big-sister talk, but it was time for a repeat performance.

"So how do I keep an eye on her without making matters worse?" Misery laced his voice.

The plastic wrap slipped through Talley's fingers and thumped on the counter. She hadn't anticipated Hope's behavior, but the girl's actions made it easier to break her latest idea to Whit. She peeked up at Whit, who was still waiting for her response. "I've been working on that." Talley rinsed the chocolate from the glass mixing bowl. "What do you think about helping out our coaching staff?"

"I'm no coach."

"But you know the game." And there was another way he could help—if he'd agree. "Maybe you could give the team safety pointers in addition to how to win." She paused, gauging his reaction. "It would be great if you could teach safety techniques."

His eyes widened.

"Just think about it," she backtracked, softening her position.

"I'm just a player," he said. "There's a science to the sport.

Aren't there credential requirements for high school coaches?"

"*Assist* the coach, not act as one. It's a win-win situation. You help the team and me. Plus, if you have a legitimate reason to be at the school ..." She held her breath, hoping to see the got-it look glistening in his eye.

"I can monitor Hope." He grinned for the first time since his sister had exited the house.

Talley breathed. "Teens talk. You'll hear as much hanging around the guys as you will with Hope."

"So, how do I talk the coach into accepting an assistant?"

If he focused on her interference instead of the idea, she'd never be able to help him or Hope. "You've already made a big impression on Coach, so ... I kind of tested the water."

The subtle expression changes signaled neurons firing in his brain. At least, she hoped so.

"You anticipated this problem?" he said.

"No." She waved her hands back and forth. "Hope totally blew me away tonight." That much was true. The ways to convince him to retire, come back to Sunberry—yeah, that was her conniving brain, but it was for a good cause. "Our team has had a rough season. Coach needs help. With Hope's latest antics, we need an inside track on high school events. It works for both sides."

With Whit, there was always a body part in motion. His constant movement energized her, made her feel alive, engaged. At present, his facial features displayed a litany of unreadable emotions. She clasped her hands in front of her to keep from gripping his forearms.

"It might work," he said. "As long as the coach doesn't expect a speech."

"Coach Cox isn't a big conversationalist." She was talking too fast, but the timing was everything. If she didn't get Whit to agree now, she might not get the chance later. "The guys will be jacked."

"Hope will be furious." His distant look sharpened on her. "Was the guy in the driveway tonight a football player?"

"Yep."

He cocked his head to the right. "What's the catch?"

Although she was prepared for questions, her shoulders crept upward. "I've sort of written an injury-prevention plan and need an expert opinion."

He crossed his arms over his chest.

"Don't dig in like that." He was just as stubborn as ever. "There's nothing wrong with making every effort to protect our students. And you know my feelings about the sport."

"How come your coach isn't writing it?" For a quiet guy, he could pick an idea to death.

"With his classes and the team, he's busy."

He narrowed his eyes. "And, of course, you have plenty of time."

"I made time." Talley squared her shoulders despite the urge to wince. It wasn't like it was a secret. Everybody in Sunberry knew her position on football. "I could use expert help."

"I'm a receiver, not a policy guru."

"But you know about the safety techniques to protect the head and neck. The best way to tackle, right?"

Instead of answering the question, he stared at her like she was an insect, and he couldn't decide if he should step on her or let her go. She figured it was a long shot before she asked. But if she didn't approach the plate, she couldn't hit the ball. She frowned. Okay, she'd used a baseball analogy when the problem was football.

"I know the technique," he admitted but didn't look all that excited about it.

"So, you could teach the players and look over my policy

for accuracy?"

He continued to stare even though she'd asked in her most persuasive tone. "I guess I could do that." One heavy brow raised. "Over dessert tomorrow?"

She blinked. Seems like her old boyfriend had learned negotiating techniques over the past five years. She'd better practice her defensive moves, or the next injured party would be her.

"But I like the idea of watching out for Hope without being so obvious."

A happy bubble almost drew her toes from the floor, and she couldn't resist brushing her knuckles across her chest. "Thanks. I thought so, but I didn't want to say anything until we talked."

When he studied her that way, she always went for her stony face so he couldn't read her thoughts. If he suspected she'd tried to manipulate him, he'd never forgive her.

"Thanks," he said. "I'm not sure how I would've handled Hope without you."

"High school years can be tough," Talley said. But college was rougher—for her. And she was repeating the journey.

When he embraced her, every rational thought, every hint of self-preservation exploded. Her instincts beat a warning against her ribs. On her present course, she might not have long with this wonderful man, so she'd better make the best of what she had.

"I can always trust your honesty, even when it hurts," he said.

*No, you can't*. But she held him close, careful of his injuries. His spicy scent combined with chocolate filled her lungs as completely as he filled her heart.

There had to be another way, a way without using Hope's problem to get him to retire. She swallowed. It was too late for regrets. She had to save him, even if it meant losing him.

# CHAPTER FOURTEEN

B efore daybreak the following morning, Whit awakened to the throb of multiple aches radiating through his body. He squinted at the bedside clock and eased his feet to the floor. Recovery was taking too long. The rookies vying to replace him bounced back in hours, not days. He had to heal by the end of the week. He'd only missed two games this season because of injuries. No way would he be out for the playoffs—not during a contract year.

His quads seized. The last thing he wanted or needed was a contract with a West Coast team. But if that's all his agent, Stan, could get, he'd probably sign. In two years, Kyle would graduate and be ready for a practice start-up. He'd help hundreds of people. If Whit helped purchase office space in Sunberry, his hometown community would have a new doc. Heck, maybe he could recruit some of Kyle's friends. Sunberry needed more docs.

Ignoring the doubts twitching his flesh, he slipped into a pair of sweats. He could get through this. Success wasn't a secret sauce. A player had to maintain concentration, a winning attitude, and avoid getting greedy.

Stan was the negotiator and swore a talk with the Phoenix team would prod the Cougars to make an offer. And Hope? A groan rumbled in his chest. His last-minute cancelation would aggravate Stan, but Hope took precedence. If Stan couldn't postpone the meeting, his agent would have to progress without him.

After a series of stretches outside under the streetlight, Whit eased into a jog. At first, his thoughts stuttered in his head. By the second block ideas flowed with the rhythm of his feet.

He'd told Nate and Kyle he had the situation under control, but Hope was as unpredictable as his feelings for Talley. Before the game, he'd been a regular player waiting to sign a contract. Now, he had sister problems, ex-girlfriend problems, and no blasted contract.

Although his movement slapped his ribs and settled into an ice pick behind his right eye, he pushed through the discomfort. By the sixth streetlight his muscles warmed to the work and renewed vigor tingled through his veins.

He opened his stride. His ribs burned like fire, but strength firmed his gait. All he had to do was square his home situation before he jeopardized his contract negotiations.

Relishing the rush of the November wind on his cheeks, he pushed harder, pumping his arms to the thump of his soles on the pavement. Instead of avoiding pain, he embraced it. He was alive. He was strong. He was focused.

Ahead, something moved. Whit squinted. A runner jogged through a vacant intersection—a jogger he could catch. Fixated on his opponent, he increased his speed. *Catch him.* Fifteen strides ahead. Ten strides. Five strides. The streetlight illuminated ... a woman.

"Talley?" His voice was breathy, hungry for air.

She glanced over her shoulder but didn't slow her pace.

He dialed up his speed to fall in beside her. "Hey."

She smiled. "Hey yourself."

Unlike his breathless rasp, her voice sounded soft and smooth in the morning silence. Her signature cucumber scent wafted around him. He matched her rhythm. She didn't glance his way, but he kept checking, hoping she'd give him that wide, interested look she'd given him last night. Crazy, but he'd missed it, missed her. Which was dumb.

At the intersection ahead, he guessed she'd turn left toward home. Too bad, he'd gladly follow her another mile— or five. It felt right moving side by side through the shadows. When she turned, his chest lifted. Yeah, it was dumb, but it was good to verify his inner imagery continued to function.

One block from her house, she slowed to a jog, then dropped to a walk after a few more yards.

"You're out early," he said.

"Couldn't sleep."

"Ditto."

She lowered her slim body to the sidewalk to stretch. "Should you be running?"

"It helps me think." He eased down beside her. "Plus, it's my job to stay in shape."

Reaching for her outstretched toe, she turned her head to study him. He adjusted his seat on the pavement.

"I saw the clip on the news," she said, her voice tight.

"Clip?"

Her brows almost met above her nose. Looks like he'd just missed something important. "The last play of the game." A hint of annoyance painted her voice.

"What's with that?" He snorted. "You were in the stands with the Scouts."

When she turned away, the hairs at the base of his skull lifted. Something was up.

"I couldn't watch the tackle. But I saw what happened afterward. You didn't jump up as usual."

"Kind of hard from the bottom of a pileup." But he doubted she'd appreciate his attempt at humor.

"Maybe, if that wasn't the only thing about that play. You had a bad headache, a concussion symptom."

*Not another sermon.* "I know what I'm doing. Besides, I've got maybe two more years left. I need to make the most of that time."

"Dead or alive?" She gave him a hard stare.

For once, couldn't they have a conversation? "I have a higher risk of injury driving to Sunberry. Besides, I'm not your latest cause."

"No, you're my ... friend." She cleared her throat. "I care about you."

"My symptoms have improved since Sunday night." Which was sort of true. He was better. Mostly. He flexed his hands to ease the need to move. But he didn't want to talk about his recovery. What was with that little pause? She didn't have speech problems. But her voice had sounded off.

*Stop, Murphy!* This wasn't the time to go sappy about her last four words. Change that—he couldn't go sappy. They were just words.

"Is that all you've noticed?" Her voice was firmer, but not her usual in-your-face interrogation.

"My ribs still hurt, but I'm stronger." He didn't have to spill his guts. But no matter how hard he concentrated, the woman had a way of getting to him. Sweat tickled his scalp. "I had some dizziness the first few days."

"So, it's worse?"

Mom would have a choice response to the curse that slipped past his lips. He stood. "The doc will check me again before the next game. I'm here to help Hope."

Dang, those big brown eyes creamed him every time. Right along with the guilt.

"How'd last night go?" she asked.

Her gaze messed with his head more than the headache. The weird thing was she'd been quick to let him off on his injuries. Talley rarely got off a hot topic—until now.

He stretched his right calf. "She wouldn't unlock her bedroom door. I told her I'd canceled my trip."

"That was just my best guess at what's bothering her," Talley said. "At least we tried."

He didn't want to talk about Hope. He didn't want to talk. At least not now. Not with the glow of the streetlamp highlighting Talley's features. He needed to get out of here before he said something even stupider. His brain felt like gauze with his thoughts slowly fumbling from one side of his head to the other. The only thing that made sense was her, how she looked. She had the prettiest mouth. And she was talking. Too bad the buzzing in his ears drowned out her words. When he leaned forward, her eyes widened, and she moved toward him. In his rule book, that meant bring it on.

He snuggled her so close he couldn't tell where her body stopped and his started. It wasn't enough. When he angled his chin and pressed his tongue forward, she accepted him. And that little pleasured noise she made roared straight to his junk.

What the— He shifted. Something sharp, probably a rock, poked his butt. It nearly killed him to release her.

"Do you know how tempting it is to have you next door?" He nuzzled the soft nook of her neck.

"Whit," she said on a sigh.

"It's only forty yards to your house, give or take. I'm betting you have a nice bed. Too bad we're in a time crunch. But later ..." He worked his brows. "After I talk to the Scouts."

He could swear she moved her head, just a fraction, but it was definitely a move. He wasn't getting lucky this morning. But in the future? *Keep the momentum.* She was moving toward the end zone. He could sense it, see it in the softening around her eyes.

He squeezed her hand. "Just don't want you to forget the offer is still out there. Dinner after the Scout talk?" *And dessert.*

"With Hope?"

He squeezed his eyes shut. Mom had left him in charge. "Now I understand the complaints of guys with little kids."

Her brows went from meeting in the middle to arching over her wide eyes. She wagged a finger at him, and he couldn't help the snort that erupted.

"So I sneak out of the house and into your bedroom." He waggled his brows again. Not because the movement did him any good, but just because it was fun.

"You're very bad." She huffed out a breath like she'd made up her mind. Holy crap! Maybe he was getting lucky this morning.

"Rachel said she could use Hope's help with the Scouts ... and offered to watch her for a few hours to give us a break." She shrugged. "You know, in payment for helping out with Parker."

Talley was always a few leaps ahead of him. He'd better keep that in mind. When he pushed to his feet, a small but firm grip stopped him.

"We're not finished yet," she said.

*Oh, heck no.* A professional athlete didn't quit just because he missed one catch.

Talley tugged his hand. "You're sore, so you've got to spend more time with the cooldown and stretching."

Stretch? He didn't want to stretch. He wanted to bury himself in her. The curve of her hip spiked his heartbeat. Of course, she was right about caring for his body. He'd worked through injuries on his own before. Pain had a way of keeping a player on the right path, which wasn't the life he wanted for his sister.

He copied Talley's position. "Hope's been talking about becoming a vet since she was in first grade. Why the sudden interest in professional sports?"

"The shiny stuff always appeals to young people."

Not to Talley—or him, for that matter. Knowing Talley, it wasn't likely to change.

"Breathe in and then exhale with the stretch," she said.

*Aw, man*. The sound of her voice shivered through him like she'd whispered in his ear. Although he'd gladly listen to her husky voice forever, he couldn't hold the stretch a second longer. When he released it, she straightened.

With his speech issues, he often stopped midway through a sentence because he couldn't always find the words to finish a thought. Most people, like his teammates, completed the sentence for him or gave him a prompt. Not Talley. She had a look that cracked him up. Her forehead wrinkled, and her eyes sort of rolled up as she tilted her head. It was a work of art. Just thinking about it made him smile—which would usually annoy her.

The more she heated up, the funnier it hit him. When the skin between her brows pleated, he held up his hands. "Sorry." He wasn't.

Whit wanted to be right about her. An affair with Talley would be complex, like an intricate play. No problem. He could be with her. He could bed her.

But he couldn't let her into his head.

# CHAPTER FIFTEEN

"Shoot me," Talley muttered, letting the storm door slam behind her. Although she yearned to look back at Whit, she didn't—not even a peek. Her resolve hung by a cobweb. If she spent one more second inhaling his masculine scent or staring at his grin, she couldn't be responsible for the outcome. No doubt, Sunberry's finest would lock her in a padded cell. Although prison might be the perfect place to reflect on why wanting her and his career didn't equal happily-ever-after for her.

Undressing on her way to the bedroom, Talley tossed her soiled clothes toward the hamper. Every article dropped to the floor.

"Nope," she muttered. "I'm not falling for him again. The definition of insanity is to repeat the same action and expect a different result."

With an angry twist, she turned on the shower. She wasn't the same college girl who had fallen head over heels. Just because the attraction between them was hotter than an overheated teakettle didn't mean she needed to act on her hormonal demands. Her heart thudded against her ribs like a caged bird despite the warm water soothing her skin.

"Just say no," she muttered. *Or yes, heck, yes!*

She'd agreed to dinner, not an affair. It was the thing to do after he'd agreed to talk to the Scouts. Parker needed help. Yep, and so did she. A nice dinner in a public place was safe. It was the after-dinner time that got murky. And an affair? She shuddered. Could she handle hot and sweaty with Whit on a temporary basis?

Because it would be temporary. He'd been honest about his plans to continue playing—in Charlotte. Honest. The word buzzed in her head like an angry bumblebee. Yep, that defining word didn't apply to her. Even if she failed to get him to retire, she'd never be able to accept his job and ignore the dangers of football.

"Earth to Talley. Devastating split with Whit, remember?"

Scrubbing at her skin, she tried to ignore the emptiness hollowing her belly. No way could she revisit that loss. A few hot nights with Whit might tempt her sexually, but the fallout would bankrupt her emotions. Once he retired was a different story. A story that filled her girl parts with want. Just what a high school teacher should focus on prior to school, even if it was a designated administrative day.

Her cell vibrated on her scarred Sunberry High desk, and Whit's name appeared on the screen. She pressed talk, her heart accelerating.

"How's your day going?" Whit said.

Thank goodness he couldn't see her face. "Any headway with Hope?"

"She emerged from her cave thirty minutes ago." He lowered his voice. "She acts like nothing has happened, and she's going to pursue a sports career just like me."

"Sorry," Talley said. "It's quiet here, but it will liven up for practice this afternoon. Oh, good news on that front. You have an appointment with Coach Cox before practice at three. Prepare to start today."

"Wow!" he said. "I'm glad you're on my team."

*If he only knew.* She pasted a smile on her face and died inside. Any other time she might've basked in his praise, but not under the weight of attempting to change his mind. It wasn't manipulation. She was merely showing him the error of his decisions.

"Can you break for lunch and give me a few pointers before I meet my new boss?"

Something told her food wouldn't be an integral part of the discussion. "I think I can break away. What time?"

"Now would work. I'm in the parking lot."

The hesitation between his words gave him away. He was worried and miserable about Hope. Talley's hands curled with the desire to hold and comfort him. But she had to stay strong.

She opened the passenger door to his truck five minutes later, and her heart tumbled. The self-talk to contain her feelings circled the drain. Dressed in a nondescript warm-up and dark glasses, he filled the truck with his presence.

"As soon as you meet with Coach Cox, you'll be official," she said.

He leaned over, placed a quick kiss on her lips, and shifted into drive. "You're like Todd's perfect pass—dead-on the numbers. I knew that when you taught me the difference between an *S* and a five." He winked. "Still, assistant coach in less than twenty-four hours."

Whit made her feel like she was winging through the clouds. One part of her wanted to rub her knuckles on her shoulder. "What can I say?" *I'm a master manipulator.*

The other part of her wanted to crawl under the nearest rock. She swallowed. "We're in a losing streak, and the coach has an offer from an NFL superstar—for free."

Whit wheeled from the school parking lot to the road. "Wish my agent worked like you."

"I wish a lot of things that can't happen."

Whit pulled into the drive-through of a fast-food restaurant. "What do you want?"

*More time with you.* She held up her canvas lunch bag, resisting the urge to pull it over her head and hide. "Unsweetened iced tea. Got the rest covered."

While they waited for his order, her thoughts spun without making traction. Sex always jacked up plans. But lovemaking?

A teen with a red baseball cap stamped with the restaurant's logo handed Whit a white bag. The greasy yet enticing smell of french fries and ground beef filled the truck. Talley's stomach grumbled. Instead of opening the bag, Whit drove away from the restaurant.

By the time he'd turned into the park entrance, Talley regretted her decision to stay with her healthy lunch. She needed comfort food to survive her memories. The towering pines lining the road swayed in the stiff breeze, and a playground swing twitched as if a child had recently vaulted from the top of it.

The park had been their go-to place. Together with Nate and Kyle, the foursome had laughed, plotted, and commiserated on the high school experience. Whit pulled to a stop to the left of the arbor where he'd first kissed her, despite her braces, her embarrassment, and her awkwardness. Although her lower jaw felt stiff and too shaky to eat, she opened her lunch and focused on something besides the fear cracking her heart.

An intense yearning curled her fingers around her sandwich. The image of children laughing and swinging in the park made her empty stomach flutter. She'd once dreamed of a child, their child.

She was an idiot.

Air trapped in her lungs. No kid dreams. No fairy tales. Besides, he couldn't be a father with brain damage, and manipulating him to retire would force him away.

She'd given her parents an ultimatum: create a home in Sunberry or leave her behind. They'd left her the same as he would when he learned how she had worked to coerce his decision.

A shiver shook her shoulders despite the warmth of the truck's interior. She'd rather lose their relationship then let him lose his life.

The crust on her peanut butter sandwich crumbled in her hand. "Whit?"

Silence. Why wouldn't he look at her? She crushed her napkin into a tight ball and suppressed the urge to chuck the rest of her meal out the window. Sweat moistened her brow. The small cab seemed to press against her. She buzzed down the window.

He finally turned toward her, and his brooding expression accelerated her heart rate.

"You always had a mission. Knew the direction of your life. Me?" The passionate spark in his gaze died, and he shook his head. "When I was little, I wanted to be like my dad. I don't remember a lot about him. But I remember thinking I would grow up to be like him, do the same job. When he died ..." He shrugged. "I was lost. I was always behind in school. When Mom married Ryan, he helped, got me into sports. Things got better, and football? I was good at it. It's the one thing my brain gets."

"Football destroys your brain, your personality, and your life." *Stop!* What was she doing? This was important, new. She'd been Whit's friend, his lover, his confidante, but she'd missed what made football so important to him. Maybe she hadn't listened. Maybe he'd never shared the truth with her.

He held up his palm. "I know the risks."

The rant battering her brain clouded her vision. She closed her eyes and scrambled for her happy image. She always visualized the day Whit handed her his acceptance letter to the University of North Carolina. Tears stung her eyes. Only happy thoughts. She exhaled and blinked. Whit's intense gaze pierced her heart.

"I wish you could see what I see." She touched his jaw, craving his warm flesh and the rough feel of stubble against her skin. "You're so much more than a wide receiver."

He froze, his breathing almost imperceptible. She'd seen the same look on her students when she covered an unpopular topic. She might as well spit in the wind because Whit couldn't hear her words. Couldn't see his family valued him far more than a paycheck. Those early years of struggling to talk and fit in with his peers had stamped "inadequate" on his soul, and he might die trying to prove his worth to himself.

"I feel good when Kyle and Nate talk about their programs." He dropped her gaze and unwrapped his lunch. "They'll be good at helping people. I have a piece of that."

Talley rolled her lips to prevent the bitter taste of failure from bringing on tears. Anger at her weakness followed. She mashed her napkin into a tight ball around the remains of her sandwich and stuffed it in her bag.

Like the massive oak outside her window, Whit held fast. The risk and the force of her argument hadn't moved him—yet. Five years ago, she'd sheltered her heart and walked away after one emotional fight. That immature tactic didn't work then and wouldn't work now. She needed to set up experiences to *show* Whit his life could be meaningful without football. With his talents, he could find his purpose. He could offer his community more than entertainment.

He had already shown empathy for Parker. Working with the Sunberry team, he would amplify the risk of the game to the players and the need for safety. If he accepted that need for the Sunberry team, he might accept he needed the same protection. But that meant she had to stay the course— regardless of her personal risks.

Despite her low mood, she made a show of checking the time and mustered a tight smile. "So, are you ready to meet your new boss?"

———

WHIT HELD open the school's glass entrance door for her.

"Coach left your badge and parking pass at the desk," she said, leading the way into the school.

"I'm a little nervous."

She threaded her arm through his. "You've already made the team, Rookie."

The whir of the floor machine replaced the usual chatter of students. Lemon cleaner suppressed the scent of cologne, aftershave, and pheromones from hundreds of hormonal teens. Located to the left of the entrance, the double doors to the administration office stood open.

"It's going to be a tight schedule with the Scouts and then dinner. We could push back dinner until tomorrow night," Whit said while they waited for the assistant to retrieve his ID.

"I can't. PTA meeting tomorrow. I'm presenting at the school."

He frowned. "Drugs?"

"Contact sports and head injuries." She cringed. So not the way she wanted to tell him that tasty morsel. "I'm on a panel with a neurologist and a pediatrician."

He tried a smile but didn't pull it off. "Still riding that white horse?"

"I'm promoting an injury-prevention plan for our school

district. However, I hope to garner enough support to ban football from our Sunberry High roster." She huffed a breath to move the hair tickling above her eyebrow. "Of course, I could use a professional review on injury prevention. Would you have time to read it for me?"

"You're serious." All hints of humor faded from his features. "Yet you're friends with the coach?"

"Changing a culture requires small steps." She got he loved the sport, even understood some of the loyalty, but ignoring the risks after Jeff's death, after the media explosion, she'd never get.

"A cheerleader can get a concussion."

*Educate, don't agitate him.* "The intent of a cheer is not to bang heads with the opponent."

"True." He stopped and pulled his cell from its holster. "Crap! That's the second time my cell dropped a call without ringing. I missed my agent. I'll have to get back with him after practice." He glanced up from the screen. "I could review your plan after the PTA meeting—unless the parents riot."

"It's not *that* contentious," she said.

"So should I arrange for dinner at your place?"

Heat spiraled down her middle. "Thursday night special—PB and J."

"I'll bring over coffee and dessert," he said.

She'd already agreed to dinner for tonight. *Make an excuse.* "Since you agreed to read my plan, I guess we can share a sandwich and dessert."

It was crazy. Asking for his help with her prevention plan was pushy enough, but flirting with heartache? She swallowed. Was heartache worth more time with Whit? At best, they'd have three more days together—if she could keep from pushing too hard. Regardless of the personal fallout, she had to stay with the plan, even if it meant ending her chances with him.

She nodded because, with the slightest provocation, a tear might leak or her voice might tremble. Her commitment had forced her to give up on a life with Whit. No way would she give up one moment of her last three days with him.

With her heart rattling in her ribs, she waited in the hall while he tapped on the coach's doorframe and disappeared inside the office.

This was as far as she needed to go. No doubt, Whit would be a good assistant like he was a good man, good son, and good brother. Her cheeks heated. Not to mention an excellent lover. She bet he'd make a fantastic husband and father. She may never know. It was her job to ensure he had that opportunity—with some other fortunate woman.

# CHAPTER SIXTEEN

Whit lowered his razor to avoid cutting his face. Why did a date rattle him? It wasn't a date. They were going to Rachel's house to talk to the Cub Scouts and then get something to eat. He called *that* a date, especially since he'd booked reservations at a nice Wrightsville Beach restaurant.

And the twitchy feeling? He didn't do touchy-feely. He also didn't do talks. As a Cougar, he visited kids in hospitals, one-on-one. He stepped into his black trousers and removed a white silk shirt from the hanger. Simple clothes for a simple man. When he talked to the kids, he'd wear a Cougar jersey over his shirt. Too bad he didn't have team shirts for the boys. He'd have to pick some up and ship them to Talley. Boys always loved team jerseys. He should buy team hats too.

When he stepped into the hall, Hope bumped against his shoulder. "If Jack picks me up for the dance dressed like that, I'm dumping him."

"What's wrong with my clothes?" Whit looked down. He hadn't dripped toothpaste on his shirt. "I paid a lot of money just for the pants."

"They're boring."

"Last time, you complained I didn't match. Black and white make it easy." Too bad his life wasn't as easy. Not to mention pleasing his little sister with her current attitude.

"Don't move," she ordered.

Before he could protest, she disappeared into the guest bedroom. One minute later, she shoved a plaid shirt and navy sweater into his arms. "Wear this with your dark jeans, the tight ones."

Tight? "This is—"

"Are you taking Talley to dinner?"

"After my talk with the Scouts."

Hope fisted her hands on her hips. "Talley deserves a nice evening. She hasn't dated anyone since she dumped that teacher from Emerald Isle. Since you're going for a one-night stand with her, you can at least dress nice."

"This *is* nice." *And Talley wasn't a one-night stand.*

But Hope had already disappeared into the bathroom. His sister could be a real pain. He stomped into the bedroom and tugged off his pants. Playing football had its hard knocks, but at least he could count on the rules. He didn't have to worry if the colors in his uniform matched. All he had to do was show up on time. Besides, Talley had never complained about his clothes. He paused on the last shirt button. Maybe she was being nice, cutting the clueless player some slack. He checked the time on his phone and kicked it up a notch. Talley might not be so nice if he showed up late.

At precisely six o'clock, he halted on Talley's porch and inhaled the crisp fall air with its hint of woodsmoke. *Game time.* He pressed the doorbell. While the muffled tune echoed inside, he shook out his arms.

The front door swung open, and one thought circled his brain—Hope had been right about his jeans. They were tight, especially around Talley. Dressed in a curve-hugging red dress and sexy boots that showcased her legs, Talley stood in the doorway. The foyer lights danced off her hair.

"Nice dress," he said, pleased his lips formed the words. And a dress meant she considered dinner a date too. Maybe. Like he could figure how women thought.

She opened the door wider, and he walked in, which was a whole lot better than standing on the porch staring at her. Man, he needed to work on his dating skills. Dating skills wouldn't explain why she looked so good. With a baller babe, he didn't have to open his mouth, just his wallet. Talley represented a whole new level of play.

She sure had a pretty smile, which was where his eyes needed to stay. Too bad that red dress dipped in front and stopped before the view got interesting.

Talley patted his backside. "You're looking pretty hot yourself."

What the ...? He grabbed her hand and spun her toward the door. "Woman, I'm trying to be a gentleman."

"Why?"

"Because ..." One thought rattled his brain, and he sure couldn't say *that*. "You're ... Talley."

"Last I checked." She extracted a key fob from her purse. "Relax, I'm not going to strip you and have my evil way."

*Tough break for him.* "I've got Mom's Pilot." He'd even swept it out for tonight.

She turned the dead bolt on the front door. "Nope, we're taking my car."

No way. "I'll drive."

"You're making an impression on seven boys. Boys are born with the hots for cars." She grabbed his hand and slapped the keys into his palm. "You were hot for my car."

*Nope, he was hot for her.* Since he couldn't say that out loud, he held up her coat for her. His gaze arrowed to her breasts, where the dress stopped, and his imagination continued to dip. So not his fault. Her breasts were just there. You couldn't take a guy into a bakery and deny him a cookie. Unaware of the detour his thoughts had taken, Talley closed the view and led him through her house to the garage.

He forced his gaze, and his thoughts, to her sleek car. "You're right. I love this car."

"Too bad it's too cold to let the top down. You should drive it along the beach in the summer."

He ran his hand along the side of the car, but the shiny red metal didn't erase the image of Talley's curves etched on his retinas. Red car, red dress, red lace underneath. He exhaled. What else would he find? Under the dress. He could care less about the car.

"Whit?" She held up her palms.

"Got it." He opened the passenger door for her, wondering how long he'd stood immobile, thinking about what lie beneath her clothes like a pervert.

She dropped into the tan bucket seat, and her dress pulled high over creamy-white thighs. He snapped his slackened jaw closed along with her door. It was a conspiracy to remind him of how they'd been together. How they could be. *In your bed, not your head.*

"It fits like a glove," he said, settling into the seat.

When he turned the key, the engine purred. He flexed his hands on the padded steering wheel, enjoying the smooth texture of the leather.

"Whit?"

Between the woman and her car, he was going to embarrass himself. "Yeah?"

No way was he going to look at her. He eased into reverse. *Nice and smooth. Ugh!* Every thought led to Talley.

*Focus. Driveway free of people, pets, and bicycles? Check.*

"Whit?"

Before he shifted into first, he turned to her. A dark, sexy gaze held his. He swallowed. He should've brought water. His mouth hadn't been this parched since summer practice. "What?"

"Stop making love to my car. It's turning me on."

He wet his lips. If she only knew. Unable to hold his gaze on her smoldering dark eyes, he focused on the gearshift. Aw man, he'd been caressing the padded knob. He stopped. Breathed. Unscrambled his brain.

"From my position, it looks like we've got two plays." He gripped the steering wheel. "Tell your friend we'll be late and take care of what's really on our minds now."

"Or?"

With the sexy quality of her voice stroking him, his right leg shook on the brake. "I love this car. It's sleek and sexy like its owner."

Her heavy brows almost merged. "What's the second play?"

Every time he was with her, her lips seemed—fuller. Or maybe he'd never seen her wear a deep-red shade of lipstick.

"Whit?"

He forced his gaze to meet hers.

"What's play two?" she said.

Words? She wasn't a baller babe. He shifted into first and released the clutch slow and easy. "I'm taking you to a place down on the water. A friend suggested it." *Pretty good fake if she'd let it go.*

"You forgot Hope."

He tooted the horn. Five minutes later, Hope sauntered across the drive and crawled in behind Talley. For once, his sister didn't comment—as long as he didn't count the smirk on her face.

"Rachel lives in the new neighborhood called Walnut Hill

on Seventy-six, about halfway between your grandmother's old place and here."

Relief rushed through him. Timing was everything. Yeah, he was primed and ready for the catch. Based on his knowledge of women, so was she. For now, he'd talk to the boys. Then he'd focus on Talley. Man, he could listen to the husky timbre of her voice and stare at the way she moved forever. Later, if the timing felt right, he'd tell her what he'd been thinking. After that? It was anyone's game.

———

THE SAME SENSE of accomplishment he felt after a winning catch filled Whit's chest. His talk with the boys had gone better than expected. He still had one more thing to do.

"Do you mind if I let Parker sit in the driver's seat for a few minutes?" he asked, opening the passenger door for Talley. "I need a chance to talk to him. He knows you, and I figure the car will distract him for a few minutes."

When her expressive brown eyes widened, he guessed he'd surprised her.

"I'm sure Parker will be thrilled," she said. "You were great, by the way."

"Thanks. I'll just be a minute. I'm going to check with Parker's mom."

Three minutes later, Whit took Parker's hand and slid the back door to the Evan's van closed. Whit's face still burned from embarrassment. He'd asked permission to spend a few private minutes with Parker and give the boy a gift. Instead of a quick yes from Parker's mom, he'd received every accolade known to man. According to Mrs. Evans, he'd earned the keys to heaven—with wings. Why didn't people understand he needed the boys more than they needed him? A fact that had solidified when he'd talked to them this evening.

Parker squeezed his hand. "I want to buy a car like this when I grow up." Whit opened the door, and Parker scrambled inside. "Hi, Miss Talley. Your car is awesome."

"Thank you, Parker."

"Is it fast?" The boy slid his hands along the steering wheel. "Mom's car isn't fast."

Whit stooped beside the door. "Pretty fast."

While Parker checked out every gauge on the dash, Whit scrambled for the best way to frame the words. "I brought you over here so I could tell you something," he started.

Parker seemed to dial into the change in his tone. Although Whit maintained his smile, his chest ached like he'd been hit by the entire defensive team. The downward tilt of Parker's eyes and mouth scored right on his heart. He recognized the signs of loss because he'd experienced them after his dad was killed in Afghanistan.

Life went on after death. Even kids got it. But at ten, he hadn't wanted to go on. Everything about going on was tied to his dad. The dad who made things better. The dad who made him feel safe. The dad who had hugged him on the tarmac and never returned.

He pulled the stone with the scratched *W* on its side from his pocket and held it in his palm. "My dad made this for me."

Parker circled the stone with his index finger. "Did he carve the W on it for your name?"

Whit's throat ached, making speech impossible, so he nodded.

"Was your dad a Marine too?"

"Yep, he fought in Iraq. When they sent his things home, there were three stones inside. One for me, and one for each of my brothers."

"Did he die there?" Parker's voice was barely above a whisper.

Whit nodded, not trusting his ability to speak. Parker

needed to know he could get through the loss of his dad. Although the pain diminished with time, it never went away. Whit hated the struggle was necessary for Parker. Kids shouldn't have to worry about losing their dads in war, but the world didn't turn on *shoulds*.

"My dad was strong and brave like yours. When I was with him, I always felt safe." Whit ran his thumb over the smooth surface. "I've kept this in my pocket since I was your age. When I feel scared or lonely, I touch it. That's why it's worn smooth in some spots."

Tentatively, Parker traced the *W* on the rock's surface. "Is it like magic?"

"Not magic, but special like our dads. When I touch it, I feel better. Like Dad's here with me, watching out for me— only I can't see him."

"My dad didn't give me anything to touch." Parker looked up, his expression so lost that Whit's gut cramped. "He didn't come home."

"I've been thinking about that." Whit placed the stone into the boy's small palm. "Marines are special men, so I think they go to a special place for people who serve their country. Marines always help Marines, like their sons help other Marine sons."

"Like you and me?"

"Yep. Like you and me. Since your dad was *especially* brave and didn't have time to make your stone, he asked my dad to help out." He closed Parker's fingers over the small talisman. "I'm all grown up now, so it's my duty to pass this on to you. Any time you feel lonely or scared, touch it right here, and remember your dad is watching out for you."

"Do you think it would help Mom?" Parker asked. "Some-times, she's really sad."

Whit swallowed. He'd give anything to bring back Parker's smile. His eyes blurred, and the back of his throat swelled. He squeezed Parker's bony shoulder. In a sudden move, Parker's spindly arms tightened around his neck. Whit's chest expanded as a tear slid down his cheek. Embracing Parker, his heart filled with ... hope? For the first time in his life, a sharp yearning flooded his system, a yearning for a son to love, and a family.

"You know," he whispered against the boy's red curls. "If you let your mom hold it and give her a hug like this, I bet it would help her."

Parker nodded and stepped out of the car. Although Whit shortened his strides on the short walk to the Parker van, his eyes were still moist when he returned to Talley's car. Yeah, getting choked up in public embarrassed him, but life happened. Players might act tough on the field, but he'd seen his share of guys break down, especially visiting kids in the hospital.

When he slipped in behind the wheel, Talley was staring out the passenger window.

"Sorry, I took so long," he said. "I wanted to answer all of their questions. And talk to Parker."

She faced him, her wide, dark eyes moist. "You were amazing."

"I loved talking to those little guys." Except talking to them reminded him of what he couldn't have, would never have—a son. "And Parker." He switched on the engine. "After all he's been through, he's thinking about his mom. Man, that tore me up."

She bit her lip and nodded. "It was all I could do to hold back sobs."

"Good thing you did." He gripped the gearshift and Talley placed her soft, warm hand over his. "I was having a hard time manning up."

"And we always thought we were so bad, back in our wild years."

He suppressed the urge to kiss her. Not because he'd been undressing her with his eyes since she opened her door, but because she'd made a joke. The diversion gave him time to control the ache in his chest and clear his watery eyes.

"What can I say?" Whit eased the car into traffic. "I'm a player. Tough on the outside, and marshmallow on the inside. Just don't tell the media. It would be a sin to wreck my tough-guy image."

"On a cheerier note, did you see the boys' smiles when you did the touchdown dance?"

"That moment will stay with me for the rest of my life. I want to order jerseys and caps for them. Do you think Rachel can get their sizes?" He shifted into third gear, ignoring the emptiness in his chest. "And t-shirts too. Would adding my number seem … I don't know, like I've got a big head or something?"

"Nah, they'd love it." Talley grinned. "While you're at it, order sweatshirts for them too."

"You're right. I'll hook them up." What a jerk. He needed to shut down the self-pity and focus on the boys. Anything to make them happy, add some cheer to their lives. The pinch in his gut eased. Making a great catch thrilled him and his fans loved it. Football gave ordinary folks a chance to win, succeed. In a tough world, people needed that. But today with the boys? He couldn't explain it. He'd mattered in a more important way, made a difference in Parker's life.

In the seat beside him, Talley shifted, the squeak of leather breaking the silence. Her palm still rested over his hand. She'd introduced him to Parker and the Scouts.

"Thanks for talking me into this gig." He winked to ease the tension. "And for the cool ride."

"You're welcome. I'm glad I got to witness this evening. Everything about it was awesome."

"Yep, awesome. And this is one sweet machine." Made even sweeter with her in the passenger seat.

"So why don't you trade in your truck?"

*Like that was going to happen.* "A man needs a truck."

"Of course, they do." Sarcasm laced her sexy voice. "Are you planning to do a lot of hauling?"

"I helped move Kyle and Nate into apartments."

"I'm a teacher, remember? This car is very affordable. You should treat yourself to one."

"I'll come home and take yours for a spin." What was he saying?

He squirmed in the seat. That sounded like a proposal, a long-distance one. His teammates Ivan and Josh had tried long-distance dating and failed. Too many available women waited for the single guys after every game, and the "player" label defined many of his teammates on and off the field.

"I read you practice twice as much as most guys on the team," she said.

*Chill, Murphy!* This wasn't the time to get a big head. It was an observation, not a compliment. But that didn't change the sappy feeling bubbling in his gut. She'd taken the time to check up on him. "You've been reading up on me?"

"Don't let your head swell," she warned. "It was the only magazine in the salon, and it takes forever to get highlights."

He loved her hair. When he cut a glance at her, a little breath escaped him. It didn't look like she'd changed the color. He wasn't sure what her color was called. It wasn't a true red or brown, but kind of like leaves in the fall. He curled his fingers around the wheel at the crazy urge to push one of those silky strands behind her ear.

He glanced at her. "I like the color, the way the sun makes it look kind of fiery."

"You noticed?"

"I notice everything about you."

Her eyes widened. Uh-oh. He needed to keep his mouth closed, and his eyes and ears open.

"That's a shock," she said, but her snarky tone didn't deceive him.

"I notice." He shrugged. "I just don't talk about it." He didn't have enough words in his vocabulary to tell her his thoughts—at least G-rated words. As for the X-rated words? Those required action, not speech.

"If we continue, you'll be in my bed," she said.

The car stuttered, and his foot searched for the gas pedal. He'd be happy to join her in bed as long as ... "You know I have to play football?"

"Got that, loud and clear. I've just never understood why you continue to play year after year."

He intended to keep that a secret. Besides, for him and Talley to work, they had to keep it light. In her bed, not in his head. "I've got my reasons."

He braked at a stoplight and glanced her way. Although lots of things separated them, he was a risk-taker, and he wanted more than one night with her. He wanted to be with a woman who wanted him, not his name, his money, or a shot on TV. When the light changed, he eased the car through the gears, savoring the upward shift of the engine, so like the feelings surging inside him.

Ideas to stay away from her and then get closer wobbled in his head. The back and forth made his vision blur and his stomach tense. It wouldn't work. Talley, a good friend to him and his family, deserved more than his lust. He had nothing to offer her. He'd seen her face with the boys. She loved being with them as much as he did. If she stayed with him, she didn't have a shot at her own family. And even if she were okay with a childless life, what could he offer besides money?

While players busted their chops at practice and flew from game to game, their wives and girlfriends spent weeks alone. Talley's life was here, not in Charlotte. Heck, Charlotte wasn't a guarantee. If the Cougars didn't renew, he could end up on the West Coast. Plus, he needed her help with Hope.

"Are you going to stay in Sunberry?" *Super play there, Whit. While you're at it, dump some salt on the wound.*

"Are you kidding?" She lifted one booted foot. "These feet are in cement."

So were his—to keep playing and provide for his family and kids like Parker.

"My friends and family are here." She made a funny face. "Change that. Your family, which I made my adopted family, is here. Who knows if Mom and Dad will retire? Or where they'll land when they do."

"Maybe you should hyphenate your name to Frost-Murphy."

Her sudden inhale echoed in the small car.

Whit cringed. *That hadn't come out right.*

When he glanced at her, she shrugged. "Caught me off guard on that one. I've wanted to be a Murphy most of my life."

He wanted to grant that wish. Always had. He was an idiot. A muddy sludge polluted his gene pool. Although he'd accepted personal risks, a man with his issues didn't father kids. Talley would make a fantastic mom. She deserved a family of her own.

"Your family is perfect." She made a noise that crossed between a chuckle and a hiccup. "Well, not perfect. Your family has such close bonds. You support one another. That's what drew me. That's what holds me here."

"They're special to me too." *And so are you.* He squirmed in the bucket seat. "I even get homesick for them—all of them. Even Hope, the turd."

Talley laughed, and this time the sound rang true, embracing him, lifting him from his slump. Her eyes crinkled and moistened with tears. The sound of her laugh buzzed through him like a shot of stiff whiskey. A grin twitched at his lips. He almost liked her laugh better than her low voice that went straight to his junk. He straightened in his seat. Nah, her laugh was second best.

"Am I rubbing off on you?" she said.

"Must be."

"A word of advice." She cupped her hand near her mouth. "Don't let Hope hear you call her a turd. She'd be on a rant for a week. That said, I totally agree."

On the road in front of them, an old pickup clogged the lane. Whit checked the rearview and changed lanes. The car's engine hummed. He needed this—fun ride, fun company.

Thirty-five minutes later, he pulled in front of a restaurant hugging the real estate between the road and the beach.

"I hope the food is good." He wheeled into a narrow parking space with room to spare. "I'm starving."

A cold, salty breeze bit his face, providing the perfect excuse to tuck Talley close to his side. Inside, they followed the hostess to a corner table for two. White linen covered the surface, and a candle flickered at the center. Outside the long bank of windows facing the ocean, the Atlantic swelled under shifting dark clouds.

He held Talley's chair.

"So, have you heard anything about your contract?" she said, surprising him.

"Still in negotiations. Stan hopes the other team offers will motivate the Cougars to move. But tonight, I want to chill. No drama."

Her cheeks turned pink. "This is lovely. I've heard about this place but haven't eaten here."

"Glad you like it." However, the way his heart stuttered

worried him. "Ivan swore by the place. The guy is a wizard when it comes to finding a fancy restaurant."

After the waiter took their order and delivered her wine and his milk, Talley motioned to his glass. "I thought players were into the party gig."

"Lots do. I don't, especially during the season."

"Because you have a lot of people depending on you?" Her softly spoken words battered his underbelly.

Parched, he should've drunk his milk or water while she sipped her wine, but the candlelight dancing in her hair mesmerized him. Memories of touching her, inhaling her scent, and sinking inside her engulfed him.

"It makes me angry," she said, the heat in her words ruining his fantasy.

"Why?" He straightened in the ladder-back chair.

"The media prints trash about you. They never show your visits with hospitalized kids or the Scouts. You're a really good guy."

That's all he needed, Talley taking on the media in his defense. "I don't read the tabloids, and I don't let it get to me. The people who know me understand those stories are crap. The reporters? They're trying to scratch out a living."

When wine sloshed over her glass to the tablecloth, he glanced up. Man she was glorious with that fire in her gaze. What would it be like if she took that same fire to his bed?

"You're too nice." Indignation flared her nostrils. "Making a living off the misery of others is dreadful."

He ran the tip of his index finger across the top of her hand. "Do you know how sexy you are when you get mad?"

She blushed and closed her very kissable mouth. Go figure. He'd stumbled upon the halt key for a Talley Quixote rant. Curious, he glanced at the time on his cell to see how long she would remain silent.

After two minutes, the waiter rescued her with their salads.

"You should set them straight." She pointed at him with a forkful of leaves.

The image of her naked, nostrils flaring, and eyes sparking fire flashed in his mind. He chewed his salad without tasting it. Maybe this would be his lucky night.

# CHAPTER SEVENTEEN

Talley chased a shredded carrot around her plate. The vegetable slipped more than her thoughts. Where was her self-discipline? Who knew she was a closet addict and Whit was her drug of choice? She was so screwed. For now, she'd fall back and regroup before she started groping him beneath the table.

The server removed the empty salad plates, and Talley excused herself and escaped to the restroom. The facilities continued with the calming driftwood and sea green decor, yet her nerves couldn't have stretched tighter if the cheer squad had tossed a three-year-old into the air. Why did important decisions and actions have to be so darned hard?

She washed her hands and tapped cold water on her rosy cheeks. She'd given up on love and Whit five years ago. Events had forced her decision, and she'd survived—until now. With a little whoosh, she slammed the linen towel into the wicker bin. She always had to stretch the limits. Why couldn't she let life unfold and enjoy her evening in a lovely restaurant with Whit? It was one night.

After a quick plump of her hair, Talley squared her shoulders and weaved her way back through the diners. An attractive woman stepped in front of her. The green hand of envy curled in her belly. Enjoying a pleasant meal with Whit did not include a cougar poaching her date.

The woman touched Whit's shoulder. "Pardon me."

Whit turned, his gaze bouncing from the woman to Talley and back. Her jealousy talons receded. Something about the stranger's bronzed skin and upturned eyes seemed familiar. Talley slipped into her seat.

"I wouldn't usually ... I mean, I'm sorry to interrupt your dinner," the woman said as her hand fluttered to the gold chain artfully looped around her neck. "It's just ... Are you Whit Murphy?"

Talley squinted at the stranger, her thoughts filtering through the past. The woman's mist of tears and her low voice clicked a memory into place like a strobe light. Holy smokes! Five years ago, Talley believed she'd never erase the image of Jeff's mother, Melanie, sobbing over his casket.

"Mrs. Rice?" Talley motioned to the empty chair across from Whit. "Please, have a seat. Join us."

Instead of sitting, the woman perched on the edge of the chair, ready as a skittish bird to take flight.

"Talley?" Melanie's hand raised to her lips. "I'm sorry. I didn't recognize you."

Whit raked his hand over his head, looking from Talley to Melanie and back. "Mrs. Rice. Good to see you." But the vibration in his voice told a different story.

"I didn't know you lived near Sunberry," Talley said.

"After Jeff ..." Melanie started with a vacant stare. "Matt and I have always liked the ocean, so he accepted a remote position. We moved to Emerald Isle a year ... after we lost Jeff." Her gaze drifted to Whit. "Do you live nearby too?"

Talley blinked. Uh-oh, Mrs. Rice didn't know. It made sense. After Jeff's accident, Talley avoided football—and Jeff had only been a friend. Melanie had lost her son. Of course, she'd avoid anything football related.

Talley bumped Whit's knee. When his brow wrinkled in confusion, she swallowed, knowing they were headed for a terrible wreck with no way to prevent it.

"I'm visiting my family," Whit said. "I moved to Charlotte after I signed on with the Cougars."

"Oh, I didn't know." The color drained from Melanie's cheeks. "We don't follow sports."

From the way Whit's gaze darted to hers, Talley guessed he'd determined her warning nudge too late.

"What's Jason up to these days?" Talley wrung her hands, hoping she'd gotten the name of Jeff's younger brother right.

"Architect," Melanie answered, but her features remained tense. "He graduated last year."

"Awesome," Whit said.

"How could you?" Melanie's eyes filled with tears. "How could you continue to play after Jeff died? You know the sport kills."

"Melanie?" The deep, masculine voice cut through the low conversations of the dining room. "Your meal is getting cold."

When Melanie straightened, Talley's internal alerts continued to blast. The older woman seemed wrapped too tight, still harboring the guilt and resentment of her loss.

Melanie's features tightened. "Matt, sorry for making you wait. You remember Whit, Jeff's college teammate, and his girlfriend Talley?"

Whit stood, and Matt Rice, Jeff's dad, shook his hand. "Good to see you. I saw you signed on with the Cougars. Glad it's going well for you." He nodded to Talley.

"I've had a good year," Whit said, unlike the experience they now shared.

Talley could usually cover for awkward lags in the conversation; however, her mind had hit the wall.

"Well, we'll let you get back to your dinner," Matt said after a moment of pained silence.

The couple disappeared and Whit gulped half the water in his glass. He wiped his mouth on his napkin. "Talk about a major blitz. I didn't recognize her."

"Don't feel bad," Talley said. "It took me a minute. She didn't use to highlight her hair."

"She didn't use to hate the game."

"Look at it from her perspective." Talley sipped her wine. *Don't go there. Just move on. Forget about the meeting.* Her hand trembled. There was so much at stake, especially with Jeff's memory so fresh.

"She blames football for taking her son," she said, her voice sharper than she intended.

"The league's made changes." He didn't meet her gaze. "They've added new rules, and they follow concussion protocols."

She folded her hands in her lap and squeezed her fingers tight enough to stop circulation. "It's not enough. And they didn't care for you. You didn't rest after Sunday's game. You hit the ground running. Still are."

"After the game, I went straight to the team doc." Whit's easygoing tone turned defensive. "He checked me over."

"They can't see inside your skull." Talley dug her nails in her palms, but the encounter with Melanie had left her raw, exposed.

"We can't stop living or playing because of a freak accident," Whit said. "Life's a risk. More people die in car accidents than like Jeff."

The server brought the House Special, grilled snapper adorned with roasted sweet peppers, and Talley's response fizzled on her tongue. She squeezed her eyes closed. Nausea tightened her stomach. Take a breath. Come at the problem from another angle—later.

"Why risk it?" The words flowed from her tongue before she could stop them. "You of all people should understand how precious our minds are."

With slow, deliberate movements, Whit placed his fork on the table, the blue of his irises flashing. "You have to push, don't you?"

"I want to understand." Because she needed something to hold on to. Something besides the fear he'd suffer dementia, emotional instability, depression, and suicide in later years.

"We live in a crazy world," he said, his words distorted from a stiff jaw. "You're a teacher and don't make squat. I play a game and make too much. If I get hurt, my livelihood is gone, forever. What if playing ball is all I can do? Guys have kids, mortgages, responsibilities."

"And what if the two to five years you play means years of dementia or worse? What about the families who live with that?"

When he closed his eyes, she focused on the ocean outside her window. In the moonlight, breakers built and rushed toward the shore like the fear she felt for Whit. Why couldn't he see the danger?

He placed his napkin beside his plate. "I wanted a nice meal with you. You know? Catch up, laugh, enjoy your company."

Didn't she want that? She forced her resistant neck muscles to nod because she couldn't risk speaking.

"I try not to think about that last night with Jeff." He hesitated. "That's a brain-cave memory."

His words stopped her thoughts. *Breathe in. Breathe out. Redirect.* "Explain your brain cave."

"Hope's invention, not mine," he said. "It's your head's black hole. I stick all the bad stuff in there."

"Jeff's accident was not your fault." She rested her hand

over his long fingers, the rough edges of healing scabs a reminder of his brutal occupation.

"It doesn't matter. If the memory torments you, in it goes. Don't you have a few?"

*Didn't everybody?* But the anguish in his gaze made her rethink her answer. He deserved a thoughtful and honest response.

"The night I told my parents I was not moving again—ever," she said.

Although she didn't want to revisit that memory, she'd forced Whit to examine the reasons he played ball. The least she could do was review the events in her so-called brain cave.

Whit folded her hand in his, the warmth of his flesh chasing away the guilt that always trailed the thoughts of her parents.

"I remember when that happened." He kissed her knuckles. "Mom sat us down for a Murphy talk. She didn't give us details, but we were instructed to be extra nice to you."

Heavens. This man, his family, had kept her afloat, given her hope and love. Of course, he would say something comforting, just like his mom. Except she didn't deserve it this time.

"I wasn't very pleasant at the time. I understood my parent's dedication to the Corps." She glanced up at him. "But I resented their service. Resented being uprooted and moved, having to make new friends, new schools. I liked Sunberry. Grandma was here, your family, my friends. I finally had a place where I belonged. I wasn't giving it up."

"You didn't."

"I was horrible to my parents." A shudder shook her shoulders. No matter what she did for her parents, she couldn't make up for that meltdown. "I told them they were the worst parents ever, and I wasn't leaving my friends behind for them. So, they left me behind." Who could blame them? She'd been an obnoxious brat only thinking about herself.

She shook her head to rid the memory, but it wasn't going anywhere. "It's taken a long time to convince my parents they didn't cause irreparable harm to their only child."

"That bad, huh?"

"I was their worst nightmare. They survived. But I said hurtful things." Was he disappointed in her? Talley peeked at him from the corner of her eye and breathed. The man was a saint. Only concern and compassion softened his gaze. Not a hint of disgust. "Ever notice how teens know the exact words to shatter a parent's heart?"

He grimaced as though he'd discovered a bone in his fish —except he'd pushed his meal aside. "I haven't had a lot of experience with kids, like you."

"Take my word for it." She forced a smile. "But enough about me. Anyway, I get the brain cave. You're right. We've all experienced traumatic events, or in my case, delivered them. It's not fun getting them out and dusting them off."

She'd fought her parents because she craved a home. Whit fought retirement because he craved success. The goals and motivations were different, but that didn't make one better than the other. Still, her goal didn't risk her life. Her chin trembled. No, her goal had risked her parent's hearts. Did she have the right to press her fears on Whit?

With Whit's big, scarred hands covering hers, she released her fear, if only for an evening. She had tonight. Sure, she wanted to be with him, side to side, flesh to flesh. But her desire was much more than sex. It was Whit. His heart, his mind. He listened to people—all people, from small grieving Parker to his lumbering teammates. He empathized and put their needs before his. He cared about feelings, needs, even flaws, like hers. She'd stepped over the line a few times, pushed too hard. He'd resisted, but not once did he judge.

The man embodied unconditional acceptance. How did that happen?

Talley froze. She'd been so careful. Endured hours of self-talk, analyzing, and planning, so she wouldn't succumb. But she had. Squaring her shoulders, she huffed out a breath. No more whining. She'd met an incredible man, gotten the chance to love him—twice.

When he leaned in and kissed her, her expanding heart fluttered against her ribs. She could continue to guard her heart, or she could show him what a future together could hold.

"You said you want to understand," he said, his features solemn. "But some things are hard to explain. Even to yourself."

"I'm sorry. I didn't mean to spoil our dinner."

He released her hand, and she picked up her fork and stared at the beautifully plated fish and peppers. "Five minutes ago, I wanted to gnaw the legs off the table."

"Me too."

Their gazes locked.

"Take-out boxes?" they said in unison.

———

IN THE DARKNESS of her car, only the hum of the engine breached the silence. Whit drove with one hand resting on the gearshift. Talley covered it with hers. Despite the cold night, his skin was warm beneath her hand. When he released the gearshift and turned his palm up, she fit her fingers between his.

"I want you to know ..." She swallowed. "I'm trying to accept the different positions of the sport. Really. I am."

He glanced her way. Since she couldn't read his expression, she waited, hoping he'd share his thoughts.

"Fair enough," he said.

"You just don't believe me?"

"I believe *you* believe it." He passed a slow-moving vehicle. "I'm grateful for everything I accomplish. Every morning I say, 'I'm working and I'm healthy.'"

Talley squeezed her lids closed. But was he healthy? Hadn't he experienced CTE symptoms?

He downshifted for a red light, and the carryout bags rustled in the back. The fragrance of fresh garlic and lemon tickled her senses.

Whit's stomach rumbled and he rubbed his hand across his abdomen. "Dinner smells good."

Her appetite had dwindled beneath her dilemma. Every shred of her soul yearned for another chance with Whit, to rebuild what they once shared, create possibilities for a future —*if* she could accept the risks he took. But life held risks for everyone, not just football players. A shiver sashayed across her shoulders. Too many people she'd loved had left her. Like her parents. Like Whit. Was she ready to risk losing him again?

His warm flesh beneath her fingers called to her. She drew circles on the back of his hand. "I could warm the food. I don't have wine in the fridge, but I have a new half-gallon of milk."

Even in the shadowy light from oncoming traffic, the heat in his gaze singed hers. "You don't have to lure me to your place with food."

"No?" She struggled to infuse her tone with a playfulness they needed.

"But it doesn't hurt."

"At least the Murphy boys won't be spying on my driveway."

His hoot chased away the suffocating tension.

"Remember when you, Kyle, and Nate ambushed me on my first big date with Jimmy Larson?"

"We were a little bad," he said.

"A little?" Talk about minimizing the deed. "You guys rocked the car, ruined my first French kiss, and marked me for life." She might have been more convincing if her snicker hadn't leaked out, spoiling her feigned indignance.

"What'd you expect? The windows were steamed up."

"Privacy."

"We got rid of Jimmy," he said without a hint of regret.

"I was so mad. I'd been chasing him for weeks. He finally asked me out, and you guys wrecked my date."

"He wasn't good enough for you."

"Really?" That was a surprising perspective.

"The sarcasm makes me hot," he said with a wink.

"What?" He couldn't possibly know she'd been daydreaming about getting him naked.

"When you get sassy like that." He shrugged. "It makes a man wonder."

She squeezed her thighs together. "Quit changing the subject. You and your brothers deliberately humiliated me to stop me from dating Jimmy."

"You were like our sister. We had to protect you."

"And who is going to protect me from you?"

He sobered. "I laid it out for you. We can get it on. See where it goes between us. But I'm going to continue with the Cougars. For now, that's all I have to offer."

Darned him for making it a challenge. Who was she kidding? Her heart had already made the decision. She'd merely chosen not to admit it.

"I make my own decisions." She removed her hand from his. "I didn't need your protection from Jimmy Larson, and I don't need it now."

"I was upfront with you."

"Like now?"

He pulled into her drive and waited for the garage door to open. "It's your play. I can walk across the yard to Mom's, or I can come inside with you. As soon as I get Hope straightened out, I'm going back to Charlotte. Football is my job. For the most part, I love it."

"If we go inside, we're not talking about dinner?"

He shook his head, and her heart hammered like a jackhammer. Heavens, he was such a beautiful man—inside and out.

A smile crept across her face. "But we're definitely eating that fish afterward."

———

**Reader's Choice:**

1- Page forward for a sweet read.

2-For a Behind-the-Door bedroom scene, type https://Book Hip.com/KKQMPSF

# CHAPTER EIGHTEEN

Standing on the sideline of Sunberry High's gridiron the following day, an image of Jeff's polished coffin blurred Whit's vision. He blinked to focus on the three high schoolers scrambling to their feet.

"Your head was too low," he hollered, trying to hide the worry from his voice. "It's called heads-up tackling for a reason."

The players weren't the only ones with focus problems. If he was going to teach the guys safer tackling, he had to keep his head in the game and out of the nightmare that had haunted him since Jeff's death. Worse, the players looked at him like he could walk on water. He played a game for a living. He didn't save lives. However, if he'd stay focused, he might teach the Sunberry team how to prevent injuries. Although the coach was trying and his heart was in the work, he lacked the specific training.

"Guys, listen up," Whit said. "Let's go through the position one more time."

Eager faces concentrated on his body movements. The

kids listened, soaking up his every word, but new techniques required practice and time. He only had three days.

While the team ran another play, Whit paced along the sidelines, rubbing his hands up and down his forearms. He could swear bugs were digging into his flesh, which was odd. Football practice usually relieved his edginess. It wasn't working today. Despite his efforts to instruct the boys, every tackle, every pass, reminded him of Jeff.

"That's better," he hollered. But was it enough?

Talley had a point. The young players liked to bang heads, which was risky. And the Cougar owners would probably birth cubs if they heard him admit that out loud. Bottom line: the boys on the team would never be professionals. They were just having fun, and he needed to do whatever he could to keep them safe.

When Coach ended the practice, Whit hustled to his truck to wait for Hope. Unlike Talley, who stuck on a position until she'd pulverized everything in her path, Hope changed like the North Carolina weather, which had returned to summer—in November.

Hope climbed into the passenger seat. Her smile didn't reach her eyes. "Are you helping Coach so you can spy on me?"

He slammed his door closed—childish but defusing, in a small way. "Considering your stunt the other night, yes."

"I'm just following in your footsteps." And she wasn't backing down. "You're so busy playing Mr. Bigshot, you don't know how the family views your behavior."

"That's not the way it is, and you know it." He cranked the engine.

"Sorry, big brother. I'm just giving my humble opinion."

*Humble, his butt.* "I don't act like some high roller. I'm just a regular guy who happens to be pretty good at running and catching a football. End of story. And that's all I can do, unlike my talented little sister."

"Seems to be working for you." She ignored his compliment. "What's wrong with me wanting the same thing?"

"We had this discussion," he said.

"But you didn't get it?"

Why did she have to be so pleasant? It was hard to argue a point with her big smile staring him in the face. He stiffened. She made him feel like a bully. But that didn't mean he'd back down. "Because you don't understand the downside."

"If it's so bad, why don't I hear you and your teammates complain?"

"People don't want to hear a guy who is making big bucks whine and moan about his job."

"So the guys who don't like the game can suck it up?" She shrugged. "I'd keep my mouth shut all the way to the bank to cash my humongous check too."

Whit dropped his head back and blinked at the small rip in his truck's roof liner—the same as the crack in his logic.

"I didn't *choose* football. I just happened to be good at it."

"I'm good at basketball," she said. "Especially if the pay's good and I don't have to spend years in school."

"Look, the money is nice, and I like buying things for my family. But I like the game and the way the guys work together as a team." He shrugged. "There are also downsides —big ones."

"I'm all ears, big brother. Tell me the sacrifices you make for fame and fortune."

He worked his jaw to relieve the cramp from grinding his molars. "We play and practice when it's one hundred degrees or one degree, rain, snow, or shine."

"Not with basketball," she said in a sing-song voice.

"The grind is constant. You can't let up because there are ten guys itching to take your slot. You're away for weeks from your family. No free time. No days off. Just go, go, go." He held her gaze, willing her to understand. "And with basketball, the season is longer, and there are more games. You can't let up. You must be better, stronger, faster. But after a while, you can't because the clock is ticking and you're aging. One bad tackle or fall and you're behind, and the next hungry rookie is waiting for his big chance. Worse, it starts taking longer and longer to recover—*if* you recover."

He'd painted a bleak picture, so why was she smiling as though he'd described an island vacation.

"Go for it, little sis." He despised the bite in his voice. But he'd run out of words to make her understand reason. "I hope you can avoid a critical injury. One that could cripple you for the rest of your life, or maybe one that damages you so badly you can't take care of yourself." For once, he didn't hide the fear. She needed to know the truth. "Enough to lose your personality and require twenty-four-hour care."

He turned the key and accelerated from the lot, cringing at the squeal of his tires. Hope, bless her, remained quiet. She'd kept a straight face, but he'd seen her lip twitch, or maybe it was one of those tics. Something had crossed her features. Maybe he'd gotten through her hard head, not a lot, but a little.

"Not every athlete suffers CTE," she said in a low voice.

He swallowed. There it was. Out in the open. CTE, the dinosaur in the living room that professional athletes tried to ignore.

He turned onto the main road. "True."

His sister was a whiz, which is why he wanted more for her than the professional-sports life.

"What about you, big bro? Do you have … injuries that haven't gone away?"

He glanced at her. Her wide eyes were intent, alert for deceit. He adjusted his seat, careful to avoid wincing from his tender side. The balance problems and lapses had eased. Based on his limited knowledge, he'd bet he'd suffered a concussion. Maybe he should tell her about his symptoms. That would pound some sense into her rosy view of sports. But he couldn't risk it. Not with an outstanding contract. If word got out and the media got hold of it, he might end up with no contract.

"What happened to the girl who wanted to be a veterinarian or an astronaut?"

The sunny smile slipped. "You should come home more often. That girl grew up. I'm almost seventeen."

"So you'd think you were old enough to have a little self-respect. Not sell yourself short to some horny player trying to score a feel."

"Jeez," she hissed. "Not only is that crude, but it's old news. You're nagging like Mom."

The stoplight turned green, but he didn't accelerate. "Don't devalue yourself that way. You've got too much going for you. Accept your talents."

Instead of responding, she tugged at a thread on her clothes. A car honked, and Whit released the brake.

"I love you." The determination he'd tried for fell flat. She'd worn him down. Dealing with Hope was like going up against a championship team, knowing you didn't have a prayer. "I want the best for you. That's all I've always wanted."

Silence. He swallowed the disappointment. What else could he do? He'd played it straight.

When his cell signaled a missed call, he squeezed the steering wheel so tightly his hand cramped. After a quick trip through the local fast-food restaurant, he drove home. Hope hopped out of the truck the minute he shoved the lever into park and disappeared inside. He pressed redial and waited for his agent to pick up. He was due some good news for a change.

———

By the time eight o'clock rolled around, the nervous energy running along Whit's limbs threatened to implode. Since Hope, his wardrobe consultant, had remained in her room, he chose a pair of comfortable jeans and a striped cotton shirt. The temperature had fallen with the sun, but he wouldn't need a coat to walk across the lawn to Talley's.

"Wow!" Talley said, opening the door. "It's only been a few hours. How'd your evening tank so fast?"

"Hope and my agent."

"Do you want to talk about it?"

"Maybe later." Although his appetite had tanked, he needed a mood elevator. Talley rarely disappointed him.

"I promised dessert," she said leading the way to the kitchen. "I've got this incredible craving for brownies and caramel a la mode. You in?"

"I'm not that hungry." But he didn't want to sound like a jerk.

He huffed out a breath. If a little bit of chocolate and caramel flipped her switch, he could force it down. Besides, a guy couldn't stay grumpy around her dressed in a black pencil skirt and white blouse. Nothing wrong with black and white, as he'd explained to Hope. The fact that her blouse hinted at white lace beneath made a guy wonder.

This was just the pick-me-up he needed at the end of a crap day—Talley.

"Step into my lair." She wiggled her index finger at him. "I know you're the big chef here. However, you've got to sample my brownie innovation."

She pointed at the counter. "Sit."

"Go ahead." He drew the line at making a fool of himself. "I've got a good view from here."

"Look." She pointed a knife his way. "I've got something I want to talk to you about, and I need to soften you up with chocolate. So, humor me."

"Hold that thought." He shoved the ends of his mouth upward into a stupid smile. "How's that? And I'd love to share dessert with you—if I don't have to sit on the counter."

Her right brow arched. "You play. You pay." She tapped the counter. "Sit."

"Why do I need to sit on the counter?"

"It's a nurturing thing."

"Nurturing, huh?" Sounded like mothering, and his ideas had nothing to do with a parent.

Although her cheeks turned one shade lighter than a Cardinal's jersey, she patted the granite countertop. "Gals have fantasies too."

An image of Talley in ten provocative poses burned through his brain. He hopped on the counter. "I'm in."

"Whit!"

He lifted his hands. "You brought up fantasies."

"Not all fantasies are sexual," she protested.

"They aren't?" He pulled her between his knees for a kiss. Coffee exploded on his tongue. When he came up for air, she looked dazed. Yep, he knew the feeling. Chocolate and the buttery scent of caramel tickled his senses. Chocolate with Talley? Oh, yeah.

When she disentangled, he reached to stop her. "I wasn't done."

She swatted at his hand. "I need to talk to you about something."

"Sorry." For what? Who knew? If she was happy, he was happy. She was so into his head. He pushed the worrisome thought aside and focused on her hands.

With practiced ease, she covered a pan with aluminum foil. Her slender fingers smoothed the edges in the same way they'd moved over him. Next time he took Hope shopping, he'd purchase new jeans—in a relaxed fit.

He fidgeted on the counter to relieve the discomfort but couldn't move his gaze to a safe place. Talley had short, low-maintenance nails, unlike the claws sported by many of his football babes. She glided a knife, thick with caramel, across the top of two brownies.

"So, how'd practice go?"

"Better than I expected," he said. "Except the players act like I have the secret football sauce."

When she licked the end of the knife, his brain exploded. Man, he could watch her all day.

"To them, you do." She arranged the brownies on wax paper. "You're a star NFL player. Of course, they're fanboying you."

"I guess. But I don't see how this is going to help me get through to Hope."

Talley sprinkled chopped pecans over the caramel. "Is she still resistant?"

"I used to think I knew my sister. But after this trip?" He shook his head. "I suck at understanding a teen's mind." No, he sucked at pretty much anything that didn't contain football.

Though he didn't have fancy words for a good speech, he spilled his guts about his talk with Hope—if you could even call it that.

"So what do you think?" But he wasn't sure he wanted to hear her analysis of his latest Hope failure.

"I think there's no working out teens," she said. "You just get through it. I talked to Priscilla."

Did he know a Priscilla? Man, he needed to open his ears and close his eyes. That would never happen with Talley around him. But he wasn't going to push his luck. He'd missed about every verbal pass coming his way.

"She's Hope's basketball coach and a friend," Talley said. "Of course, Hope is a talented player. Priscila said a Coastal recruiter asked about her."

"Just what I need," Whit said.

He'd always wanted the best for his siblings, but life would've been simpler if Hope were only smart. Too bad she'd also gotten the athletic gene the same as he had. Only difference? Football was it for him. There wasn't a smart gene on his entire strand.

And if Talley didn't stop licking her fingers, he was going to embarrass himself or go caveman on her. Oblivious to his gutter detour, she sucked caramel from her index finger, her cheeks hollowing, then released it with a subtle smack. His vision blurred, and his jeans pinched his flesh.

"Misery loves company," Talley continued. "My night at the PTA turned out to be a bust too."

Although sorry her plan hadn't succeeded, his hearing had turned off.

*Kiss her*, raced his thoughts. Stop her talk. Cover her pretty pout before she tortured him blind.

"That's tough." His voice was as rusty as an old hinge. "But I've got a diversion."

"Trying to change a social norm isn't easy." She turned to wash her hands in the sink, but she was also avoiding eye contact. "Parents don't consider football dangerous."

Crap, he was ready for bedroom gymnastics, and she was winding up for a rant. Talley on a cause was more lethal than a lineman mowing down every man in his path.

With her tongue peeking from between her lips, she sandwiched the caramel and pecans with the other brownie.

"The dads are the worst." She wrapped her tongue around the knife, licking off the residual chocolate before dropping the utensil into the dishwasher. "What does pain tolerance have to do with masculinity?"

He'd like to take a shot on that one, but she'd probably swat him with a spatula. "Nobody likes a whiner. Players suck it up. Get the job done." His skin started to itch. He needed to move, but he'd promised to sit. "Want me to put those in the oven for you?"

"Microwave." She punched in the time and turned with her hands on her hips. "But I would like you to make a YouTube video."

He hopped to the floor. "No way."

"Think about it. We could reach kids everywhere. They would listen to a famous football player, and so would their parents."

The more he shook his head, the more she jutted out her chin. When she did that, she was about as immovable as Ivan on the line.

"We're the perfect team, like in college." She beamed at him as if he'd agreed to her crazy scheme. "I'll write a script. Simple, to the point. Nothing that will trip you up."

He placed his hands in a *T* two inches in front of her nose. "Time out!" The echo of his voice seemed to bounce off the walls in all directions.

She blinked, and her brows moved together. He hadn't meant to shout. He wanted her to stop talking. But she didn't look receptive to a kiss.

"I'll donate." He lowered his voice. "But no media. You know why."

"Wait until you try these." She removed the pan from the microwave. "Pour two glasses of milk."

A fake. He knew the play. Distract the opponent and then blindside them. But he was ready for her. There was no way she'd stop, and he wasn't going to give in. Not on this.

She rounded the counter and slid a saucer with two brownies toward him. "Be careful. The caramel will be hot."

Caramel oozed from between the chocolate layers. But he didn't want to eat. He also didn't want to talk. She bit into a fudgy square, and the tip of her tongue traced her lips. He swallowed.

She caught a crumb with her palm. "Aren't you going to try it?"

He'd rather try her. "I'll ... watch you."

She blotted her lips with a napkin, spoiling the image. "What?"

"I was going to help you with the cleanup," he said, unable to take his gaze from her mouth.

"I've ruined you." She pointed a finger at him. "One night in bed and all you think about is going back for more."

Absolutely. He still had a few operating brain cells. But she didn't want to hear that. She wanted him to eat. He bit into the rich chocolate and creamy caramel with the added crunch of pecans.

"Mm." It was almost as good as Talley. Caramel coated his lips, and he felt like a dog trying to manage a glob of peanut butter.

Talley's lids drooped, and her eyes turned smoky. "Let me help."

She moved closer and ran her tongue along the outline of his lips.

"Don't poke the bear," he whispered, his throat tight.

Holding his gaze, she took another bite with a flash of white teeth and pink tongue. She'd turned sorcerer. He swallowed and mimicked her actions. Their gazes still locked, they chewed, slowly.

"Clean up," she murmured.

He was all over that. When he finally released her, she

was watching him, her gaze filled with interest and something else.

"So, would you at least consider my proposal?" She grinned.

"Owners balk on videos telling parents and kids the sport is dangerous."

Did she have any idea what one lifted brow could do to a guy?

"Think about it," she said.

His thinking cells were the problem and he'd let his little homecoming get out of control. Time to man up. The longer he put it off telling her his latest news, the harder it would be. They'd had a good run, but it was time to end the fantasy.

"I heard from my agent," he said, his voice flat of emotion. "He got me two more years ... with the Phoenix Rattlers. I have to return to Charlotte on Monday. Fly to Phoenix soon." A nice city, but not where he wanted to live.

She stilled in his arms. "Too bad it has to end."

Aw man, he didn't want to hear "too bad." He was dying inside. Not that he wanted her to go postal and beg him to stay. They'd both known the rules long before the start of the action.

"It doesn't have to end." He stiffened his jaw but couldn't resist running his hands along her toned arms.

*Let loose, Murphy.* He couldn't save this, them. He was just causing a slow death in place of a quick end.

Determination burned in her gaze. "We both know that's not true."

It wasn't supposed to be like this. In her bed, not in his head. But she wasn't just in his head. She'd invaded his body, his soul, his heart. When she trembled against his side, he stroked her back, holding the memory of her tight.

"I've fallen again." The soft stir of her whisper raised gooseflesh along his chest.

When she scrambled away and clapped her hand over her mouth, a sharp pain pierced his chest. He didn't want her to hurt like he did.

"You know I can't be the man you need." He winced, hating the words, but didn't hold them back. "The man you deserve."

His fingers twitched to touch her, soften his words. Comfort her. Tell her how he felt.

Her hand fell away from her mouth. "Retire," she whispered.

Every muscle in his body froze, exposing the truth. He was a fraud. A pro football player going for the quick fling.

"I shouldn't have given up on us the first time," she whispered. "I couldn't move on after Jeff's death. Didn't." Her hand curled into a fist. "I'm afraid I'll lose you like Jeff."

"I'm not Jeff." He stepped back, increasing the distance from her pain, her temptation. Because he wanted to tug her into his arms and tell her he'd do whatever it took to make her happy.

"We need to step back for a while," he said, the words slicing his throat. "Focus on getting Hope straightened out."

"Please," she whispered.

She needed to stop. Words couldn't fix him, or them. But she continued to talk, and the hum of her voice buzzed in his head.

"There's something I need to say," she said.

"We were friends from the start." He shook his head, hoping she'd stop torturing them. Her ruthless determination to resolve a problem used to annoy him. Now, it was slowly shattering his insides. But he couldn't let her talk him out of it. "For now, that's where we need to stay."

"I gave up on you because I was afraid of losing you." She ran water into the baking pan stained with chocolate. "I was wrong. Hope will come around. Once she does, I ... I don't want to lose you, what we have. We can work through this. I'll be there for you, go to your games, if that's what you want."

For years he'd dreamed of that promise. But it was wrong and there was nothing he could do to make it right. He could live with a lot of things, but he couldn't live to destroy Talley's spirit and give her nothing in return.

"I'm going to play as long as I can land a contract." He loved her, had always loved her. But he swallowed the admission. "My family needs my help, and I need to give it to them."

She touched his forearm, her fingers cool. A drop of caramel glistened on his shoe. If he looked at her, he was doomed to fail.

"Help me out here," she said. "Do we have a chance? Can you at least meet me halfway?"

*Hold her, kiss away the desperation in her tone.* But if he did, they'd both be lost. He couldn't live with that outcome. Couldn't live with her hurt and disappointment when he failed her expectations. She was already paying the price for his selfish desire to be with her.

He rubbed his forehead. "Some things can't be changed. I accept my limitations."

"What limitations?" The recessed lighting caught the sparkle of tears in her eyes. "Look at what you've accomplished with the Sunberry team and the Scouts. You're a great teacher. You could go back to school. Finish your degree. I'll help like I did in college."

This was the Talley Quixote he remembered. He should thank her for the reminder. With a steadying breath, he dredged up the old anger. "No one is ever enough for you. You can't accept people. You have to push, test." The words spewed from his lips like the boil in his gut. He was a top athlete. He earned the big bucks. People recognized his face.

And it wasn't enough. No matter what he did, it would never be enough. "I thought I was the only one with the learning problem. You don't get it."

"I get that you're afraid you can't do anything besides risk your life for football."

"When you love someone, you will do whatever it takes to make them happy." He hadn't meant to shout. His ragged breaths echoed in the room.

"I get that," she said.

"Really?" he said. "Do you know why I signed with the Cougars?"

She dried the counter in harsh, angry strokes. "To make money for your family. To build your self-esteem."

He laughed, and the bitter sound raked his throat. "Remember the first night I told you I loved you our freshman year? We were eating pizza at the Rathole."

"How could I forget?" Her chin trembled. "It was the best day of my life."

Man, they really were worlds apart. "How did you respond?" *Shut up, Murphy. Go home!*

"I told you I loved you," she murmured.

"You said a lot more than that." He couldn't stop the hurt he'd hidden for so long. "You also laid out our fantasy life as teachers and the three children we'd have."

Although he detected her confusion in the way she kept biting her lip, he couldn't let her get to him. If she did, he'd never be able to end this tonight. He had to end it.

"I thought ... you wanted to teach and coach," she said, starting and stopping the same way he did under stress. "As for children? Sure, someday."

"Things I can't give you." He turned away from her hurt and disappointment.

"That doesn't make sense." She hurried to his side. "You

were all I wanted. I wanted a simple life with you, here, near our friends and family."

"You still don't get it." He removed her hand from his arm. "I wanted you to be happy. I left so you could find a man who could give you those things."

"You have so much more to offer. You're more than some gladiator in a ring."

He shook his head. "Really? 'Cause from my view, I fit the profile for you. You can't fix me. I wish you could but add me to one more person who couldn't measure up."

She trotted after him. "Whit?"

He shrugged off her hand and reached for the door handle. "No, Talley. Let it go. Be my friend. Help me with Hope. But there will never be a you and me. That was a dream."

His cell hummed in his pocket as Irish bagpipes filled the room.

"Are we getting texts at the same time?" Talley checked her phone. "Whit?"

An electrical charge raced up his spine, lifting the hairs at the back of his neck. "It's Mom. She's called a family meeting here tomorrow."

"Now, I'm really worried," Talley said.

Mom wouldn't schedule a family meeting unless she had serious news, especially when Kyle and Nate were due home next week for Thanksgiving.

Another text vibrated his phone. "It's Nate."

"Does he know what the meeting is about?" she asked.

"Nope. He pointed out that Mom's text was limited to you, me, and Nate."

"Kyle was excluded?" She was biting her lip, her eyes wide with fear. "So he already knows the reason for the meeting."

# CHAPTER NINETEEN

This night had not just happened!

Talley waited until Whit disappeared from view. Ava would be okay. She had to be. They all depended on her to keep them grounded, comfort them, guide them through the train wreck of life. In the meantime, she would not catastrophize the reason for Ava's meeting. It would be important, but they'd weather the crisis, regardless of its source. Ava had more energy than most of the kids in her class. If something were wrong, she'd overcome it. Besides, Kyle would ensure his mother had top-notch care. Until Ava told her a different story, her surrogate mother was A-OK. Whit was not.

He'd signed away his life to make hers better. Talley rubbed her fingers through the condensation on the storm door. Head down, hands in pockets, Whit disappeared inside the Murphy home. Cold, fat raindrops splatted against the windowpanes. All this time, she'd never figured out what had driven Whit. Hard to do when she'd been too busy being right.

Tree branches rustled against the house. Talley shivered

and pushed the door closed while her mind flipped through memories, searching for clues she'd missed.

Whit was the second born of four. He liked kids. Fought with his brothers, but that was normal. So, when had he decided against children, and why hadn't she known? Because she was always on a mission, always going to accomplish a goal, save a kitten, succeed. Just like her parents.

She trudged to the living room and sank into the sofa cushions. She hadn't listened, couldn't hear what was clear to everyone else in the universe. Mercy, everyone else in her circle had twenty-twenty vision, and she'd been wearing blinders.

She wasn't an educator or a savior. She'd modeled her Marine parents. Except her missions didn't take her out of the country. Her missions targeted Sunberry's social issues, like a little boy who'd lost his Marine dad or a high school football team in need of an injury-prevention policy. Her work helped people. However, there was a downside to blindly setting a course based on her sometimes-questionable knowledge. Once she'd set her path, come zombies and an apocalypse, she'd march to completion. This time, it was right over the top of Whit.

"That's me." She huddled beneath the soft blanket. "Blinded by the light."

She'd screwed up and lost Whit, again. But she wasn't giving up. After they dealt with the latest Murphy crisis, she'd find a way to change Whit's mind, even if she had to beg.

The following morning Talley paced her living room. Whit would need help preparing the afternoon meal. Ava had asked him to arrange catering, but he'd cook. That's what Whit did in place of exercise. Would he want her help? The meeting centered around her relationship with the Murphy family, not Whit. She pushed the curtain aside to check next door. Nate's car sat in the drive.

She stuffed her phone into her cross-body bag and hurried to the Murphy's. With the youngest brother as a buffer, she was helping out, regardless of Whit's opinion. At the front door, Talley's shoulders curled inward, and her courage fizzled. She took a steadying breath. She'd been walking through the Murphy door for over ten years. It was her second home. Besides, Ava occupied the house, not Whit. And he'd said they needed to maintain their friendship.

She opened the front door and forced her unsteady feet forward. "Anyone home?" Talley hoped her voice stayed even despite the trembling in her throat. "Talley reporting for the meeting."

"Kitchen," Whit said.

Anger didn't taint his voice; but anger indicated feeling. His indifference would be far worse. Talley shook out her hands, trying to reduce the pressure coming at her from all sides. The Murphys were a family, and she'd been included within their unit. Something was threatening that unit, but together, they had a chance to withstand any assault. Now, as many times before, they'd huddle and share a meal.

Ava Murphy loved her. Ava included her. Ava had asked for her presence, and Talley would never betray the woman who had comforted, sheltered, and guided her.

The aroma of coffee, cinnamon, and something she couldn't identify led her to the kitchen. With sandy hair and blue eyes, Whit was the anomaly of the Murphy siblings. Tall and dark-haired like Hope and Kyle, people often mistook Nate, the youngest of the brothers, as the oldest. Maybe it was his size. Nate had a good two inches and probably fifty pounds on Whit. But Talley attributed it to his perpetually solemn gaze that exuded maturity. Today, the same anxiety eroding Talley's stomach reflected in Nate's dark eyes.

"Did I interrupt a family moment?" Talley said, depositing her purse.

"Hey, our hooligan neighbor." Nate nearly cracked her ribs with his bear hug. "I bet you see kids following in our footsteps every day."

"More like *your* footsteps," she said. "I was the saint of the foursome. How's the physician assistant program going?"

"It's going. And you were far from a saint." Nate turned to Whit. "Need any help with the meal?"

Whit closed the oven door. "Set the table."

"You're the tactician of the group," Nate said. "Any ideas about the pop meeting?"

Talley retrieved the plates. "I'm here at least three times a week. I haven't noticed anything out of the ordinary, other than Hope."

"You can't blame this on me." Hope entered the kitchen, her curls tamed in a messy bun. "Mom's been hiding something for over a month."

Despite the surge of energy bouncing through the room, only the hum of the refrigerator disturbed the quiet. After a glance at Whit and Nate's stunned expressions, Talley turned to Hope.

"What?" The teen snagged a bag of chips from the pantry.

Whit took the chips. "I've been cooking all morning. Why didn't you say something?"

"I haven't had a chance. You've been too busy playing helicopter brother and sniffing after Talley."

This wasn't the time to rerun their issues with Hope. Based on the heightened color on Whit's face, he was ready for a confrontation.

"What makes you think she's hiding something?" Talley asked.

Hope did the sullen-teen shrug, but her gaze shifted away.

"We're in this together," Talley said.

"She got a phone call a month ago. We were making sweet

breads for a bake sale at school. Anyway, she got real still, and I could tell something was up. Then she said she felt fine."

"And?" Nate prompted.

"And nothing," Hope said. "I asked her, and she said they'd messed up on a blood test, and she had to get another one."

When the sound of the front door creaked, conversation ceased.

"I hope you ordered something good," Ava called. "I'm starving."

"I guess we'll find out soon enough," Whit muttered. "Mom always says a good meal could fix almost anything. Looks like we're going to put it to the test."

Nate hugged Ava. "Kyle isn't here yet."

"Yes, he is," she said. "He came in behind me. He's sitting in the drive, talking on his phone. If he doesn't show up by the time the food is on the table, you can drag him in here."

When Ava turned to her, Talley expected her usual side hug, but Ava embraced her, held her tight, squeezed harder. Tears moistened Talley's eyes, and she bit on her lip. She'd been wrong. A catastrophe awaited them.

Ava released her and rounded the counter. "You didn't have to cook."

Whit removed the stainless-steel roaster from the oven, and the heavenly aroma of seasoned beef and cooked vegetables filled the house. Although Talley hoped for a hint of what lie before them, Ava picked up the matriarch reins, firing off instructions and keeping everyone busy with last-minute meal preparations. Whit whipped potatoes, Nate cut the warm soda bread, and Talley and Hope fixed drinks.

Kyle, the oldest, slipped into the mix with little fanfare. Talley chewed her bottom lip. It wasn't hard to miss the narrowed gaze Whit shot his brother. Instead of addressing it, Kyle turned to her and hugged her. Kyle never hugged anyone. He might cuff her on the shoulder or try to give Nate, who was almost twice his size, a noogie, but he didn't hug. However, his brotherly affection provided an up-front view of his bloodshot eyes, indicating long, hard hours and too little sleep. The news Kyle and Ava were sheltering was not going to send the family a warm, cozy feeling.

They sat around the large table, and Kyle shared details about med school. Ava picked up the conversation thread during Kyle's lapses, but everyone else remained on alert. The moist meat didn't require a knife, the seasoning on the vegetables tasted perfect, and not a single lump ruined the creamy mashed potatoes, but the wonderful meal tasted like cardboard on Talley's tongue.

Across the table, Whit had cut his meat and buttered a slice of bread but had not lifted his fork. Nate took too long creating a gravy well in his potatoes and Hope cut her vegetables into tiny pieces. After loading their plates high with food, Kyle and Ava ate with gusto, which was also suspect. Brainiac Kyle, with his dark-framed glasses, usually ate like he thought, intentionally and selectively. Clearly, the impending news wasn't as challenging as delivering it.

"You outdid yourself, Whit," Ava said. "This is delicious."

Nate pinned Kyle with a steady gaze. "How can you sit there and eat?"

As teens, Nate had been the follower and rarely challenged his older brothers, especially Kyle and his know-it-all attitude. Nate's gaze narrowed and roved around the table. When he came to Talley, he nodded.

She squared her shoulders. "Maybe we'd have an appetite if we were included on the reason for the abrupt family meeting."

For once, Kyle didn't have something to say. Instead, he looked to Ava.

"Fair enough," Ava started. "I've been diagnosed with Chronic Myelogenous Leukemia, CML."

Talley blinked. Although Ava had rattled off a long medical term, *leukemia* pulsed in her head. Blood cancer. Ava was dying? How could that be? She looked healthy, her golden-olive skin supple and almost wrinkle-free.

Hope's fork clattered against her plate. "Are you going to die?"

"Of course," Ava said. "We're all dying, but probably not from CML. According to my oncologist, if you have to get a blood cancer, this is the best one to have."

Talley gulped her water. Probably, it *probably* wouldn't kill her. Neither would a fork, but she'd released it just in case her brain exploded. Unstable people shouldn't be trusted with sharp utensils.

"That's not comforting," Nate said.

Talley licked her lips. Was Whit breathing? She'd never seen him so still. Whit was constantly in motion.

"Duke scientists developed the first drug used to treat CML." Kyle's voice hummed on about a drug she couldn't pronounce.

Ava and Kyle continued to smile as if they hadn't lobbed a bomb at the table. Nate was nodding. She'd bet her car that her face looked exactly like Whit and Hope's: shell-shocked.

"I'm sorry if I've caused needless concern," Ava said. "But I didn't want to worry you until I had the facts. I've talked with two people who were also diagnosed with this condition. One has been in remission for twelve years. The other gentleman, like me, was diagnosed this year."

"How long have you known?"

Talley turned to Whit. If she hadn't seen his lips move, she wouldn't have recognized the hoarse whisper as his.

"Two weeks." Ava cut a slice of beef. "There's no reason to

think I won't respond to treatment, and so far, my labs have shown that."

"I had her come to Duke for a second opinion," Kyle said.

"Everything is right where it needs to be," Ava said. "So I'm going to continue with my oncologist here in Sunberry."

"Guys," Kyle said. "Come on. Shake off the morose stares. Mom's going to be fine. If she doesn't respond to the first drug, there are four other drugs that work with CML. But she'll probably respond to the first one. All indications point in that direction."

"Says the guy who has had two weeks to process the news," Nate said.

"Okay, okay," Ava said. "We'll handle this the Murphy way. Let's go around the table so each of you can express your concerns. Whit, please start."

"I feel betrayed," Whit said. "We're a family. We don't keep secrets. What about Dad? Does he know?"

"Yes," Ava said.

"And don't lay the secret guilt on us," Kyle said, pointing his fork at Whit. "You had a concussion from that last tackle, and you didn't share it with us."

"I play football. Everybody here knows the risks."

"Whit?" Ava said, concern lacing her low tone.

Whit's eyes narrowed. "It's a brain bruise, not cancer!"

Talley stiffened in her chair. She'd witnessed her share of past Murphy disagreements, but she'd never heard Whit raise his voice, especially to his mother. He gulped his milk.

"Nate, go ahead," Ava said.

"It would've been nice to be included, especially since I'm also in medicine."

"First year," Kyle said.

Talley cringed. Leave it to Kyle to ratchet the tension with his condescending tone.

Ava smiled and squeezed Nate's forearm. "I'm very proud

of you, especially after my experience. I was so lucky to have a physician who not only talked to me but listened to my concerns. You're going to be a fabulous provider."

Nate glanced at his plate. "Since we're confessing truths, I'm not continuing with the program. My girlfriend Sharon's been pushing the pharmacy program. She's got this big plan that we should open our own pharmacy."

Talley slapped her napkin to her mouth. Whoa, she'd missed that clue. When Nate told her his program was going, he'd meant it literally. As in bye, see you later. Just what Whit didn't need—another reason to extend his career.

"Wow," Ava said. "I wish you had discussed this with Ryan and me before you made a decision."

"I didn't figure it out until recently," Nate said.

"Kyle, anything you'd like to share?"

"It's not like Mom's known for weeks. Genetic tests take a while. Until the results came back, she didn't have a diagnosis." Kyle's dark gaze roved the table, waiting for a sibling to challenge him. "I've got an offer to partner with a Hillsborough practice. It's not exactly what I had in mind, but I won't have the practice start-up costs."

"Oh, Kyle. Ryan and I have been putting aside some money to help you," Ava said. "Sunberry needs good physicians."

Kyle crossed his utensils over his empty plate. "Thanks, Mom. I haven't signed on the dotted line. But it's an offer I've been considering."

"Talley?" Ava said.

Talley shifted. "I feel stupid. I live right next door, and I'm over here almost every day. I had no idea you were sick. Now this ..." No wonder Hope had lost her mind. The teen knew something was up and had bottled it up inside. Since she'd refused to talk about it, she'd acted out.

"I'm sorry," Ava said. "I know how it feels when

someone you love is diagnosed with cancer. When my mother told me she had lung cancer, I was devastated. Worse, I felt powerless. I was trying to protect you from the helplessness of not knowing, at least until I received test results."

"You told me you can't protect the people you love," Whit said.

Ava nodded, her eyes moist with unshed tears. "I did, and I believe it. But I can't stop my feelings, so I try my best. Just like with you. You want to play, and every time you go on that field, I hold my breath. But I don't let my fear prevent you from doing what you love."

"I appreciate that," Whit said. "I know my career doesn't save lives like Kyle's and Nate's, and it doesn't teach kids like Talley's, but it allows me to do special things for the people I love. You don't have to move to Hillsborough, Kyle. I'll help you set up practice. Nate, if you want to switch to the pharmacy program, I can help with that too. Little sis, I really hope you decide to go into veterinary medicine because you've wanted to do that since we lost Joby. You pick out a vet program, and I've got your back." Whit looked away and then steadied his gaze on Talley. "To do those things, which make me happy, make me feel like I'm contributing to our family, I'm going to play as long as this body can run down the field. It's just going to be from a field further away. My agent got me another two years with the Rattlers. I'm moving to Phoenix."

Hope pushed to her feet with so much force the table shook, causing utensils to clatter against china. "You're leaving too! What about me? Don't you want to know how I feel? Or do you already know? Mom, you lied to me. I knew something was wrong. Every time I came home from school, I wondered if you'd be okay or if you'd be slumped on the floor. Every time I left in the morning, I wondered if you'd be home when I returned or would you be like my first dad. Kiss me goodbye and never come back."

Her bun bounced on her head with the violent pivot of her head. "You're all leaving. Kyle's moving to Hillsborough, Nate's going to Jacksonville with his girlfriend, Talley's going to follow Whit, probably to the West Coast, and Dad's deployed. Have you ever thought about me? This is my home, and it used to be yours. I don't want to leave." Tears spilled down her cheeks. "What happens to me if you die and they leave? What happens to me?"

Ava stood. "Hope, honey."

"No! You don't get a say about me." She jabbed her finger at Ava. "Not after you lied to me."

Whit reached for Hope's arm, but she shook him off and hurried out of the room. The bang of the front door shuddered through the house.

Kyle stacked his plates and stood. "We missed the mark on the results of this meeting."

Whit stood. "I'll get her."

"Wait a few minutes," Ava said. "Give her time to process this. I had no idea she guessed there was a problem with me. I'm sorry. I was scared too. I have a wonderful family. I was afraid I wouldn't see Hope graduate, or see Kyle and Nate in their white coats, or watch all of you fall in love and walk down the aisle, hold my grandbabies." She blotted her tears with a napkin. "So I kept it in, and I'm sorry. But we're going to get through this, and I'm going to be okay. Yes, I may have side effects from the drug. But I'm going to achieve remission and live a long time. Because I want to witness all of those amazing milestones with all of you."

THIRTY MINUTES LATER, Talley cornered Kyle and Nate in the kitchen. Kyle closed the dishwasher, and Nate raised his cup. "Kitchen mess is cleaned up. I just brewed a fresh pot. Want one?"

"What I want is a private huddle with you and Kyle," she said. "My house. Five minutes."

Without waiting for a reply, she spun on her heel and left. It nearly killed her, but her rant didn't include Ava. As for Kyle and Nate, watch out!

She opened her front door for Kyle and Nate six minutes and thirty-two seconds later and tapped the face of her wristwatch. "You're late."

"Jeez, I didn't—"

"Living room." Talley pivoted without waiting for Kyle to finish. Nate had the good sense to keep his trap shut. She'd had it up to the tops of her boots with their whining. When she pointed at the sofa her finger shook with an impending rant. This was one of those times she should stop and count to ten, run around the block, or perhaps chew nails because she was going to lose her mind. Which was too bad for her surrogate brothers.

Kyle crossed his arms over his chest. "What the—"

"I've got something to say." She glared at him.

"Like that's new," Kyle plopped down in the corner of the couch.

"Is it Whit?" Nate asked.

Talley forced her hands to unfold from fists and dropped to the edge of the chair. "Ding, ding. You get the prize. Of course, it's about Whit."

Nate's forehead wrinkled. "He hasn't come back yet. I guess he and Hope are having a heart-to-heart."

She leaned toward the sofa. "You two think you are so smart. But either you're *really* stupid or you choose to be obtuse."

"Hey." Kyle held up his hands. "We get you're upset about something. You want to help us understand why?"

"Whit's worked his butt off to help your family."

"That's true, and we've told him so." Kyle contorted his features into a what-the-heck look that made her want to thump him on the side of his head—hard. "He's a big boy. He doesn't need you to go off for him."

"Of course, he doesn't." She pushed to her feet, anger heating her belly. "But you two do. While you bury your head in your books, Whit sacrifices everything to hold this family together."

Kyle leaped to his feet, his face red with indignation. "For your information, I'm holding up my part. I made sure Mom saw the best Duke has to offer. They facilitated her tests, so she didn't have to wait so long. Besides, it was her call on keeping her health a secret."

"And what's Whit's part?" She leaned into Kyle's personal space and jabbed her finger to his chest. "Finance your every need? Sacrifice his dreams for yours?"

"Hold it," Kyle said. "I thought you were ticked off about Mom keeping her diagnosis from you."

"Who told you to think?" Talley said. "I'm talking about your dependency on Whit. Both of you."

"I don't understand." Nate's easygoing tone went edgy. "We didn't ask Whit to pay our education. You heard him. He likes to do things for his family. That's Whit. He's always been that way. And it's not like it's a stretch. Jeez, he makes a ton of money."

Talley whirled in his direction. "Risking his life. Both of you knew about his multiple concussions, yet you don't say anything. You don't want to cut off the gravy train."

Kyle moved forward. "I've never asked him for anything."

"You're his brother. He risks his life so you can drive new cars, go to fancy schools, and have health insurance. In the meantime, the two of you know exactly how dangerous his work is. Instead of educating him and making him see reason, you come up with more ways he can give you money."

Kyle studied his shoes. "It's not like he's hurting for money. He makes my tuition in one game."

Talley dropped back into the chair. Holy crap. How did she get through to them? They loved him. And they were clueless.

"No, Kyle." She kept her tone low and purposeful. "He's risking head injuries so you can set up a debt-free practice." She glared at Nate. "And so you can finance your dream career if and when you figure it out."

Nate stiffened. "How many concussions has he suffered?"

"I don't know. But that tackle last week hurt him. Even if he's saved enough, he needs your support. He worries that he can't do anything else. Why does he think like that?"

"He's always been a little slow," Kyle said. "It's okay. He's our brother. We never let anyone put him down."

"But *you* did," Talley said, embarrassed that the catch in her voice signaled her disappointment. "He's not slow. Do you know how intricate those plays are? Have you ever noticed how he can anticipate maneuvers? His mind works differently, not slower."

"I may have screwed up." Kyle adjusted his glasses to avoid meeting her gaze. "But I love my brother. He's always been there for me."

"Me too," Nate said.

A resigned smirk stretched the tight lines of Kyle's mouth. "Okay, Talley Quixote. You always have a plan. Let's hear it."

# CHAPTER TWENTY

He thought he was fast. Whit rolled through another intersection, checking all directions for Hope. His sister must have grown wings on her feet. She only had ten minutes on him—unless some guy had picked her up. He grabbed his phone to text Talley and then put it down. He and Talley were history. Yes, he was moving to Phoenix, but unlike Hope's prediction, Talley was staying in Sunberry. He rubbed his chest to soothe a muscle spasm.

Though the temperature hovered in the high forties, he turned up the heater to ease the chill shaking his shoulders. Mom. Was she really going to be okay? Was remission a thing? What about the drugs she needed? Were they covered? What if two years wasn't enough?

When he slowed for the next intersection, his brakes squeaked. He couldn't think about Mom, at least not until he located Hope. Poor kid was so confused. If he never had football, his teen years would've been a disaster. More accurate, Talley had smoothed his teen years. Talley had smoothed his life. A car behind him honked and sped past.

He pressed the window lever, and the cold air slapped his

cheeks. The scent of rain and damp pine filtered through the fog enveloping his thoughts. When the right tire dipped into a pothole, the answer hit him with the same certainty of a well-planned play. Hope was hurting with a need that friends couldn't soothe. Like him, she'd find a place to submerge and wallow in her misery. He gasped for air.

A tear rolled down his cheek, and he didn't bother to wipe it away. Funny how a guy lived thinking life went on forever. Except it didn't. Mom took care of herself, lived a good life, helped others, kept the Murphy clan together, and bam. She had leukemia. He'd never heard of a good leukemia. Crap, that was like a good tackle. If you were on the bottom of the pile, good didn't apply. Pain did.

With the sound of the engine rumbling through the cab, he drove toward the high school. He'd give anything to take on Hope's pain. She was a mixed-up kid, and he, Mom, and Talley hadn't realized the real reason for her behavior. They were too fast to apply the drama queen and a druggie labels on her. But no one saw the fear she was hiding. She just wanted to finish high school in her hometown and feel safe with her parents. Who didn't? No kid wanted to move from place to place.

He jammed the gearshift into park and stepped to the school parking lot.

"Hope!" His voice echoed in the gloomy afternoon. Silence. He took a deep breath, but it didn't ease the trembling along his limbs. She could be hiding, suffering alone. He broke into a jog, the worry and angst more tolerable with the movement. His muscles warmed, and he opened his stride and circled the school grounds, starting with the soccer field. As he ran, his gaze swung in an arc to the right, center, left. No sign of her, but she was here. This is where he'd go.

Ahead, the gate to the football stadium stood ajar. He veered toward the entrance and picked up speed on the downhill to the track, feeling his way to her. The cold air stung his cheeks and chafed his throat while blood hummed through his veins.

After the first lap around the track, he opened his stride more, pushing to his maximum speed. No longer at an easy pace, his heart and lungs labored to fuel the constant motion of his legs. The trees around the perimeter of the school grounds blurred. The slap of his shoes on the track pounded to the rhythm of his heart. Where was she? She had to be here.

He approached the metal bleachers for the home team, slowed, and dropped to a walk. Hot from the workout, he unzipped his jacket. With the low-hanging clouds dimming the afternoon sunlight, the bleachers stood in shadow.

A splinter of peace eased the ache in his chest. Kyle was a pain in his backside, but his brother was whip sharp. Although their secrecy hurt, Kyle had ensured Mom received top care. To Kyle, remission was a done deal. Big brother might have a big mouth and a big head, but he wasn't a liar. Mom would be okay. Kyle had done his part, ensuring she had the right drugs and care. He'd do his part and pay any lapses in her military coverage.

Right now, he had to find Hope. No way would his sister find peace—not without help. Once he found her, he'd take her home, so they could heal together.

His gaze tracked up one section of the silver metal bleachers and down another with only his heavy breaths cutting the silence. If Hope were hiding, she was aware of his presence, had watched his run around the track.

A frigid breeze chilled his chest, wet from exertion. When he zipped his warm-up jacket, movement beneath the stands flicked in his peripheral vision.

Perfect place. Why didn't he think of it ten minutes ago?

He walked toward the end of the bleachers, face forward,

eyes shifting to the right as if faking a play, and typed a group text to Mom, Kyle, Nate, and Talley:

*Found Hope. Be home soon.*

When he moved forward, the shadows changed. Hope huddled beneath the fourth row, her knees hugged to her chest, watching, waiting.

His stomach clenched. He'd give every cent to his name to change the events of the past three days spent doubting and badgering her. Too bad he didn't have that kind of power. He moved parallel to the bleachers until he reached the end, then walked toward the concession area until he reached the fourth row. Bending so he could move beneath the metal, he wove through the support system. Hope didn't meet his gaze.

He sat beside her and folded his legs, hoping the right words would come to him when he needed them. Every few minutes, she sniffed. He didn't think the cold air caused her sudden congestion.

Tears clouded his vision. Although he wasn't ashamed of showing emotion, he rarely cried. He felt. He hurt, but misery, disappointment, and anguish came out in other ways. His hands locked, his right foot tapped, and the pressure mounting inside him continued to build.

"How'd you know where to look?" Hope murmured.

He took in a breath, exhaled. "It's where I would go."

"I guess, in some ways, we're alike."

He nodded.

"You don't have to worry about drugs. I wanted something to stop being afraid. They worked fine until I woke up."

The back of Whit's throat burned. She sounded so lost. He'd always been proud of his brothers but never envied them. Right now, he wished for Kyle's vocabulary or Nate's sensitivity.

"The bad thing is—" Hope hiccupped. "I don't know why I feel like this."

He wrapped his arm around her shoulders. When she shuddered, another piece of his heart died.

"I know." His words shocked him, but they settled like gospel in his mind.

She turned her head toward him. "How?"

"I've been there." And he had. Until now, he hadn't realized the truth.

"You never lose your cool, until today," she said. "You were mad. Your face got really red."

"I used to get jacked up like that a lot."

Her shoulders brushed against his in a shrug. "I've never seen it."

"It was before you arrived on the scene."

"That doesn't count," Hope said. "You were a little kid."

"It has nothing to do with age." His words were coming in spurts and stops, but they seemed right. "Sometimes, people get confused."

"She's never lied to me."

"People do crazy things to keep their loved ones safe," he whispered, struggling as much with his emotions as the words. "I'd do anything for you guys."

"I just want us to be together. I know we can't live in the same house." A faint smile tipped her lips. "That might be dangerous."

He bumped against her. "You got that right. I might have to pound my big brother."

"He's okay," Hope said. "He can't help it if his brain and his mouth get in his way."

Whit snorted. "That's priceless, little sister. I wish he were here to hear it."

"His sense of humor sucks." She shifted on the gravel beneath them. "Will you come back to Sunberry after you retire? Nate's a lost cause. No telling where he'll end up."

"Give him a little time. He'll figure it out. He may fool you and move in right next door."

"That would be okay as long as he doesn't bring Sharon with him."

He squinted at Hope. "Have you met her?"

"No, but I'm not going to like a girl who doesn't want to live in Sunberry."

"If she's in love with him, she'll go where he goes."

"Why does the girl always have to be the one to move?"

"You're right. If they love one another, they'll figure it out."

The gravel beneath his backside dug into his butt like tiny knives slicing through his jeans, but he wasn't going to shorten the moment. Soon his sister would be going out in the world. It might be a dry spell before she gave him the time of day.

Hope drew in a long, shuddering breath, and he squeezed her shoulder. Her strawberry-scented shampoo filled his senses and brought memories of Mom with razor sharpness. The anger he'd harbored toward his little sister hardened and fell away. Hope had so much of Mom in her—the same shampoo, same hair, and the same hint of mischief lit her eyes.

A tear leaked down his cheek.

"What's going to happen to us when she dies?" Hope asked in a hoarse whisper.

She'd been reading his mind. "That won't happen for a long time." At least that's what he kept repeating over and over in his head.

Her head moved against his shoulder. "It could happen any minute, to any of us. Even kids die, and so do football players."

"Nothing's going to happen to me." He pushed to his feet. "Except for the rocks punching holes in my butt."

"You need more padding."

He laughed and pulled her to her feet.

"Whit?" She wove her arm through his on their way back to his truck.

"Yeah?"

"Come home. Kyle and Nate can make it without your money. Don't move to Phoenix."


EARLY THE NEXT MORNING, Whit stood motionless in the drive as one and then the other taillights from Kyle and Nate's vehicles disappeared around the corner. His brothers were returning to their lives, but he didn't know if he could do the same.

The fear of death gave a guy perspective. His career meant nothing compared to the loss of his mother or any of his loved ones. Around Mom, he'd always felt like a super-hero, like he could do anything. Through it all, Mom, the Murphy rock, had supported him, supported all of them.

Although his body ached the same as after a bad game, he shook out his muscles. A splash of red and orange along the eastern horizon filtered through the pines and emphasized the gray clouds overhead. With a little luck, the offshore winds would clear the skies. He yearned for the sun. He stretched in the driveway, ignoring his body's complaints.

"Getting old," he muttered.

But in some ways, that was a good thing. He started out at a slow, even pace and slowly increased his speed. The knots in his shoulders eased. His thoughts cleared. No dizziness. No confusion. Not even a struggle. He snorted at the irony. All this time, he'd worried about his stupid contract and protecting his ego, protecting the game he loved.

Big football star born with screwed-up brain risks perma-nent brain damage to provide financial security for his family. That's what he'd told himself. Though true, there was more.

"Face it, pal. You do it for yourself."

The big secret was him. When he walked onto the field, made the catch, scored, he felt strong, successful, like a man. He needed that feeling, craved it. That's why he fought for the next contract. Off the gridiron, he was the same kid cringing when bullies called him dimwit. Off the field, he didn't feel like a man— a man a woman like Talley needed him to be. Worse, he'd taken that decision away from Talley.

He pushed for more speed and the words. "I ... get ... it."

His legs resisted the same as his ego once had. But years of training took over, and his stride eased and opened. With the pound of his feet on the pavement, his next actions crystallized in his mind.

Energy pumped through his veins, fueling his speed. The cold air stung his skin. *Bring it on.* The slap of his shoes and the beat of his heart drove him forward.

Talley, competent, loving, and so goal-oriented, had always been there for his family, and for him. Yesterday, she'd been there for them the same way she'd always been there. Yeah, she could beat a horse to death with her mission-fever. But most of the time, that horse would stumble to its feet and run a little further—like him.

So, big man, are you ready to trust her?

He hoped he wasn't too late.

# CHAPTER TWENTY-ONE

W hen the doorbell echoed through the house that evening, Talley clasped her hands together in silent prayer, which was dumb. Whit wasn't going to forgive her. He wouldn't even talk to her. In the past twelve hours, she'd left numerous messages on his cell, lurked around the football field, and even enlisted Hope's help. Whit hadn't responded.

Maybe he needed time to lick his wounds, let the dust settle. Or maybe he was busy. It wasn't like his world existed around hers—as hers did around his.

She yanked open the front door, and Hope stood on her porch with a folder clutched in her hand.

"Don't tell me. Restraining order?" Talley forced a stiff smile.

Hope shook her head, a grin twitching her lip. "I didn't open it. I just promised to give it to you."

Talley swallowed her last hope. Although she'd stepped over the line, she'd hoped... The beam of truck lights swept across the door and Hope turned to give a thumbs-up.

"Well, here we are." Hope's breath made a small cloud in

front of her face. "Nate and Kyle returned to school before dawn. Whit's off to Charlotte. Mom's painting."

Talley's shoulders drooped. Whit deserved the best life could offer. She wasn't it.

Hope held out the folder. "This is for you." She moved past Talley to the kitchen. "Whit red-penciled the injury-prevention plan for you. I helped him write steps to help Coach Cox."

*What?* Talley trotted to catch up with her.

"There's two of them," Hope continued. "Something called a Head's Up Tackle technique and a Dip-n-Rip." Hope opened the pantry door. "I thought it sounded like a Whack-a-Mole game and potato chips. Do you have anything sweet?"

Talley blinked. Maybe tonight she'd be able to sleep because her life felt more like a dream. Or a nightmare.

"Guess he got the contract he wanted." Talley lifted a carton of egg substitute. "Scrambled-egg night."

Hope shook her head and pulled out a stool at the counter. "Whit and I talked. We're cool. I'm sorry I was such a mess. But I was right about Mom being sick. Who knew there were blood cancers that people lived with?"

"Not me. I'm just glad you and your mom are okay." The yellow liquid spread in the pan with no direction, like her life. But at least Hope was okay. "Next time, talk to me. You're not alone in the world."

Hope picked at her blood red nail polish. "Sometimes it feels that way. You aren't moving, are you?"

Talley stirred the congealing eggs and turned off the burner. "This is my home. I went through a lot to stay here. I'm not leaving."

"He's not retiring." Hope trudged to the refrigerator and returned with the orange juice bottle. Instead of grabbing a glass, she unscrewed the lid and sipped from the almost empty container.

Talley dumped her pale eggs on a plate and raised a brow at Hope. The teen shook her head and drank from the bottle. Although Talley's appetite had tanked, she needed something in her stomach. Her nose wrinkled in protest. The yellow stuff might be an okay substitute for eggs but not for Whit.

She carried her pitiful excuse for a meal to the stool beside Hope and sat. Where had she gone so wrong with Whit? He loved his family. The fact he'd consider moving west to continue his career made his priorities clear. The sad thing is she'd wrecked their friendship trying to get him to change.

"Sometimes life sucks," Hope said.

Talley couldn't lift the food to her mouth. Her eggs rated up there with Hope's opinion of life. "How long have you known Whit didn't want children?"

"Since like forever," Hope said, her teen-speak devoid of the usual attitude.

Talley placed the silverware on her plate and pushed it aside. Maybe she should jab the fork in her eye while she was at it.

Hope sipped her drink. "He said he wouldn't pass on speech problems to kids."

"I didn't think his problem was a big deal," Talley said. "I mean, I know it was tough in middle school. But Whit was respected and liked in high school."

"Because of sports."

"Because he's a caring, generous man."

Hope shrugged. "That too. But it still bothered him. And then there's Kyle. He's a hard act to follow. Trust me, I know. All I hear is how smart Kyle was. Every teacher is like, you're Kyle Murphy's little sister. He always got A's in my class. Blah, blah, blah. No one seems to remember he was a stinker when we first moved here."

Talley laughed despite her dismal mood. "Only Mrs. Turnbull is left from Kyle's days. His other teachers have since retired."

"Lucky me." Hope tapped her phone. "When Whit and Nate attended, Kyle's teachers were still working with excellent memories. Do you know how that feels, especially for Whit?"

Although Whit had been self-conscious about his school performance, Talley hadn't understood the depth of his feelings. Once again, she'd been too involved in her objective to help him pass a test to notice his pain.

"I wish someone would've knocked me on the head, told me to wake up, get a brain," Talley said.

"We figured you knew. You were smart. Not like Kyle, but smarter than most kids." Hope returned to the pantry. "Do you have any snacks?"

"Graham crackers."

Hope did the teen eye roll. "Regardless of the sugar grams, crackers do not count as dessert. Don't you have any chocolate? I thought you made brownies."

"Your brothers polished them off. As for chocolate candy, I don't trust myself with it in the house."

"I don't trust you with Whit's heart."

Talley winced. "I guess I deserved that."

"Ya think?" Hope grabbed the box from Talley's hand.

"I thought you didn't consider those dessert."

Hope unwrapped a pack. "A dessert attack calls for desperate measures."

"So does a broken heart." Talley snatched a cracker and bit into it. Hope was right. Tonight called for candy, preferably chocolate or caramel.

"Any chocolate at your house?" she asked.

"Nope." Hope sighed. "Whit and I cleaned it out last night."

"Sunberry Fast Mart?"

Hope held up her half-eaten cracker. "These are growing on me. Kind of like you did."

When Talley turned, Hope was grinning, her long arms extended. Talley stepped into the hug, blinking back the hot sting of tears.

"You grew on me too. Kind of like your entire family. That's why I wanted one just like yours."

"We are pretty awesome." Hope disengaged and popped another square into her mouth.

"Without a doubt."

The refrigerator hummed in the silence.

"Do you think he'll ever forgive me?" Talley said, fearing the answer.

"He's already done that once." Hope removed another cracker from the sleeve. "Do you think you deserve a second —no, third chance?"

Talley closed her eyes, almost afraid to consider.

"If I were Whit, I wouldn't give you one." Hope stuffed the last cracker into her mouth.

Talley's shoulders slumped. She'd always liked Hope's forward approach to life, except when it cleaved her heart.

"I can't imagine life without Whit," Talley murmured.

"I can't imagine a life without any of my family. I don't remember my real dad, but I still think losing one parent is enough for a kid. Do you think Mom will be okay?"

Talley nodded. "Don't sell Kyle short. When he lets his brain get jumbled up in the facts, he can be a jerk. But behind all those brains, he loves and worries the same as the rest of us. Worse, he takes Ava's care personally, and that's some heavy lifting. If he missed something about her care, he'd never forgive himself."

Hope studied a cracker before chomping down on it. "I came to the same conclusion. I just hope he doesn't disappoint us."

"Not as bad as he does." Talley tossed her napkin into the trash. "He hates being wrong."

"Don't we all?" Hope's squint sent a chill down Talley's spine. "Could you get over his career choice?"

Talley removed the milk from the refrigerator and cringed at the sell-by date. She removed the cap and sniffed. It wasn't fresh but didn't smell as bad as her day was going. She could feel the heat of Hope's stare, yet she focused on the milk.

"Want a glass?" She lifted the carton. "It hasn't curdled yet."

"I'll stick with the juice. One food risk a night is my limit."

Talley retrieved a glass, avoiding the teen's gaze. Except she couldn't avoid an answer that she didn't have.

"Whit hasn't totally given up on you." Hope smashed her cracker into smaller pieces. "But he still wants you to come to his press conference. I have no clue why."

Milk sloshed over the edge of Talley's glass and puddled on the counter. With trembling fingers, she set down the carton before she made a bigger mess.

"When? Where?" Talley slapped her hand over her mouth to stop her inane stuttering. He'd asked her to witness the conference, and the reason for the request terrified her.

"Seven p.m. tomorrow at the Sunberry Opera House."

The words echoed in Talley's head, loud and then soft. Whit didn't do media. How many times had he emphasized that point? This wasn't good news, and this wasn't news she wanted to hear, certainly not in a public forum.

She ripped off three paper towels and swiped at the spilled milk. A press conference in Sunberry didn't make sense. Whit was in Charlotte. The Opera House attracted older artists who could no longer fill the large-capacity city venues. Sunberry didn't even have a local TV station. Although the heat of Hope's stare burned her left cheek, she didn't turn. Right now, she'd give anything to climb the oak down by the creek, sit in the branches, and cry.

"Talley?"

Talley blinked Hope's features into focus. "Got it. Seven tomorrow."

"I don't know why he didn't call you to ask." A note of sympathy touched Hope's statement. "I don't even know what he's going to say."

Talley gripped the edge of the counter. She'd made such a mess of their lives, especially hers. Did she try to fix it or slide under a rock out back? No more fixing things. The back of her eyes tightened, warning her of the threat of tears. She willed them back but couldn't speak—unless she wanted to howl like a kid whose ice cream fell in the dirt. She rolled her lips and nodded.

"I don't have plans tomorrow night." Hope rattled the paper for the last cracker. "Do you want a compadre to go with you? We could go to the Sunberry diner. They have a big-screen TV, and you know the networks will pick up on it."

She hugged Hope's neck. When the girl hugged her back, a few tears leaked despite her blinking.

"Thanks, li'l sis." She held Hope tight, struggling to regain control. "I thought I'd lost you too."

"Are you losing it?" The girl's attitude was just what she needed. Hope pulled two tissues from the box on the counter and handed them to her. "You can't lose family. You get mad. You quit talking. You swear you're going to slowly dismember them. But in the end, you forgive them."

Talley laughed. Well, maybe it was more a cross between a sob and a laugh. But some of the sadness slipped from her heart.

Hope stood. "I better go. Mom had Bennie bring over a wooden chest to paint."

Talley wiped her eyes. "I didn't know you painted."

"I don't, but Mom's going to teach me." Hope wadded the empty wrapper and stood. "If you change your mind ..." She cocked her head to the right. "About going it alone tomorrow. I don't want you blubbering in front of everyone in Sunberry. This is a small city, and Whit's the local celebrity. If he announces the signing of his new contract ..."

Talley pressed her fingers to her lips. A flash of Jeff's smile cut into her. Two more years of professional ball. She straightened her shoulders. "Thanks. I'll probably need the moral support." Because she had a terrible feeling about Whit's news conference.

# CHAPTER TWENTY-TWO

Whit turned into the Sunberry Opera House parking lot an hour before sunset the next day, his thoughts spinning. In his dreams or wide awake, the scenario didn't vary. The pigskin spun in the air, heading right at him for the big play—except he ran to the right, and the ball went left. That was it. One minute, he was at the top of his game. The next, he was unemployed, another washed-up player, one of those guys who'd lost the moves.

Worse, the story applied to his professional and personal life. Time had come to toss the coin. By the end of the day, he'd be the same jock clinging to the spotlight or running down the field in an entirely different game.

Although cars filled the lot, an attendant directed him to a vacancy near the back entrance. His agent always covered the details, right down to special parking. Except for today, surprised fit him better than special. Why did the Sunberry residents care about his press conference? Sure, he was an NFL player, and people were curious about the hometown celebrity. But a press conference? Boring for most and intimidating for him.

He blew out a breath, stepped from his truck to the uneven pavement, and noted the neon-green feather clinging to his knee—probably from Hope's Halloween costume hanging in the guest room closet. The silky plume tickled his fingers, releasing some of the tension pinching his shoulders. He stuffed the feather in his jeans pocket.

The Cougars contracted people to dress players for public appearances, but Hope had rescued him once again, selecting the jeans and plaid shirt he'd worn to take out Talley. Things were still awkward between Hope and him, but the discomfort would iron out. It always did. He'd jacked up his life, more than once. Hope deserved another shot, the same as everyone, even him.

A northerly breeze stirred the naked tree limbs causing the skin along his shoulders to pimple. He drew the cashmere sweater over his head. Nothing like a crowd to intimidate a guy. But today he had to be on his game. No penalties, no fumbles. Right from the snap of the ball until contact. When he turned toward the entrance, a small image made him hesitate. He'd know that red cowlick anywhere. A grin eased his jitters.

He turned to Parker and his mother. "Hey, Parker. Mrs. Evans. Good to see you again. Didn't expect to see so many people here. The Sunberry grapevine must have progressed to six-G speed."

The boy's mother met him with a thin smile that looked as out of place as he felt. He never had a talent for quips.

"I hope you don't mind." She studied the pothole near her foot. "Parker insisted that he speak to you first thing."

"No problem." He turned toward the boy. "What's up, buddy?"

Silently, Parker took his hand and led him beneath the naked limbs of an old oak.

Whit squatted so he was eye level with the boy. "What's on your mind?"

Parker held out his fist. "I heard them talking on the news. I would be really sad if you have to be on a team far away."

Surprised as much by Parker's words as the sudden sting of tears, Whit nodded. Parker placed his dad's rock into his hand. The familiar shape nestled in his palm like the last piece in a puzzle.

"It helped Mom and me feel better." The boy folded Whit's fingers around the stone. "But I think you need it for a while."

Unable to speak, Whit traced the crude *W* scratched in the smooth surface. His thoughts slowed, and he let the cool stone warm in his palm. No matter how much his hand had grown, the small talisman always seemed to fit. He shook his closed hand and nodded to Parker before placing it in his pocket.

Whit straightened and inhaled the crisp air. The kid had a way about him—straight to his heart. But he couldn't accept the talisman, especially after what Parker had gone through. He glanced at the sincerity shining in the boy's gaze.

"Thanks for thinking about me." He squeezed Parker's small bony shoulders. "I've got a hard job coming up, and this is just what I need to get me through it."

Parker nodded, his expression belying his tender age.

"But I can take it on one condition," Whit said, recognizing how hard it was for Parker to give up the talisman. "It's only a loan. You know, like lending a ball mitt to a friend during a game?"

Parker's gaze lifted from the ground to Whit's face, and the beginnings of a smile smashed Whit's heart and cut off his breath. No matter where he had to go or how far he had to travel, he'd stay in touch with Parker. He could never replace the boy's father, but he'd be there for him.

"You're the keeper of the stone." He ignored the hoarse rasp of his voice. "See, that's the way it works. You can loan it to people who really need it."

"Like Mom?"

"Yep, like your mom. And now me."

"But you might need it longer. Moving far away might make your tummy feel icky." Parker's gaze moved past Whit's shoulder. Probably to Mrs. Evans. Poor little guy. He'd lost his dad, and the kid needed stability. No doubt, change terrified him.

Whit blinked hard to clear the film clouding his vision. "You're right. Moving, changing jobs, having to make new friends is *really* hard. But big guys get over things faster," he lied. "I'll give your mom my phone number. So no matter where I have to move, you can call me. If you need me, I'll come back to see you. And you know what else?"

Parker pursed his lips and shook his head, the sadness on his face ripping at Whit's resolve. "I visit my mom a lot, and every time I come home, I'll stop by your house to check on you. Deal?" Parker nodded and touched Whit's fist with his small finger. "You hold it as long as you need to. I'm getting bigger, and I'm strong."

Whit managed a watery smile. "You sure are. I almost didn't recognize you."

When Whit turned back toward the entrance, Parker nestled his hand in Whit's. Whit straightened his shoulders. Crazy that a little kid could make him feel like a better man. Hand in hand, they walked to Mrs. Evans. Parker glanced sideways through brushy orange lashes. Whit winked.

"Mrs. Evans, if it's not too much trouble, Parker and I have a little business to conclude after the conference. Can you meet me by my truck?"

They made the arrangements, and Parker squared his narrow shoulders. Whit didn't know whose chest puffed out more, his or Parker's. The kid was special. Anybody, including a wide receiver, could see that. He hoped someday Mrs. Evans would find a good man. Parker deserved a worthy father, and any man with half a brain would want to claim the boy as a son. He sure would. He was grateful just meeting the boy.

Inside the Opera House lobby, Whit blinked at the sea of faces surrounded by ornate red walls and gold trim. Ten reporters had traveled to Sunberry to hear him fumble for the right words. He sipped the water placed on the table near the microphone. A press conference was big news for Sunberry, and a chance to showcase its historic Opera House. However, he didn't expect *he* would be big news, at least not to this extent. He was one Cougar player. Yeah, he was a pretty good wide receiver, but so were a lot of guys. The Duke rookie would dominate the news next season if he stayed healthy.

Whit tried to roll the tension from his shoulders, but it didn't stop the electrical charges firing along his muscles. When he sat at the long table facing the room, his heel tapped a frantic tattoo on the red carpet. Five minutes. That's all it would take to say the lines he'd practiced. Too bad he couldn't ask for Talley's help. But he could do this. The execution of a few words was no different than a game play.

Except he wasn't moving, and he wasn't outside. The walls of the historic building closed around him, and the cacophony of voices expanded in waves. Sweat beaded on his flesh and dripped down his torso. He fidgeted before removing his navy pullover.

He leaned toward Stan, seated to his right. "Let's get started."

Dressed in a suit and tie that probably cost more than one of Hope's typical shopping sprees, Stan held up his hand.

Didn't the guy ever sweat? The cramped lobby of the Opera House felt hotter than the practice field in July.

"ESPN is en route," Stan said in a low voice. "I promised to give them five minutes."

Behind the front row of reporters sat Coach Cox, Rachel, Parker, Mrs. Evans, and two boys from the Scouts. Whit blinked, and his breath stuttered in his chest. They'd all come. In the back, five Cougar teammates stood along the wall, shoulder to wide shoulder. Ivan was at the end, his big face solemn. When Whit met his gaze, Ivan moved his fist to his chest and tapped. Whit swallowed. His teammates had his back. Time to execute the next play.

Stan continued to read some document like it held the keys to a bank. Whit scanned the walls. No clock. If a guy needed the time in the stadium, all he had to do was look up at the scoreboard. The Opera House had a clock tower; it was also outside. He'd give his next paycheck to walk around the perimeter. Anxious, he tapped the screen on his cell phone.

"In three minutes, we're starting," he whispered to Stan.

Cool air swirled through the room when Talley squeezed in and settled behind the reporters. Whit's heartbeat bobbled, and his breath hitched. She'd come. He'd hoped she'd attend but expected her to watch on TV. Now that she was here, the urge to exit for the men's room rattled him. Instead, he straightened in his seat and stared into those big brown eyes. The noise, the lights, the musky-scented air faded, and Talley filled his vision. As long as he drew air, he'd never tire of looking at her.

Her lips twitched, but she didn't look upset. She looked hot, and not as in overheated—although he could do sweaty with her right now. The wind had messed her hair and given her that just-loved look. However, what he needed for the next five minutes was her tenacity—if she'd hang with him for a few more minutes, maybe ...

Stan leaned toward the microphone, and with a few moderately spoken words, his silver-tongued agent commanded the attention of the auditorium. Cameras clicked and bulbs flashed while Stan gave a brief introduction, then turned the mic to Whit.

He huffed out a breath. *Game time.* Whit sipped his water, but his lips felt glued to his teeth. He blinked at the unfamiliar faces directed at him.

"Thank—" He cleared his throat and closed his eyes. He'd practiced what he had to say in front of the mirror. So spit out the words. It didn't matter if he screwed them up.

Sweat inched down the side of his face and sent a shudder through him. The scrolled wood trim between the wall and ceiling moved like a golden snake on some weird video. The bright lights burned his eyes.

He pointed at the microphone. "Does this thing move?"

A technician stepped forward. "Sir?"

"Can I carry this thing around? I'm better when I move."

Within moments, he stood before the cameras, the microphone clenched in his hand. His muscles still rippled with nervous energy, but he could breathe now. The place was hot as the beach in August, which enhanced the musty smell of the old wood.

"Most of you know I'm a better runner than I am a talker," he said.

A murmur parted the heavy curtain of silence.

He blew out a breath. "I appreciate your coming out on such short notice. Sunberry is not easy to get to, but it's a nice place."

*Quit rambling, and tell them what you came to say.* He paused and grabbed his water bottle from the podium. The cool drink didn't ease his dry, rusty vocal cords or loosen the band squeezing his chest.

"I love football." The three words echoed in the silence,

gave him courage. "Everything about it, the workouts, the running, the competition, the guys. My teammates—" He swallowed. "We work together to win. I don't have the words to explain how that feels"—he thumped his chest— "here, inside. All I know is when I race down the field, and that ball is spiraling right where it needs to be ... Man, it's everything."

He swiped at the sweat on his face with his shoulder. "You see, I couldn't talk when I was a kid, and I wasn't good in school. So, football ... football made me feel good about myself. I could do something without a lot of help. Pretty awesome for a guy like me, for any guy who has always been behind.

"Some of the guys on the team are super smart, so the plays come easy for them. Not me. I struggle to get everything right. When the throw is off, and I have to outmaneuver the opponent, and I succeed?" He shook his head. "Nothing better than that."

He stopped and drained the last of his water before turning back to the reporters. They probably wondered where he was going with all this.

"Football is just a game, but there's something about this game ..." He paced to the end of the seats and retraced his steps. Cameras clicked, and video recorders hummed.

"My bet, the fans feel that way. Maybe they had a bad day or are worried about the bills. For a couple of hours, they get caught up in the game. During that time, they struggle with the team. When we win, the fans win too."

He found Parker's small turned-up face. "Maybe on the inside, they're still little kids too. The one that needed help, or fell behind, or didn't meet the standard. Maybe that's what the game does. Because when I make a catch that seems impossible, that little-kid feeling vanishes. I feel strong. I've accomplished something. Not for me, but for the team, the community, the kids out there who are struggling like I did."

A flash darkened his vision and buzzing hummed in his ears. Nameless faces and glaring lights filled his vision. His next words faded. He blinked and tried to swallow. Talley's face focused. A stiff smile curved her lips, and she nodded. He sucked in a breath.

"Because of my brain problem ..." He shifted his weight from his right foot to his left. "I ... I know what it's like to struggle to do things most people don't think about. I know how important my brain is. That's why I can't risk beating it up anymore."

Talley's eyes seemed kind of sparkly. Not sparkly, but teary. His eyes watered. He cleared them with his index finger and thumb.

"Football has given me everything. I can't thank enough the Cougar organization and all the folks who helped me become the player I am. Also, the fans who supported me, made me feel special. But it's time for me to stop. Better to stop on the way up than the inevitable slide down."

A flush of embarrassment heated his neck and cheeks. He hadn't meant to mention the kid part. He moistened his lips. Shook it off, changed directions.

"The game brings people together. The guys on the team are different, different talents, races, backgrounds. But together, when everything kind of clicks, we make it happen. A bunch of regular guys work hard to do something incredible. For the last five years, I got to be a part of that. It's been one heck of a ride."

A cough interrupted the silence, and he realized he'd stopped pacing in front of the long table and stood staring at Talley. Busted, he grinned despite feeling as though he was on the line, waiting for the snap. Instead of sprinting to make the catch, he was racing for Talley, for his life.

"I'm ready for the next part of my life. That's kind of scary for a guy like me. Bring on a free safety or even a three-hundred-pound lineman, but a good woman, maybe a family?" He winked. "Scary stuff."

"You're retiring?" a young reporter blurted out.

"Yes, sir. But you better bet I'll be in that stadium cheering on my team." He raised his fist. "Go Cougars."

## CHAPTER TWENTY-THREE

How long could she hold her breath without passing out? Talley exhaled, hoping more than fresh air kept her knees locked in a standing position. Was she Whit's good woman?

Whit's agent was talking, but Talley couldn't hear his words for the roaring in her ears. She had to think, assess, work out what she'd just heard. The room was so hot sweat beaded her upper lip. She clawed at the scarf around her neck. With her heart thundering in her chest, she pushed through the crowd. An exit sign blurred near the ceiling on her right.

She extended her arms and cleared a path like a swimmer pushing through the water. With her lungs bursting, hungry for air, she slammed through the door. Cool air bathed her face. Her ragged inhale cut through the silence, and she bent at the waist with her hands on her thighs.

Whit's words circled her mind and her heart. Now, she understood the true meaning of blindsided. Whit's confession had blown her away. Shattered everything she believed about him, them, what was possible. On wobbly legs, she walked toward Main Street to where she'd parked her car.

"Talley!" Whit's voice echoed in her ear.

"Not enough time, not enough time." She fumbled with her purse, the key fob, and the door handle. Her stiff fingers ignored the directions from her brain. With a terrifying jangle, her keys dropped within inches of the street grate. Talley snatched them. Her pounding heart had little to do with almost losing her keys and a lot to do with the man approaching her.

She'd known Whit since high school. He'd been her pal, her compadre, her brother, and her lover. But she didn't know the beautiful man who had addressed the crowd. The compassion, the wisdom of that man deserved far more than the quivering mass standing in the street. At a loss for words, she stood shy and unsure like a schoolgirl on her first date.

"I thought you'd need more time with the press," she said in a voice that sounded more like a Minnie Mouse cartoon.

"Nothing more to say." He buried his hands in his pockets. "Stan can handle the details. I just had some last-minute business with my teammates and my buddy Parker."

A smile fell into place despite her nerves. Cute Parker. She should've known he'd insist on coming to see his favorite Cougar. She followed Whit's gaze up the tree-lined walk leading to the downtown area.

He extended his hand. "Walk with me."

*Earth to Talley.* She blinked at his long fingers, his scabbed knuckles, and the blood vessels roping his hand. Although her body trembled, she touched her fingers to his, settling into the warmth of his palm. Home. Home with Whit. Home in Sunberry. Maybe. She stiffened.

Doubt didn't seem to affect Whit. He drew her across the street to the sidewalk separating the quaint shops from the row of antique streetlights.

"I've always liked this street," he said. "It's timeless. No matter how far I go or how long it's been, this place is waiting for me."

Talley stumbled and recovered. Whit's sentiments sounded like … hers. "I … I thought you liked Charlotte."

"Charlotte's a great city." Whit shrugged. "It's just not home."

"You made Sunberry proud of you today." Talk of her hometown eased her logjammed words. "You made me proud."

Although the heat of his gaze burned her face, she couldn't meet it. At least not yet. Her world had shifted on her, and she hadn't regained her footing. She'd thrown away so many chances. She had to get this right. Step wrong, say the wrong thing, and her opportunity might evaporate.

"A lot has happened over the past week." He maintained his usual brisk pace. "I've spent the past two days wrapping my head around it."

His conversation, like his stride, made her struggle to keep up. Their roles had reversed. She needed to tell him to slow down. Explain. Clarify. Because her thoughts tumbled around in her head. She bit her lip. Whit always waited. She could too—if he didn't go *too* fast.

They passed a restaurant with twinkly lights winding along the balcony.

"I was pulling away from you," he said.

Her heart cringed and struggled to pump air to her ambushed brain.

He kicked at an acorn, sending it skittering to the curb. "I've got this thing about protecting people. I guess it came from losing my dad at a young age. Anyway, I was trying to protect you from a childless life, and you were trying to save mine. Mom always said you can't protect people, only love them."

"When you love a person, you accept them for the way they are." That didn't sound right. She had to say it right, make sure he understood what was in her heart. "I'm learning too."

"And forgiving?" His heavy brows lifted.

"I don't know how you can forgive me. I can't forgive myself." She blew out a breath. "I was so busy saving you, I failed to listen to you."

"I've been thinking about that too."

She could hear the smile in his voice, but at this point didn't want to push her luck. Besides, there was nothing funny about a person who admits they lack personal integrity.

"No matter what happens, you always hold the course," he said. "I figured if you could hang in there, I could. It was pretty ugly."

"I'd say you slayed your demons, on national TV."

"Yeah, it feels pretty good now that it's over."

Talley swallowed. "Is this where you tell me we're over … for good?"

The clicks of her boots on the sidewalk filled her head. Just say it. Don't ease off the Band-Aid. Rip it off fast. She gulped a big, steadying lungful of air and glanced to her side. Whit wasn't there. She turned. One hundred feet behind her, he waited, grinning, his head cocked.

"W-Whit? Why are you smiling?"

"Why would I leave a woman who wants to save me from me?" He held out his hand for her. "I could be wrong, but it sounds like you care about me."

The way her pulse pounded in her neck, Whit was no doubt sending her blood pressure through the clouds. He understood? He didn't think she was pond scum?

His smile faded. "I know you want children. You'd make a great mom. But I don't know if I can give you one. Besides my exposure to CTE, I probably have a bent gene," he added.

"We all have bent genes. They're shaped in a double helix."

She stopped and turned to him. Whit stood rooted to the sidewalk, his feet wide apart, slightly bent at the waist and knees. He was always ready for action. That's why he was an NFL star. But she didn't work that way, especially after his announcement coupled with his present shy smile. Her heart performed a soft-shoe against her ribs.

"I'm probably making a mess of this," he said. "I figured it would be lame to ask you to help me practice this speech." He took her hands, and his intense blue gaze shivered through her. "What do you see when you look at me?"

She opened her mouth to speak. *Get it right.* Silence. She nipped her lip. "I see ..." Well, she could see just fine, but her vocal cords seemed to have gone on strike. She cleared her throat. "I see ...I see a remarkable man with heart, courage, and an incredible capacity to love."

He closed his eyes and released a long breath. "Messed that up."

She pressed her hand against her lips. Her heart pounded so hard in her ears, she couldn't think.

"*I* messed up, not you." He touched her cheek as if she were a fragile piece of art. "I planned to ask that question early in my talk. Right after I told you I love you."

"Whit!" The words came out on a sob, which was so wrong. She didn't cry. It was just that she'd worried she'd lost him. Because she should've lost him.

His voice and gaze warmed her shoulders better than her favorite blanket. The critical self-talk humming nonstop in her skull ceased. She dropped her forehead to his chest, absorbing the steady rhythm of his heart. This. She needed the quiet to think. Strong, gentle hands forced her chin up.

"Hey," he said. "You already know my scars and fears. I think I've loved you most of my life. I'm just a little thick."

"A girl can't hear that too often," she said, her voice stuttering.

He grinned. "I'm a little thick?"

She tried for a stern look, but her stupid grin wouldn't budge. "I love you."

"I love you, Talley. A guy can't say it too often." He wiped a tear from the corner of her eye with his thumb. "Don't get all dewy-eyed on me. I'm not done."

She sniffed. "Sorry."

When he started walking again, she pressed her fists to her temples. *Come on.* She couldn't take his dribble of information for freaking ever. He had to spit it out, tell her all of it, everything going on behind his heavenly blue gaze. But he was already six feet in front of her. She hustled to catch up.

"I was going to walk away because I couldn't give you children," he said the moment she caught him. "Hope called me an idiot. We can go to a genetic counselor and see what they say. Anyway, I need you on my team, need help planning our lives together, and weighing the risks. At least, if you want to sign a contract with me."

Holy smokes! She planted her feet but didn't release his hand, so he had to stop with her. "Are you asking me to marry you?"

He glanced at her from the side. "I'm making a mess of it. I almost asked Nate to help me. Kyle would crack a joke. Nate would understand."

She grabbed his shirt and pulled him close. "Kiss me and make it better."

He gave her a salute. "Yes, ma'am."

She poured her love and frustration into her kiss, and Whit seemed to pick up on it because he hugged her to him. His tongue swept into her mouth and dueled for dominance with hers. The warmth of his hot hands cupping her bottom burned through her slacks.

When he let her up for air, his grin reappeared. "I'm a better kisser than I am a talker." He glanced to the right and then to the left of them. "We're kind of exposed here. I don't want my teacher to get into trouble."

"You should have rented a room." Her words sounded raspy, but she couldn't seem to draw in enough air.

"You haven't answered," he whispered.

She was getting to that. He kept surprising her, and then there was the attraction thing. Her man was just too sexy for her own good.

"Loving you isn't the problem."

His grin faded. "It's the kid thing?"

"No, Whit, it's me. I love my job. And now I understand how you love yours. I'm afraid for you. But my fear shouldn't influence your decision to play. And my fear doesn't justify my manipulation. I love you, and I'll walk by your side—" She squeezed her eyes closed and swallowed. "I'll walk by your side regardless of your occupation. So if you need to play, those reporters haven't left yet."

He shoved his hands in his pockets, studied his shoes, and nodded. "Thank you. But I've made my decision."

When he peeked up at her, she knew their lives might hit a few bumps. But they were going to make it through.

"Are you on my team or not?" he said. "Because we're seeded dead last, and unless we enlist new recruits, it's only you and me."

She giggled. It was so inappropriate, but Whit caused her to do crazy, unexpected things. Using his shoulders to springboard, she jumped up and wrapped her legs around his waist. He caught her like she knew he would. The man had great hands and even better instincts.

"I have no idea how this will go." He turned in a slow circle, but her head spun like her heart. "I know I want you by my side."

"I want you to be happy," she said cupping his chin with her hands.

He eased her feet to the ground. "I am ... with you."

"But you love the game." And she didn't want him to hate her later for forcing him to leave it.

"Yeah, I do." He dropped his gaze. "I'll always love it. I could live with a bum knee or ankle. But a brain injury? Something they can't fix?" He shook his head. "I know what that's like. I'm not willing to take that risk anymore."

"But you've worked so hard to speak, get through school, and now with the MVP within reach, this decision. I'm so sorry. I should've trusted your decisions."

The crooked smile that made her fall in love with him eased the tension in his features. "I'm not. It's time to stop playing and start working. There are a lot of kids who lost their dads. I want to help them. I can't do that without you by my side. To be honest, there's not too much I can do without you by my side." He took her hand and turned back. "Do you think you could lobby to get me a job working with the Scouts? I'd like to be a counselor. I'm not qualified yet, but I figured you could help there too—if I can get into school."

"Really?"

"I kind of liked working with the high school team, but I don't want to promote tackle football to kids." He shrugged. "Figured you had the in on that one. Maybe flag football?"

"I'll see what I can do."

She squeezed his fingers, matching the way his words squeezed her heart. Or maybe it felt tight because Whit had made it grow a couple of sizes.

"It's never going to be easy for us," Whit said.

"I kind of worked that out too." She shrugged. "You know me, I kind of go for the hard causes."

"Good thing. I come with a lot of baggage."

"Whit?" She moistened her lips.

His gaze swung back to meet hers, and all the reasons she loved him, had to be with him, had risked running the Murphy gauntlet settled into an ironclad resolve.

"I love you. Some things are hard to change. But I can and always will support you."

"I kind of like the way you are." He stopped and wrapped her in an all-body-contact hug that left no doubts about his commitment. "You keep coming up with those plans, and I'll keep managing you."

"Managing?"

He feathered kisses along her jaw. "Managing my feelings for you."

"And he scores," she murmured before sealing the pledge with a kiss.


the end

# BE FIRST TO KNOW!

Do you love being first ? Like getting all the information so you can make the best decisions? **Turner Town News**, my monthly newsletter, gives you the inside scoop. Plus, if you subscribe now, you'll get a FREE download of the **Clock-tower Romance Character Map.** With my character map you can scan my books to find and track your favorite characters. I've made it super easy for you. Just click 'I WANT TO STAY IN TOUCH' below, provide your email and first name, and you'll get the character map. That's it! I never share your information with anyone and you can unsubscribe at any time. So what are you waiting for? Click now.

## I WANT TO STAY IN TOUCH!

Subscribers get everything FIRST. Yes ma'am. That includes the following:

- Turner Town News,
- Stories behind the stories that I only provide to subscribers

- Video clips
- Book sale alerts - I run specials every month. The next one could be the book you've wanted to read.
- Fun contests with prizes (Did you know my subscribers helped me choose a cover, a title, and a pet for a book character? So don't miss out on adding your voice!)
- Cover reveals-you'll see it first
- New releases
- Health tips
- Recipes
- More free stuff

————

I'm thrilled that you decided to spend time in my Sunberry world. I hope you enjoyed the Murphy family. If so, you'll want to read the following:

- Home to Stay - Award-winning Murphy Clan Beginning
- Murphy's Secret - Whit Murphy's romance
- Murphy's Cinderella - Kyle Murphy's romance
- Murphy's Choice - Nate Murphy's romance

I love hearing from readers! You can connect with me and support my work in the following ways:

1. Like my Facebook fan page, BECKE TURNER AUTHOR
2. Visit my website: www.Becketurner.com
3. Join my private Facebook group Becke's Book Mates
4. Read my health tips blog on my website.

5. Leave me a review and follow me on Amazon, Goodreads, and Bookbub.
6. Refer me to a friend.

Keep scrolling for the following special gifts:

- Home to Stay excerpt
- A Sunberry Christmas excerpt (Dec. 9, 2022 release)
- Caramel Filled Pumpkin Blonde

# PLEASE LEAVE A REVIEW

If you have enjoyed this book, please leave me a review on, Goodreads, Amazon, and Bookbub.

Reviews help readers find books from people who have enjoyed a story and help me improve my craft. Yes, your opinion matters. If you can spare just five minutes to leave even a one or two line review, it would be so helpful in this book's success.

- **Goodreads Review:**
- Click on the link: Goodreads, click on **Murphy's Secret** cover and rate and write your review.
- Or go to Goodreads.com, type **Murphy's Secret** in the search field. Click on the title, scroll down and click on the Write a review button.

- **Amazon Review:**
- Click on the link: Write an Amazon review, scroll down to the write a customer review button on the left side of the screen, and fill in the box with your review.

- Or go to Amazon.com, select Kindle Books from the Amazon menu at the top of the page and type **Murphy's Secret** in the search field. Click on the title, scroll down the left side of the page, and click write a customer review button.

- **BookBub Review:**
- Click on the link: Bookbub, scroll down to the review button, click and leave your review.
- Or go to Bookbub.com, sign on, type **Murphy's Secret** in the search field. Scroll down to the red Write a Review box. Click the box and write a review.

One or two sentences to say I liked a character, it was a page-turner, or I laughed at the dog is all it takes for a review. I'm into easy. Thanks so much!

———

Page Forward for

- HOME TO STAY Excerpt (Book 1 Award-winning Murphy Clan Beginning )
- A SUNBERRY CHRISTMAS Excerpt (December 9, 2022 release)
- Caramel Filled Pumpkin Blondie Recipe

# GO BACK TO WHIT'S TEEN DAYS!

## Award-Winning Murphy Clan Beginning in Home to Stay Book 1

If you enjoyed Murphy's Secret, read an excerpt from **Home to Stay**. This award-winning romance marks the beginning of my career and teen Whit's introduction to Sunberry.

———

## Chapter 1

6:30 P.M.

Her boys couldn't be missing. Not today. Ava Robey checked the lane leading from Sunberry Road to the house. They weren't missing. They were late. And she had good news. They'd made it to the final round in the lease competition. If they won, Robey's Rewards would open in the only available commercial site on Main Street. One month of after-school and weekend work separated them from opening their new business.

But where were they? Her hand shook so hard she made the cut too short. One six-inch piece of trim and the laminate floor she'd installed would be complete. Her eyes moistened.

Breathe. Don't panic. They'll be here.

Hope, her five-year-old daughter, stepped over the toolbox and stood with her chubby hands fisted on her hips. "Where are my boys? The barn light is on."

Ava shoved an errant tendril into the Marine bandana tied around her head. "They're with a new friend. They'll be here soon."

Careful to keep her trembling fingers away from the saw's edge, she cut another trim piece. Most days the wood scent, the smooth texture of the surface, and the dramatic transition of the project relaxed her. Not today. The pungent odor of the construction adhesive blasted through her sinuses like a lethal toxin.

Hope waited by her side until the scream of the saw died. "I don't like Kyle's friends."

"That's why we moved to Gran's farm," Ava answered, careful to hide the tension from her tone. "Kyle is making nice friends, now." She hoped.

Once she'd installed the final piece, Ava loaded her tools into Grandpa's hand-made box, wishing for his assurance that everything would work okay. So, what was keeping her three sons? They knew today was special.

6:35 P.M.

Ava straightened with a hand to her back, ignoring the aches brought on by hours on her hands and knees. Outside the front window, the leaves stirred along the desolate lane. She swallowed past a thickening in her throat. They're okay. Any minute, Kyle, Whit, and Nate would burst through the door with a hare-brained reason for their delay and hungry for dinner.

"We need to go get them," Hope demanded, her high voice indicating near melt-down mode. "They're going to miss Daddy's memory party."

"No, munchkin." Ava bent on one achy knee. "They won't

miss it. They'll be here soon. Why don't you throw the ball for Toby?"

The black lab sleeping near the pantry lifted his head and drummed his broad tail against the new wood floor.

Hope stomped a booted foot. "I want to eat!"

"I'll make dinner in a little while."

"Two minutes?" Hope held up two stubby fingers.

*Breathe. It's not her fault the boys are late.* "In ten minutes you can help me set the table for the party."

Hope brightened and raced to the throw pillow in front of the TV screen. "Jiffy is ready for my memory." She held up the battered stuffed pig. "See? I gave him a bath last night so he'd be pretty and clean."

"Good job."

Before her daughter noticed her tears, she picked up the toolbox and exited through the back door, the hinges creaking from her hasty retreat. Keeping her back to the doorway, Ava deposited the toolbox along the wall, pulled a wadded tissue from her pocket, and blotted her eyes. The last shards of daylight dropped behind the trees and darkened the orange and yellow leaves. Twilight blanketed the old farmhouse like depression had blanketed her life five years ago. She'd survived those dark years, like she'd survive her boys' teen years. Because after tonight, they'd be grounded until graduation!

"You need to call my boys and tell them to come home right now." Hope said, startling Ava with her proximity. "I see stars."

Ava shuddered. Why had she taken Kyle's cell phone? Because he'd left her no choice. And why hadn't she questioned him about the new friend when he'd called for permission? He had a new friend, and he'd called to ask. She'd been thrilled by his consideration. Two hours ago.

Keeping her head turned from the intense scrutiny of her

daughter, she opened the cupboard door, and removed six plates. How did she fix this? She couldn't call the friend, couldn't drive to the house. She couldn't even call the police. What would she say? My boys are late for dinner? What if they'd been abducted?

Don't panic. They weren't little kids. All three had topped her five feet seven inches over a year ago. Sunberry, a small city located near the North Carolina coast, had its share of small-time crime. But who would pick up three boys? Not one lone child, who could be overcome and intimidated, but three good-sized adolescents who had seen the better side of far too many disagreements.

The dishes clattered in her trembling fingers. Had Kyle found trouble in Sunberry already? She'd hoped he would grow out of his rebellious streak, focus on his schoolwork. He was smart—and angry. Had he done something bad? Led his two younger brothers into trouble? A memory of Kyle's dark eyes once bright and loving faded into his current dark-edged gaze.

Hope tilted her head to the side. "Are you going to cry?"

Ava closed her eyes, inhaled, and then blew out a breath. "Not if I can get a hug from you."

Plump arms encircled her neck. She couldn't lose Hope or her boys. Ava hugged Hope close to her chest, careful to avoid squeezing too hard.

"Ooo," Hope cooed.

Heavens, she loved that funny sound, the tickle of her daughter's silky curls, and the scent of her strawberry shampoo. But her heart continued to race.

6:50 P.M.

Headlights illuminated the lane and Ava shifted for a better view through the front window. Her heart pounded *lub-dub, lub-dub* in her ears. The boys had ridden their bikes to school this morning. A big black SUV bumped through the lane ruts, bouncing the beam of light across the living room wall. Thank goodness, it wasn't a police car. Although all traces of saliva abandoned her mouth, she swallowed past the constriction in her throat. *Never show weakness.*

The SUV stopped in the drive behind her aging Ford Explorer. When the headlights blinked out, the outlines of multiple passengers moved beneath the interior light. However, the tinted glass obscured the occupants' identities. The driver's door opened and a large man, dressed in desert fatigues, straightened in the dim light from the porch.

A memory sent a chill racing along her spine. The set of his wide shoulders seemed familiar. When he looked up, her heart skydived to the pit of her stomach and she slapped her palm over her mouth. No! Not now, after so long. Captain Murphy, a man she thought she'd never see again, moved toward the back of the SUV. Her three missing sons trailed behind him.

"Why you?" she whispered.

While Toby whined from his position at the front door, Captain Murphy helped lift the boys' bikes from the cargo area of the SUV.

Hope stepped beside her. "Are my boys with a stranger?"

Ava gripped the window ledge. How did she explain to her children the man in her driveway had given their father his final, fatal orders?

When she jerked on the doorknob, the door scraped against the threshold announcing yet another item on the repair list for Gran's old house. Now her sons had joined that list. Looking guilty as sin, they stood behind the Captain, their gazes fixed on the weathered porch boards.

From the other side of the screen, the Marine stared at her. "Ms. Robey."

Ava stepped back. "Come in. From the looks of the boys, your story will require time and a meal."

Fifteen-year-old Kyle shot her an uneasy glance but moved forward.

Whit, her second son, followed, his bright blues moist with unshed tears, a gash bisecting his right brow. "Sorry, Mom."

She reached to inspect his face. "Are you okay?"

He ducked out of her grasp. "It's nothing."

Ava lowered her hand. This wasn't the first time one of her boys had suffered a cut or had come home late. But they'd never done it on November third.

With the tattered pig clutched under her arm, Hope gave her three brothers a fierce look. "You made me wait for Memory Night. I'm not coloring any more pictures for you!"

"Shh, honey." Ava moved Hope aside to let them enter. "Let Mommy handle this, okay?"

"I've been waiting forever." Hope's pouty bottom lip trembled.

"Thank you for your patience. Now, go feed Toby so I can talk to this gentleman." Ava gave her sons a no-nonsense look to let them know they were in deep trouble. "We'll talk later. Clean up for dinner."

She met Kyle's angry brown eyes, so like his father's. For a moment, her resolve wobbled. Near the cusp of manhood, Kyle tested her authority at every opportunity. She squinted. Was his jaw swollen? When he glared back at her, she pointed toward the hallway. "Ten minutes and we're sitting down for dinner."

With her breath held, she waited. *Come on, Kyle. Don't display the family wrinkles in front of the Captain, even if we aren't military anymore.*

Fourteen-year-old Whit, the family peacemaker, wrapped one arm around Kyle and the other around twelve-year old Nate. Together, the boys started down the hall, two dark heads surrounding her fair-haired middle son. After two steps, Kyle looked over his shoulder, anger still glittering in his glance.

"He always has to get in the last word," she muttered.

"He's smart," Ryan spoke from behind her. "Men like Kyle make good Marines. *If* you can turn that anger into a constructive outlet."

She whirled to face him. "You can't have him. You can't have any of my sons."

Unlike Kyle, Ryan didn't break her gaze. Standing at well over six feet tall, he filled Gran's small entryway. Sorrow, not rage, however, glistened in his eyes. Compassionate eyes—the same as her second born.

Heat flashed up her neck and face. "Sorry, it's—" She motioned toward the adjacent kitchen. "Please, come in and sit down. Coffee?"

He pushed away from the doorjamb and followed her. "Don't go to any trouble on my account."

"You brought my sons home. Coffee is the least I can do." She placed two white mugs on the counter. "I hope decaf is okay. I avoid caffeine after noon."

She placed the coffee in front of him, noting the stiff set of his features. Ryan Murphy had a bigger than life presence, dwarfing her country-style kitchen. Even sitting at the long plank table built for a family of eight, his wide shoulders and long legs seemed too large for the bench her three sons usually occupied.

She glanced at him before removing the pitcher of batter from the refrigerator. "I've been laying new floor, so I mixed pancake batter before I started. Three growing boys are hard to fill. I always make a double recipe and have plenty."

He looked like he had a bad case of poison ivy and didn't know whether to scratch or suffer. At least that was her take. She'd never been able to read him. He'd been from a prominent Sunberry family. She'd grown up on the farm. Although her husband Josh had liked and respected Ryan, she'd only been around him in later years at functions like the Marine Corps Ball.

While he sipped coffee behind her, she prepped the grill and poured syrup in a saucepan to warm. After ten years as a military wife, the rules remained stamped in her brain. Josh was enlisted. Ryan was an officer. She'd never seen Captain Murphy attempt to link the gap. In all fairness, the military wives often bridged the ranks and Ryan was single. At least he used to be.

When she sat at the table, he straightened. "So, you installed the floor by yourself?"

"The boys help me on the weekends. I finished the living room about ten minutes before you arrived." A burst of pride flamed in her chest. She'd done a good job once she'd figured out how to cut the corners.

"A woman with tools? I'm impressed. My sisters might have hung a few posters if I wasn't available." He smiled, and his features underwent a startling transition.

Her hand drifted to her chest. Amazing how a simple expression changed a man's looks.

She shrugged to hide her unexpected reaction. Must be the dimple on the right side of his mouth.

"Gran's house is rough. No one's lived here in years. When Mom and I opened the door that first day, we almost high-tailed it back to Charlotte."

"Sorry to hear about your mother."

Her breath hitched. Despite the leaking roof, deteriorating floors, and molding walls, she and Mom hadn't given up, hadn't given in to weakness. They'd laughed so hard they'd cried. Ava blinked. They'd had a good run. She wiped the tear at the corner of her eye and sipped her coffee, letting the warm liquid soothe her the same way Mom once had.

She blew out a breath. "So, what's the story on my boys?"

The man wasn't model material. His nose had a bump in the middle and his chin-line bore sporadic pock marks from teen acne. Still, he had a confident look—like a man who knew and understood himself and his world. A jab of resentment poked at the back of her mind. He hadn't known too much about Afghanistan. Otherwise Josh would still be alive.

"They were in a fight. I broke it up. Afterward, I made a deal with them. Based on your approval, of course."

The thought of being obligated to the man caused her fingers to curl around her mug. "Captain Murphy."

"Major now, but please, call me Ryan."

"Ryan." His name rolled off her tongue smooth as hot syrup on cakes. "Thanks for bringing my boys home. There's light traffic on our road, but I don't like them riding their bikes on it after dark."

He held up his palm. "I'd like to give your boys time to tell their side of the story before we talk. There's nothing worse than having a grown-up rat you out before you get a chance to come clean." He paused, opened and closed large calloused hands. "I mean if it's okay with you." He dipped his chin. "Sorry. I'm used to making decisions."

*Big surprise, there.* Still, she liked the idea. Not because it was his. Truth be known, she wanted *not* to like it.

"If there are any..." He held her gaze. "Holes in their account, I'll bring you up to speed afterwards. Since I'm involved, I've also got an idea about consequences—at least how I want to be repaid."

Repaid? Okay, she *really* didn't like that, especially when they were close to acquiring their dream. What the dickens had her boys gotten into? She sipped the decaf and released a slow breath. The time she'd charged into the principal's office to find her boys had told her *part* of the story flashed in her mind.

"Fair enough." She stood. "Boys! Five-minute warning."

When she topped off his cup, the steam swirled upward. "Family dinner time is important. That's when we talk. How many cakes do you eat?"

He pushed to his feet. "I'll come back after dinner."

"Don't." Blood pounded in her ears. "Dinner is my way of thanking you for bringing them home. Don't take that away from me."

His gaze sparked with an emotion she couldn't read. "Three big ones or six small ones."

When she removed the griddle from the pan drawer, the metal clanked grating against her already frayed nerves. Darn her boys for putting her in this situation. She wanted them to like Sunberry, make friends, be normal. Heat flushed her cheeks. This better not be the new Robey normal.

Major Murphy remained ramrod straight, his sleeves rolled up his forearms, but his gaze flicked around the area. Josh used to do that. He never missed a thing. She sprayed the marred surface of the grill to keep the pancakes from sticking. Everything about the scene was flawed—like Gran's rundown place, her holey jeans, faded Marine t-shirt, and her hair tied beneath one of Josh's old handkerchiefs. At least the new floor looked good.

The gas burner on her range sputtered and then flickered to life along with something long buried within her—awareness of a man. Her scalp tingled, and guilt churned her stomach. She'd buried Josh five years ago and not one time had she thought of a man—any man. Right, like a widow with four children and a sick mother had time to think about a social life. Heck, she hadn't even seen an eligible man in the last year—unless she counted Bennie, the handy man she used for jobs exceeding her skills.

"Mom and I moved back to Sunberry because Kyle kept making the wrong kind of friends in Charlotte."

The batter hit the griddle with a sizzle, breaking the silence.

"Whit tries to talk Kyle out of getting in trouble. Nate doesn't challenge anyone. He follows his big brother." Stop babbling. The man didn't need to know about her family problems. But one thing he *did* need to know.

She turned to gauge his reaction. "Tonight is Memory Night."

Silence. Within seconds he stiffened with a slide of his boots and a widening of his eyes. Her breath hissed through her teeth. He knew the significance of the date.

"Every November third, we share a memory to remember and honor Josh." Her voice, rusty at the start, sounded stronger. "We'll all share a memory about Josh. You'll go last. I'm sure you can come up with something to tell them about their father. After that, the boys will explain why they were late."

When he started to push to his feet, her blood heated.

"Josh was a good man." She glared at Ryan. "You owe his sons at least one story about their dad.

Get Home to Stay

# BOOKS BY BECKE TURNER

Clocktower Romances are set in fictitious Sunberry, NC and the characters throughout the series are friends or relatives. There are no cliffhangers and each book can be read as a stand alone and in any order of publication.

———

## AWARD-WINNING MURPHY CLAN

- *HOME TO STAY* ( The beginning, Ava and Ryan Murphy)

- *MURPHY'S SECRET* (Whit Murphy's romance)

- *MURPHY'S CINDERELLA (Kyle Murphy's romance)*

- *MURPHY'S CHOICE (Nate Murphy's romance)*

- *MURPHY'S STANDOFF (Marriage in crisis, Ava and Ryan Murphy)*

### Coming Fall 2024

- **MURPHY'S RESCUE** *(Hope Murphy's romance)*

### SUNBERRY FRIENDS & NEIGHBORS

- *CAROLINA COWBOY*

- *LOVING TROUBLE (companion novella to CAROLINA COWBOY)*

- *THE PUPPY BARTER*

- *A SUNBERRY CHRISTMAS*

- FLIGHT WITHOUT WINGS

Want a bigger bang for your buck? Choose a 3-book collection!

THE CLOCKTOWER ROMANCE COLLECTION

- *HOME TO STAY*
- *CAROLINA COWBOY*

THE MURPHY MEN COLLECTION

- *HOME TO STAY*
- *MURPHY'S CINDERELLA*

THE MURPHY BROTHERS COLLECTION

- *MURPHY'S CINDERELLA*
- *MURPHY'S CHOICE*

THE FEEL GOOD COLLECTION

- *HOME TO STAY*
- *THE PUPPY BARTER*
- *MURPHY'S CINDERELLA*

# SNEAK PEEK OF NEWEST MURPHY FAMILY SAGA

## MURPHY'S STANDOFF

Pain uncovers strengths and reminds us of a life well-lived.

Ava Murphy stretched her taut muscles cramped from a day of slumping over her latest artwork and let her mother's words warm her aching joints. After a deep, calming breath, she pushed back and reviewed the tranquil farm scene decorating the long Parsons table. A wooly lamb by the fence would perfect the piece. The wall clock over the entrance to her work room ticked a protest. Ryan would arrive soon and despite his retirement from the Corps, he insisted on punctuality, especially for his mother's family dinners.

Like the scenes she painted, her life held a storybook quality, and she never failed to whisper a prayer of gratitude every morning. Smiling, she cleaned her fine-tipped brushes, her memories tumbling through her mind like the soft bristles against her palm. Her evolution from a broken widow with four grieving children to a happily married business owner and artist still amazed her. And the kids? Oh my goodness. She couldn't be prouder. Her friends and neighbors were probably sick of hearing about her three fabulous sons and—

Ava capped her paints. Hope, her only daughter and the youngest, was still in the mixing-the-paint stage. But she'd soon graduate from the University of South Carolina and join her successful and happy brothers. Healthy and happy. Ava tidied her work area. That's all a mother wanted for her children.

As for Ryan and her? Hello, golden years. Even more satisfying, her business, the shop she'd built and nurtured like a struggling garden, continued to prosper and grow. Shoot, even her dog Irish was the perfect fur baby. Speaking of Irish, she hoped Ryan remembered to let him out and give him a snack. Their family dinners tended to run late into the evening.

Excitement refreshed her flagging energy. She couldn't wait to see her three sons, their wives, and their little ones.

When the familiar toot of Ryan's horn filtered through the shop, Ava grabbed her purse and switched on her silenced phone.

The device vibrated and the screen illuminated with a text from Hope.

Hey Mom,

U of PA offering a new Artificial Intelligence major!

Can you believe it? Applied today.

Talk soon,

H

*What!* Ava slammed the back door to her shop, unaware of the setting sun and the low idle of Ryan's pickup. Did her daughter think money multiplied like bunnies? If Hope changed majors again, she'd lose credits and delay, yet again, her graduation date.

*Beep!*

Through the truck window, Ryan tapped his watch.

Ava marched to the truck and yanked open the door. "I just got a text from Hope."

Ryan's grin faded. "Is she okay?"

Ava jammed her seatbelt locked. "Not a word from her in almost a month and then—" She swallowed, her mouth dry, her thoughts jumbled. "She's been working on a new career path. New as like in the tenth one."

"Six," Ryan said, his voice barely audible above the heater's fan.

Ava huffed. Like the number mattered. "But this major is special. It not only requires different classwork, it requires a different university!"

Ryan shifted the truck into gear with a little jolt. "I thought she liked Carolina."

"She also likes to spend money because she's moved up to the Ivy League, no less. Do you believe that?"

The squeeze on her hand stopped the rant building in her mind. She glanced at Ryan's strong fingers surrounding hers and then found his gaze. His calm demeanor wriggled beneath her fried nerves and lit a fire.

"How can you be so chill? Six years! Six stinking years and nothing!"

"Honey, breathe. She's healthy. She's smart. She'll figure it out."

*Breathe?* Ava's stiff fingers curled into a fist. How could she relax while their daughter floated from one idea to another with no thought of growing up, taking responsibility?

Ryan backed onto the asphalt. "I'm not thrilled with her choices. But there's no sense in losing your mind over a text. You know Hope. She probably heard about the program from a friend and the idea lit up in her brain like the dog in the movie. Remember, squirrel?"

Ava clamped her jaw shut before she said something she'd regret. But her husband had missed the point. They were discussing their daughter, not a children's movie.

"Once she has time to think it through—"

"Hope said she's already applied." Ava cringed. She hadn't meant to cut him off just like she hadn't meant her tone to be so shrill. But Ryan could be too laid-back, especially when it came to Hope.

Nervous energy vibrated through her hands. Although she could feel his gaze on her face, she didn't turn. Couldn't. One look at his patient features would send her over the edge. She wasn't interested in patience. She wanted him to rant and rave with her. Just because he retired from the Marines didn't mean he'd forgotten how to battle. This was war!

Ava huffed out a heated breath. Well, maybe not war. She was starting to go off the deep end like her daughter. Good thing they were going to the family dinner. After Hope's text, she *needed* a diversion. Because every cell in her body called for her to jump in the car, drive to Columbia, and strangle Hope!

Ryan drove at a snail's pace to his mother's home. Which was a good thing for her family members. By the time they motored across town and parked behind her second son, Whit's car, her blood pressure had fallen from the red zone. However, Hope's text continued to circle her thoughts like a tornado on steroids. Every revolution sent bolts of energy skittering beneath the soft fibers of her sweater.

Ava squeezed her lids closed. Inhale, hold, exhale. Thank goodness Whit, Talley, and her granddaughter had arrived before them. With an iron will, she forced an image of her precious granddaughter to replace Hope's latest bomb. Ellie would lift her spirits. There was no better feeling than her grand's chubby arms tightening around her neck. Ellie's hugs always filled her heart—even when worry burdened its beats.

With Ellie's big grin, mischievous gaze and blonde ringlets firmly fixed in her mind, Ava stepped onto the curved Murphy home driveway. Winter continued to grip the North

Carolina air, sending a shiver through her. Ava embraced the chill brushing her heated cheeks. When Ryan's long arm stretched around her shoulders, she leaned toward his solid presence. Over nineteen years of marriage hadn't dampened her reaction to his touch.

"Let it go." His lips brushed her forehead. "Just for a few hours."

She nodded.

"This"—he waved his arm to take in his mother's two-story brick home with its festive Valentine's wreath decorating the double-door entrance— "is our happy place. Four generations of Murphys have found comfort here."

"I can't count the times I've thanked your mother for showing me and our children the importance of family. I love our monthly dinners here. It's a good tradition and I'm proud our sons follow it and bring their families. My boys." Her voice hitched. "That's what Hope always called them. I haven't heard her use that reference in some time."

When he squeezed her arm and glanced away, a lump formed in her throat, and she clenched her bag to keep from touching his tear with her thumb. Her big, strong Marine had a soft underbelly for his loved ones.

"They're men now." His voice wobbled. "Good men. Who knew the mouthy teen I picked up after a street fight would grow up to be a doctor?"

Who knew her steady Marine would learn the perfect timing to interject a heartfelt comment?

Ryan took her hand at the steps to the front door. "Kyle's more than an oncologist, he's a good husband and a wonderful father to Dana's Sam. Man, she's a cutie. She reminds me of Hope when I married you—sassy and full of herself."

"Sam's adorable." Ava battled her building anger.

Hope was still sassy, immature and full of herself, but Ava swallowed the criticism. Time to focus on positive thoughts. Besides, she didn't want to dampen family day with a Hope intervention—even though her youngest was overdue.

"I'd love another grandchild." The thought of another Murphy curved her lips. "Dana mentioned she was considering it, and Sam's so good with Ellie. She'd make a perfect big sister."

"Don't give up on Whit and Talley," Ryan said. "Ellie needs siblings to play with."

A bubble of laughter escaped her. "Our granddaughter is on fire! Whit doesn't have to worry about staying in shape. Chasing Ellie is much harder than catching a football."

The front door swung open and Ryan's mother, Stella, opened her arms. "Come in, come in. Everyone's here and we're almost ready to serve." Stella hugged Ava. "Whatever troubles you, family comforts."

*But not this time.* Ava blinked back her tears, surprised her mother-in-law's words had struck such a melancholic cord. "I always feel comforted in your home."

"Exactly my intent." Stella's smile flattened. "You're usually the first to arrive. Is everything okay?"

Ryan's gaze shifted toward Ava. "Can't complain."

Although she understood his nonverbal plea, she guessed Stella had seen through the ruse. When it came to family problems, the Murphy matriarch had a second sense.

"Chaz did the cooking honors today." Stella took Ava's coat. "Or should I say her chef Otis did. It smells delicious. Nate's about to chew my table leg waiting for you."

"Of course he is," Ryan said. "I've never known him to miss a meal. Marrying Chaz and getting a back door into Gina's Eats and Treats was the best decision he's ever made."

"If that's Mom and Dad, chop chop!" Nate's voice filtered

from the kitchen. "Starving people inside. Enter at your own risk."

"Poppy!" A whir of blonde ringlets streaked between them.

Ryan snagged their granddaughter halfway through her giggling takeoff toward the dining room. He stole a kiss below Ellie's chubby cheek.

"Poppy, go!" Ellie said around her giggles.

"Nana needs a hug," Ava said.

Ryan suspended Ellie near Ava's face and their granddaughter stopped wiggling long enough to give Ava a slobbery kiss.

The remnants of Ava's emotional upheaval evaporated. "Mmm. Thank you, sweet girl."

Ellie squirmed for freedom. "Ice cream."

Whit expertly caught Ellie's dive toward his chest. "Right at the numbers!"

Ellie squirmed. "Down, Daddy."

"Daddy needs a breather. I've been chasing you since we got here." Whit delivered a raspberry on Ellie's tummy and set her loose on the floor. "And she's off!"

A snicker vibrated in Ava's throat and she reveled in the sheer joy of sharing her granddaughter's antics with family members.

Whit hugged her. "How long does this phase last?" he whispered.

"If she's anything like you," Ava wrinkled her nose. "You're in for about nine more years."

*If Ellie takes after her aunt, twenty.* Ava patted her second-born's slackened jaw. With his light brown hair and blue eyes, he looked nothing like the rest of her family. But his heart was pure Murphy gold.

"Please tell me you're kidding," he said.

Although his pleading gaze tugged at her heart, she couldn't lie to her son. "Sorry. I'm just giving it to you straight. You were in second grade before I started breathing again." And she still wasn't breathing when it came to Hope.

Ellie squealed and Talley streaked past them.

"We'll talk later." Talley waved. "I'm hot on the trail of your spirited granddaughter."

"Carry on," Ryan said, his rich laugh echoing in the entryway.

Ava gazed at the ceiling, willing her tears of joy to recede. *Thank you, thank you, thank you. Help me through the next thirty days.*

Another month should give Ryan adequate time to transition from the Corps to civilian life—she hoped. In the meantime, she'd deal with his shadow following her around the house and the shop. The man needed a mission, and she wasn't it! As for her daughter...? Ava swallowed. Her youngest might require thirty years to get her life together. She prayed it happened—soon.

Although she loved Hope, she didn't love her inconsiderate and immature behavior. At twenty-five, Ava was married and raising Kyle and Whit, mostly solo because their father was also a Marine—a deployed one. Hope couldn't put together a life plan let alone be responsible for little ones. Thank goodness her daughter didn't have a steady boyfriend. Ha! Like anything in Hope's life was steady.

"Are you okay?" Kyle's wife, Dana, her expression worried, stood before Ava.

Ava embraced her to avoid her scrutiny. "I'm much better with all of you here. Thank you for integrating into our family. I'm so happy Kyle chose you."

Moisture filled Dana's pretty blue eyes. "I get far more than I give. Your beautiful family has filled the one I lost. I feel close to Mom and Robin here. When Stella offers her prayer, I send them a message that Sam and I are safe and loved."

Ava dabbed at her eyes. "And you've reminded me of the gifts in my life. It's so easy to let small things mess with your mind." *And spirit.*

"Family helps me shoulder life's messy obstacles." Dana's gentle squeeze emphasized her words.

"Coming through." Stella lifted her hands filled with a large serving dish of pasta.

The aroma of tomatoes, spicy meat, and fresh baked bread awakened Ava's appetite. Following behind Stella, Nate's wife, Chaz, held a large bowl brimming with spring mix.

A blonde lock highlighted with peacock blue swept across her right eye. "Otis outdid himself again." She winked at Nate. "I'm so glad my amazing husband convinced me to keep Gina's."

"Survival instincts run strong in the Murphy family." Nate held up his beer. "Wine or brew, Dad?"

"I think this is a beer day," Ryan said.

Ava's heart thumped harder. Even with the gray peppering his temples and laugh lines framing his dark eyes, her man still looked fine—mighty fine. However, he hadn't been himself since he'd severed his Marine ties. That worried her. He didn't need the extra burden from Hope's escapades to hinder his transition to civilian life.

Unaware of her growing angst, her family gathered and took their seats. To her left, Ryan's gentle grip held hers, his thumb rubbing back and forth against her flesh. She relished the simple gesture, letting it ease her questions about their union.

To her right, Kyle, her first born, gently squeezed her

fingers. He'd always been sure of his way and was settled with an admirable commitment to his family and community. Again, she closed her eyes against the sting of tears.

During good times, the get-togethers spent listening to her family's challenges and successes filled her with pride. In stressful times, the nearness of her loved ones sustained her.

Stella's gravelly tone cut through the silence. "I love our blended family and I appreciate that you give up one Sunday a month to join me. You could have settled anywhere. Like with my daughters, I would accept that. Although I enjoy traveling to see their families, it's not the same as joining in our family home."

She paused, letting her thankful gaze touch each family member. "Thank you for staying in Sunberry, for raising your families where I raised mine. I love sharing this house and this community with all of you.

Now, let's enjoy Otis's latest creation. If it tastes as good as it smells, we may have to fight Nate for our fair share."

"Really?" Nate muttered. "Am I ever going to live down my infamous appetite?"

Kyle raised his hand. "Own it, Bro. You're the Murphy with a hole in his belly and I'm the Murphy wise guy. Be glad you have special people who care about a handle."

"I'll gladly own mine." Whit spooned green beans onto Ellie's tray. "It means I have a place at this table with the people I care for." He waved his index finger at Ava. "No tears. We're lucky to be together."

"Daddy!" Ellie clapped her hands.

"Eat fast, Dad," Talley said. "Your darling dervish will be finished in 1.5 minutes—if she's hungry."

Whit groaned. "She must eat. There's no way she can sustain her energy levels without refueling."

"Normal milestones don't apply to Eleanor Murphy," Talley said.

"We understand." Kyle extracted a warm roll from the bread basket. "At two Whit could climb the front of the refrigerator like a spider. If Mom wouldn't let me have a yogurt, I'd send Whit to get one for me. Shoot, I couldn't even open the door. Super Bro swings on the door like a monkey, pulls it open, climbs the interior shelves, and grabs a snack for us. Yogurt was one of his first words."

Talley stopped chewing. "That better be a Murphy family legend."

Kyle raised his right palm. "Nope. Absolute truth. And—"

"Don't strike terror into my wife," Whit said. "I'm trying to talk her into another baby."

The table quieted for thirty seconds and then Stella pumped her fist. "Yes!"

A green bean sailed over Whit's shoulder and landed upright in the mashed potatoes like a flag standard.

"Yay!" Ellie raised her arms in the air.

"And she scores!" Chaz said.

Ryan chuckled and Ava sucked in her cheeks to stop the grin. Ellie didn't need encouragement, but she was such a cute little stinker.

Whit eyed the bean, probably considering if he should retrieve it or let it stand. After all, how many times did one lob a bean in the potatoes and have it stick straight toward the ceiling? It had to be some kind of record.

Talley's gaze narrowed on Whit and Ava covered her grin. She knew exactly how Talley felt.

Her thoughts spun to a halt and her smile faded. She'd been so excited when she learned she was carrying a little girl. Hope had been a beautiful child with her big brown, interested gaze. But mercy, her boys had turned her darling daughter into a huge diva and now— How could she help her daughter navigate adulthood?

Ryan's gentle poke drew her back to the conversation. She straightened. "Did I miss something? Sorry, memory lane."

"I just pointed out that you had Nate and Hope after Whit," Ryan said.

"I did." Ava's heart swelled despite the constant guilt about her mothering skills after Josh's death. "Nate was an absolute angel and Kyle was the perfect big brother. He gets the credit for raising Nate. Their bond was instantaneous. The moment Nate could crawl, he followed Kyle. Kyle potty-trained him, taught him the alphabet, taught him to ride a bike, and probably taught him a few things a mother doesn't want to hear about."

Kyle pointed at Nate. "He was the perfect gopher—until I got into high school."

"No pressure, Talley." Ava waved her hands. "A spirited child makes a mom cautious. Josh begged for months before I considered having another child. But it was worth the challenge. Look at the fine men I've raised."

"Thank you, Mother." Kyle bowed his head toward her.

When Ellie pointed at the mashed potatoes, Sam scooted out of her chair and plucked Ellie's bean from the center. "There you go. You can eat beans with mashed potatoes if you want, but they're better dipped in ketchup."

Ellie's garbled two-syllable word made Ava pause. Was that an attempt at thank you... or a cuss word? One never knew when it came to firecracker Ellie.

"Mom?" Sam climbed back into her chair and shook Dana's arm. "Can we get a baby sister? Buddy said he's getting a new baby this summer."

Ava stifled a giggle. Sunberry Water should test their product for a fertility enhancer. Regardless, the looks on her daughters-in laws' faces shouted they weren't ready to launch into motherhood and neither was her eldest son.

Kyle's fork hovered in the air in front of his open mouth, but his wife was focused on her daughter.

"Hey, sweetie." Dana cleaned a dollop of ketchup from Sam's cheek. "That's a private conversation. We'll talk about it at bedtime, okay?"

Chaz glared at Nate. "Don't even go there."

If Stella's smile widened, she might split her face. "Like Dana so expertly put it, we've veered into private conversation territory. However, before we change the topic, I'd like to second Sam's vote, and that goes for each of my three grandsons. I'd love more great-grands." She pressed her palms together and dipped her chin. "When you're ready."

Ava's fingers tightened around her glass, which beat cheering her mother-in-law's performance. Of course it was easy for the grandparents because they were in the share-and-spoil stage and not 24-7 coverage.

"Thank you, Miss Stella." Chaz finger-waved from the end of the table. "I've only had a few months to enjoy my new salon. In the future I might reward my husband's fabulous building skills with a child. But *not* yet."

"Congratulations." A rosy hue from Sam's indelicate question continued to stain Dana's cheeks. "Two of the clinic's nurses were raving about their new cuts."

Chaz rubbed her knuckles against her chest. "I aim to please."

"How's the Martinez project?" Ryan asked.

Ava hid her snort in her napkin. Ryan's question wasn't fooling her a bit. Her husband had stepped in to change the topic to safe mode. Her daughter had also mastered diversion by watching Ryan and her sons. Although Ava admired the trait, she did *not* admire Hope's questionable decision-making and what lurked beneath it. This time her daughter had crossed Ava's line. Worse, Ryan tended to shelter his only daughter. But Hope's latest announcement had been the last straw for Ava. At twenty-five, it was time for Hope to stand on her own. The Murphy men had sheltered Hope too long.

Although she'd been proud of her sons' protective natures, she'd never predicted Hope's present outcome—five years of college, two years of community college, and no direction. Heavens, her daughter had become a professional student. Too bad teaching didn't interest Hope.

Her daughter needed to learn a beautiful smile and weaseling wouldn't always resolve life's obstacles. Flawless skin wrinkled. Bone and muscles weakened. When that happened to Hope, she and Ryan wouldn't be around. But her sons would be. Ava squeezed her eyes closed. Which was Ryan's position.

He didn't understand the importance of independence for young women. A woman, the same as a man, needed to have her own achievements. If a woman piggybacked her dreams and desires on another, she'd miss the joy of accomplishment. The memory of opening day at Robey's Rewards still expanded Ava's chest with pride. She'd done it. Was it wrong to want her daughter to experience that feeling?

Was she overcompensating because of what happened after Josh was killed? A shudder shook her shoulders. She'd known Josh was gone the minute she'd opened the door to the chaplain and Ryan standing on her porch. She hadn't known what that loss would do to her life. Although Ava couldn't prevent life's events, she'd do whatever it took to prepare her daughter should a similar experience occur.

Beside her, Ryan cleared his throat, pulling her back to the dinner conversation.

"I ran into Gracie Butler at Gina's this week," Whit was saying. "She said she was going to let Jack use her new house as a model. Sunberry needs more single housing. I'd be interested in supporting that endeavor."

Ava stiffened. Whit continued to fill Hope's college fund

regardless of her academic performance. She had good grades, just never enough credits in a single discipline to graduate. Maybe it was time to stop the steady flow of funds. Whit could well afford it but should he?

Ava blinked. The conversation had stopped.

"Mom?"

She turned toward Whit. "I'm sorry. I didn't sleep well last night." If she were honest, sleep had eluded her for months. Every time she closed her eyes, her mind filtered through ways to help Hope or ways to keep Ryan busy.

"I got a low-funds notice on Hope's account," Whit said. "Do you know how much she needs? She hasn't answered my calls."

Silence blanketed the dinner table. Beside her, Ryan stilled. Ava had only gone hunting once, but she still remembered the way granddad's dog had frozen on its target—like its life depended on it. Like Ryan finally realized how far Hope had gone.

"More money?" Kyle said. "I thought she was finally going to graduate."

"Not everyone is sure of their path," Talley said. "You knew you wanted to be a doctor, but Nate changed his mind."

"No one said she couldn't change her mind." Kyle bunched his napkin and set it on the table. "But there's a limit to flexibility."

Whit made a T with his hands. "Time out. The money's a nonissue. I just need an amount so I can cover her needs."

"She's drained it?" Ava's stomach knotted. Hope should have paid the spring semester's tuition months ago. Whit would've known the amount, which meant Hope had used all of this semester's spending money in less than thirty days. Whit avoided eye contact. Sometimes Ava wished she didn't know her sons so well.

But she understood this drama because everyone had lots

of practice—over five years of Hope's drama. And that didn't count her diva daughter's sideshows that were not academic related.

"Sounds like it's time for a Murphy intervention," Kyle said.

"Son." Ryan's tone brooked no argument.

"It's too much, Dad," Kyle said. "We all know it. We've had her back, hoping she'd figure it out. She hasn't."

Nate wiped his mouth with his napkin. "I'm with Kyle on this one. I think she needs help with this decision. I've been in her situation. I can talk to her."

"I talked to her last month." Talley shushed Ellie and added a roll to her tray. "She was excited. Said she'd found something that really interested her."

Ava sipped her tea to soothe her dry throat. "Was it artificial intelligence?"

Talley shook her head. "Exercise science. But she wouldn't tell me the details. She wanted to surprise us."

"We're surprised," Kyle said.

Ava placed her napkin on the table to stop wringing it. Either Hope was lying about her major or had changed it twice in the last month.

She forced a pleasant smile despite the tension in her lower jaw. "Thanks for your input. But it's time I scheduled a lunch in Columbia."

"Honey?"

She bristled at the edge of steel in Ryan's tone. They'd followed his wait-n-see approach for the last two years. Kyle was right. Enough was enough. Although Ava didn't expect Ryan to agree, she expected him to give her ideas a try. Especially after Whit reported Hope had drained her account. Drained. Empty. Like Whit's sacrifice was nothing. This would not stand. Hope was her daughter and she'd determine the next action. Not her sons and not her husband. Not while she was still drawing air.

———

**Is this the beginning of the end for Ava and Ryan's marriage?**

Click the link and continue the Murphy family saga today!

MURPHY'S STANDOFF

# CARAMEL FILLED PUMPKIN BLONDIE RECIPE

In MURPHY'S SECRET, Talley stress-baked brownies to soften a tough conversation with Whit. Although she used a boxed chocolate brownie mix, I've tested something much better. I hope you enjoy them. This recipe originated from Lauren's Latest. You can check out her fabulous recipes at her site. www.laurenslatest.com.

I decalorized and simplified her recipe by substituting brown sugar with Truvia Brown Sugar and the bag of caramels and cream with Smucker's Sugar-free Caramel Syrup.

**Brownie Ingredients**

- ¾ cup butter, softened
- 1 cup packed brown sugar (I used ½ c Truvia Brown Sugar Blend per package directions)
- 2 eggs
- 1 teaspoon vanilla extract
- 1 cup pumpkin puree
- 1 teaspoon cinnamon
- ½ teaspoon nutmeg
- 1 ¾ cup all-purpose flour
- 1 teaspoon baking soda
- ¼ teaspoon salt

**Filling Ingredients**

- ½ cup chopped nuts (optional)
- ¼ cup semi-sweet chocolate chips (my family prefers dark chocolate)
- 11-ounce bag of caramels, unwrapped (substituted as indicated below)
- ¼ cup heavy cream (Substituted as indicated below)

**\*\*Substitution**

Omit cream and caramels and substitute with Smucker's Sugar-free Caramel Syrup. The syrup eliminates unwrapping a bag of caramels, doesn't need a cream thinner, nor does it require melting. I simply squirted it on top to cover the brownie layer. Easy-peasy.

**Instructions**

1. Preheat oven to 350°. Spray 9x13 pan with nonstick cooking spray and set aside.

2. In large bowl, cream butter and sugar until light and fluffy.
3. Stir in eggs, vanilla, and pumpkin until combined.
4. Combine dry ingredients and stir to combine.
5. Incorporate dry ingredients into wet ingredients, scraping sides to ensure smooth batter.
6. Spread 2/3 of the batter into prepared pan.
7. Sprinkle with chocolate chips.
8. Squirt a thin layer of caramel sauce over chips and spread evenly with a spatula or butter knife.
9. ** If using caramel candies, place caramels and cream into a microwave-safe bowl and heat until melted, stopping every 20 seconds to stir.
10. Pour melted caramels and cream mixture over chocolate chips and spread evenly.
11. Place dollops of remaining batter over top of caramel. Smooth dolloped batter over top to cover.
12. Bake for 25 minutes or until edges are golden brown.
13. Cool completely before serving with a dollop of whipped topping.
14. Enjoy.

# ACKNOWLEDGMENTS

To use one of Dad's favorite euphemisms, writing fiction is *a hard nut to crack*. This story, along with the countless others I've created, was a labor of love. Without the support, information sharing, and advice of the following, this book would continue to reside in an external drive folder:

- The amazing women in Georgia Romance Writers (GRW) for sharing the highs and lows of my writing journey.
- My 2019 Golden Heart Award class, The Omegas, for sharing my best Cinderella conference and providing ongoing support.
- A critique partner extraordinaire and personal cheerleader, Peggy Anderson.
- Ginny Copeland for plugging my plot holes.
- My son for his military review and his continuous question, *when's that book coming out.*
- My daughter who had the wisdom and the courtesy not to ask.

A special thanks to my husband, who persuaded me to attend my first writing conference, never complains about his Honey-Do List, and never questions the time and resources required to follow this dream.

# ABOUT THE AUTHOR

## Updated 3/15/24

Becke Turner retired her healthcare data analyst hat to write contemporary romance full time. Like Lacy in FLIGHT WITHOUT WINGS, she was bitten by the horse bug at an early age. Her parents finally surrendered to her constant harassment and bought her pony, and another pony, and another... After years of breeding, training, and showing, Becke and her husband still make their annual trek to Wyoming for a week of mountain riding.

Although her stories reflect her varied interests in medicine, horses, and adventure, every story shows the character's journey to find a home filled with love.

Becke married her hometown honey during her first year in college and they're still riding trails together. After moving to eight different states, they call Blythewood, SC home. Two adult children, four fabulous grandsons, and one diva granddaughter complete their tribe.

Murphy's Secret

Written by Becke Turner

Cover Design by Special-T Publishing

Edited by JJ Kirkmon

Copyright @ 2022 Becke Turner

This book is a work of fiction. Names, characters, places, and incidents either are products of the author's imagination or are used fictitiously. Any resemblance to actual persons, living or dead, events, or locales is entirely coincident.

Published by Special-T Publishing, LLC

ISBN - 978-1-953651-05-1

Library of Congress Control Number:

First Edition

First Printing --

Made in the USA
Columbia, SC
25 September 2024